TRICK OR TREATS

TALES OF ALL HALLOWS' EVE

SPEED CITY CRIME WRITERS

Edited by
DIANA CATT

Edited by
TONY PERONA

SPEED CITY PRESS

ALSO BY SPEED CITY SISTERS IN CRIME

Racing Can Be Murder

Bedlam at the Brickyard

Hoosier Hoops and Hijinks

Decades of Dirt

The Fine Art of Murder

Homicide for the Holidays

Murder 20/20

Trick or Treats: Tales of All Hallows' Eve

CONTENTS

ST. CECELIA'S GHOST

BY TERI BARNETT

"Seriously, Mom. I'm fine."

"You don't sound fine, Izzy. You sound stressed. Are you eating too much Halloween candy again? You know what it does to your blood sugar."

Isabella 'Izzy' Martel may be forty-eight years old, but her mom still sometimes saw her as an awkward teenager who needed extensive mothering. Not that Izzy didn't appreciate Jane Martel, just the opposite. She loved her mom dearly and was grateful she was still around and vital at seventy-five. Izzy sighed. Truth be told, Jane had way more energy than Izzy could ever hope for.

"Okay. I might be a little stressed. And I may have eaten way too many chocolate peanut butter pumpkins last night. I have to meet with the construction project manager at the church remodel today and I'm not looking forward to it."

"Well, you should just move back home then." Jane huffed. "You can have your old room."

Izzy blew out a breath. Even though she'd lived in Indianapolis since moving here straight out of college to get her MFA in interior design, whenever trouble was anticipated, her mom would try to get her to move back to Detroit. "Mom, we've had this conversation. More times than I can count."

"Well, you can't blame an old bird for trying, now, can you? I miss you."

Izzy laughed. "No, I suppose not. And I miss you too." Her wrist buzzed and she checked her smart watch. "Hey, Ma, I gotta go. Henry is waiting for me downstairs."

"Oh. *Henry*. Remind me again how old he is?" She heard Jane take a sip of tea. "Is he *interesting?*"

"Lord, Ma, he's twenty-three and he works for me. Even if he was date-worthy—which he's not because, for starters, way too young—he has an adorable girlfriend who happens to be a chef at one of the up-and-coming restaurants in Broad Ripple." Her watch buzzed again. "Love you, Mom! I'll give you a call tomorrow!" she said and disconnected the call.

Izzy grabbed her tablet and stuffed it into an oversized rectangular black leather purse, tossed on a gray and black plaid jacket over a deep purple dress, and topped it off with one of her crocheted creations—a burnt orange shawl with a hint of gold sparkle—and fastened it in place with a large silver skull pin. It *was* two days before Halloween, after all. Time to get into the spirit of things. She checked her look in the mirror, tucked a strand of short silvery brown hair behind an ear, and said to her reflection, "Okay. Let's do this."

"Tell me you brought coffee," Izzy said to her intern, Henry Joseph, as she exited the heavy brass doors of the restored garment-factory-turned-condo building she lived in downtown. Henry had been working for her for three months now and had a great eye for design. She was hoping he'd want to stay on at least part time when his internship ended. He was good at his job and she liked his energy.

"Good morning to you, too, boss." Henry pushed his tall, lanky frame away from where he was leaning against his car and smiled. "In keeping with the spirit of the season, we have pumpkin lattes," he said, opening his door and sliding into the driver's seat. Izzy walked around to the passenger side of the bright blue seventies GTO, got in, and closed the door behind her.

She snapped on the seat belt and lifted the coffee cup out of the center console. *Oh, the spicy cinnamon smell was heavenly!* Izzy took a sip and sighed. "Good morning. Tell me again how you afford this amazing resto-mod on what I'm paying you?"

"Stolen from dad's collection. Not that he would notice. I mean, who keeps fifty-six restored cars in a warehouse on the southside and never drives them?" He patted the dash. "Blue Goat here was dying for some action." He pulled away from the curb, tires squealing.

"Yeah, well, let's save the action for the job site." She took another sip. *Autumn in a cup, that's what this is.* "The contractor gets a bonus if they finish ahead of time so I'm expecting some push back on the change orders I'm considering."

"What's the client thinking about changing?" Henry asked.

"Possibly removing any walls which were not part of the original construction. Also restoring the earliest color palette. They asked for estimates before finalizing any decisions."

"Gotcha." Henry took a drink and turned north on Meridian Street. "I've been digging into all that historical research you gave me to do. Did you know hundreds of St. Cecelia parishioners have filed reports over the years saying strange things have happened to them there? The consensus is the building is haunted."

Izzy shot him a look out of the corner of her eye. "*Sure* it is."

"No, really. I mean, it is over a hundred and fifty years old. Anything that age would have a ghost or two, don't you think?"

"Henry, if I'm not mistaken, you're studying interior architecture, not mythology, correct?"

Henry frowned. "I believe a society's mythos plays into their inter-pretation of structure. While ghosts may or may not actually exist, they *are* part of our myth. And, if enough people believe something, it eventually becomes a societal truth."

"Okay, professor. I can't disagree with that particular observation."

Izzy motioned with her free hand. "Looks like there's a parking spot just up ahead, on the east side of the street."

"You're pretty much a naysayer, aren't you?" Henry huffed as he maneuvered into the parking spot and exited the vehicle. "You're a creative type. Where does your imagination lead you?"

Izzy slid her business credit card into the meter, logged the hours, then responded, "My imagination is reserved for my design work. Well, and the occasional crochet project. Beyond that, I prefer to focus on what's in front of me. The things I can see and touch."

The pair crossed the street and walked through an alley to the old church. They entered through a side door which had been designated the construction entrance. Izzy usually specialized in office design, but one of her clients had referred her to the church board. The client had been happy with the transformations she'd made to his office suite and thought she could help out here. She was grateful for the project and loved the bonus of all the historical research. But it was a huge task and, thankfully, she had Henry to do a fair amount of the investigative work for her.

Izzy and Henry stopped inside the door. Sun flooded the stained-glass windows and cast colorful patterns over the checkerboard limestone floor. They slipped on their hardhats and scanned the job activity. Construction sounds echoed loudly throughout the chamber. "The project manager is over there. I'm going to go talk to him," Izzy shouted over the din. "You want to come along or stay back here and check things out?"

Henry snorted. "Are you kidding? I wouldn't miss this conversation for anything."

Izzy shook her head and left in the direction of the PM, Henry following close behind.

"Chad? Chad!" Izzy tapped him on the shoulder, and he turned toward her.

"Oh, hi, Izzy. What are you doing here? We don't meet today."

"I know. I'd like to go over some possible change orders."

"Women, always changing their minds." Chad rolled his eyes and looked over at Henry. "What exactly are you wanting to do now?" he asked the younger man.

Henry shrugged and pointed at Izzy.

"Hey, I'd appreciate it if you'd address your questions to me."

"What?" Chad looked at Izzy blankly.

"For Pete's sake. I'm the client's rep, remember?" Izzy tamped down her anger. This was definitely not the first time she'd been talked down to, disregarded, assumed to know nothing by a contractor and it likely wouldn't be the last. Never mind she'd been designing and managing large scale, multi-million-dollar renovation projects for the past twenty-some years. *Misogyny was alive and living quite well within the construction industry.* Huh. That'd make an excellent tweet. She'd have to remember that for later.

She pulled a stack of papers out of her bag. "Would you please go through these and give me some estimates for the work? The client wants to understand costs before implementing any additional changes."

Chad thumbed through them. "It's going to take a couple of days." He glanced at Henry. "How about you give me the gist of it before I put any time in."

Henry shook his head and pointed at Izzy again.

For heaven's sake. "We're considering taking down the newer construction, those rooms built into the transept on the east side," Izzy explained. "Since St. Cecelia's now has a community center, they no longer need those spaces."

"I came across a note during my research that there are bodies supposedly hidden in the walls. Possibly the bones of a church saint," Henry said.

Chad laughed and clapped Henry on the back. "No bodies so far, buddy boy."

Henry straightened. "Don't call me 'buddy boy.'"

Chad held up his hands. "Did y'all skip breakfast this morning? Feeling a little hangry?"

"More like disrespected. What is wrong with you anyway?" Izzy asked. "Your HR rep should send you for some sensitivity training."

She looked at Henry. "C'mon. We need to get to our next meeting." She glanced back at Chad, her mouth in a firm line, and shook her head as they walked away.

Izzy's phone buzzed next to her head, where she'd dropped it on her bed at some point during the night. Right after tweeting about what an idiot that contractor was. No names, of course, she was a professional, after all. Just a full-on rant about how women are treated by the construction industry in general and certain project managers in particular. She rubbed her eyes and looked at the clock. *Who calls at six a.m.?* She checked the caller ID. "Henry? What's going on? Why are you calling so early? Is something wrong?"

"Oh my god, boss. It's the contractor. The one we met with two days ago? Chad? It's on the local news."

"What? Look, you just woke me up so I haven't had any coffee. I need short and direct sentences."

"Chad has disappeared. His wife filed a missing person's report. No one has heard from him since we met with him."

A frizzle ran through Izzy. She sat up and pushed her hair out of her eyes. This, unfortunately, wasn't the first time someone had vanished from one of her job sites. Just late last summer, a structural engineer—who was missing for a couple of days—had turned up dead in the basement of a northside commercial office building she was working on. She'd decided to do some investigating of her own and ended up being the one to find the body, knife sticking out of his back. Revenge for dissing the mechanical engineer in front of the client. She shuddered with the memory.

"I wonder if the church ghosts got him."

"Geez, Henry, we've had that conversation." She rubbed her eyes. She was going to need a lot of coffee. Extra strong. "I'm going to head over there and have a look around."

"Want me to come along?"

Izzy hesitated. If something fishy was going on at the job site, she didn't want to get him involved. On the other hand, he was observant and may see something she didn't. "All right. Pick me up in an hour?"

"See you then. I'll grab coffee. And muffins."

"You're a good man, Henry," Izzy said and hung up the call. She sat in bed for a few moments. What were the odds of another death on one of her projects? She shook her head and laughed at herself for even considering such a thing. *Pretty much zero, right?*

THE CONTRACTORS WERE USUALLY on site around seven a.m. and here it was, almost seven-thirty, and no one was working. Tools and sawhorses and building materials all left in place. Izzy and Henry slowly walked down the main aisle, their footsteps on the worn limestone floor echoing through the sanctuary. "It's too quiet. Like a ghost town," Izzy said. Then added, "Poor choice of words."

Henry chuckled. "You're coming around. Do you think they shut the job down because of Chad?"

"Probably. I hadn't thought of that. If he was last seen here, the police might not want anyone near the site until they've investigated. Which means we shouldn't be here, either." Izzy shrugged. "You know though, as long as we are here, we may as well have a look."

"Can I help you?" Both Izzy and Henry turned at the sound of a deep male voice.

"And you are . . . ?" Izzy asked.

The man, late forties-early fifties, graying hair and wearing a navy-blue suit and black Chucks, approached. He put his hand in his pocket, pulled out his wallet, and flashed a badge. "Detective Felix Antonelli."

Izzy opened her mouth to speak but the detective cut her off with a wave of his hand. "Yes, just like the cat and yes, I am Italian. On my father's side, anyway."

Henry snickered.

Izzy shook her head. "That's not what I was going to say." She extended her hand. "Isabella Martel. Izzy. I'm the interior designer. This is my project."

"Well, you just made my work easier."

"What do you mean?"

"Your name is on the job records, so you are on my list of people to talk to. Do you have a moment?"

"Yeah, sure."

"Good. Let's have a seat." He motioned toward the oak pew just in front of them.

"If you two don't need me, I'm going to go look around. I'm working on the theory that one of the church ghosts got hold of Chad. It is Halloween, after all, and the veil between the worlds is thinnest today." Henry considered that for a moment. "Maybe they possessed him. Or dragged him into hell. Huh. That leaves a picture in the mind." He turned on his heel and headed toward the transept to the east.

"That's Henry Joseph, my intern. He specializes in Overly Active Imagination," Izzy said as she watched Henry for a moment. She turned to the detective. "How can I help you?"

"Tell me about your relationship with the missing project manager."

Izzy considered the detective. She knew from past experience she should choose her words carefully. "It was professional."

"That's not what his assistant says." Felix pulled a small notebook out of his chest pocket and flipped through the pages. "He said you two were often at odds and that Chad disappeared right after arguing with you."

"We were not arguing," Izzy said. "He was being obtuse, implying I couldn't possibly know anything about construction by virtue of being female. I simply corrected him."

"You run into that often?" Felix asked.

She sighed heavily. "More than I'd like."

The detective checked his notes again. "Seems you had another person turn up missing on one of your projects. Building north of here. You found the body."

"Yes, that's true, but I don't see how that incident is connected to this one." Izzy's eyes narrowed. "Wait a minute. Are you suggesting I did something to Chad?"

He held up a hand. "Really, I'm only trying to sort out the facts of this case and rule out any possible connections to the other one. You are a common denominator."

Izzy relaxed a little. "Okay. I apologize. I'm obviously on edge about all of this."

Felix nodded and continued, "No worries. Now, I did see your tweet last night about a contractor who gave you a hard time. You seemed pretty angry. Were you referring to Chad?"

She stared at the detective. Green eyes. How'd she miss that detail? She was all about details.

A scream rang out and reverberated through the building. *What the hell?* They both jumped up and ran in the direction Henry had gone. "Henry? Henry! Where are you?" Izzy called out. No answer. And no Henry. They entered one of the transept rooms the client was considering removing. Izzy turned a full circle in the twenty-by-twenty-foot space. *Nothing out of the ordinary.*

"Maybe he found one of his ghosts," Detective Antonelli said.

"Oh, not you too?"

"It is Halloween." He shrugged. "Leave no stone, or possibility, unturned."

"There has to be a simpler, more logical explanation than a ghost hauling Henry off into the great unknown." She planted her hands on her hips and surveyed the room again. There was a thin layer of construction dust everywhere. "Hey, look at this." Izzy walked over to a wall, stopping about five feet short of it.

Felix walked up behind her. "What do you see?"

She squatted down and pointed at the floor. "These footprints. They end at the wall."

"Huh. Like someone walked right into it and vanished." The detective pulled a pair of nitrile gloves out of his back pocket and slipped them on. He reached out and tapped against the panel in front of him. "Seems solid."

"You have to wonder, though, if there's a hidden door here some-where," Izzy said. She studied the wall again, looking for anything out of the ordinary. The craftsmanship was beautiful, and the trims and edges all matched up perfectly. She made a mental note to reuse the paneling elsewhere if they ended up demoing this room. "I suppose maybe there could be one, but I don't recall seeing any references to such a thing in the old construction drawings."

A rattling sound, like chains clanging together, came from behind the wall. Izzy and Felix stared at each other. "Um. Did you hear that?" she asked.

"I thought ghosts with chains were more of a Christmas thing," Felix said.

Izzy braced her hands against the wall panel in front of her and leaned forward, listening. Her weight caused the wall to shift slightly and she heard a click. She stood back and watched as the panel slid into a pocket to the right.

"Well, I'll be damned," Felix said. He pulled a flashlight out of his jacket and peered into the dark opening. "Look at this." The light hit a heavy set of ropes running the length of what appeared to be a three-foot-by-three-foot square shaft. "What do you suppose it is?" He moved the light beam back and forth. "Pitch dark. Can't see the bottom."

Izzy stepped back and considered the location within the overall structure of the building. "A shaft like this with thick rope cables? I'd bet it was a dumbwaiter. Though I don't know why there'd be one in this church. There's only the main floor and attic." She turned on her phone flashlight and pointed it up. "See the pulleys? The ropes start here, they don't even go up."

Felix snapped off his flashlight. "Fascinating."

"Henry!?!" Izzy shouted down the shaft. "Are you down there?"

Her shouts were met with silence and a cold blast of air. The hair on the back of her neck stood up. *No. No ghosts. I don't care if it is Halloween.*

"How do we get to the basement?"

"That's the thing. According to the old blueprints, this is it. No basement." The hidden door started to close, and Izzy lodged a piece of scrap wood between the panel and wall, holding it slightly open. "Let's go take a look at the drawings. I must have missed something," Izzy said as she led the detective to where the now missing Chad had set up his office area. She dug through the layers of plans until she found copies of the original blueprints. "Here." She pointed to a building cross section. "See? There's nothing beyond an extremely narrow crawl space." She crossed her arms and tapped her chin. "This makes no sense. There's really no place for a dumbwaiter, or Henry, to go. Assuming he even fell down there."

"Boss! Thank goodness you're still here!"

Izzy spun around. Henry was walking toward them, covered in dust and cobwebs. "Henry! Are you okay?"

He paused and patted his arms and torso, blew a cobweb away from his eye. "Pretty sure I am. But you both have to come with me. You won't believe what I found."

Felix and Izzy followed Henry into the room with the hidden dumbwaiter. Izzy pointed to the opening in the wall. "We thought you fell down there."

"What? No way." He peered into the void. "Though that is cool. Do you remember telling me about the possibility of an old lost staircase leading to the attic?"

Izzy nodded. "Yes, of course."

"Well, I found it, but it doesn't go up. It goes down." He nodded toward a secondary doorway on the other side of the room. "It's back there, in the sacristy. I came to get you guys to look at it with me. I am not going alone."

"You screamed," Izzy said. "We thought something happened to you."

Henry gestured the length of his body. "Do you see all these cobwebs? I had a spider on me as big as my hand."

As if on cue, a long groan echoed up through the dumbwaiter shaft.

"All right, Shaggy. Let's go," Felix said.

"Shaggy?" Izzy asked.

"Tell me this investigation isn't feeling a bit *Scooby-Doo*." He gestured to the open panel. "Hidden dumbwaiters and secret staircases? Ghostly moaning?" Felix shook his head. "All joking aside, I am hoping this is all somehow connected to our missing project manager."

Izzy snorted. "Right. And I suppose you're going to pull off a mask any minute and shake your fist at us 'darn kids' for thwarting your evil plans." She considered the detective. "You're a little cavalier about all of this. Maybe *you* did something to Chad." Felix stared at her and she felt her stomach flip. "Okay, fine. I take that last part back. Show us the staircase, Henry."

Henry led them to a large vestment closet. The back wall panel was open, revealing a narrow stair leading down.

But to where?

Groans and more chain rattling.

"It's the church ghosts. They've claimed Chad and they're coming for us," Henry stage-whispered. "You two go on ahead. I'm going to hang back and look around up here. Possibly by the exit."

Izzy laughed. "Coward."

"I'm big on self-preservation." He called over his shoulder. "Scream if you need me."

"While you're in self-preservation mode, how about you go take a look through the documents in Chad's office again? The detective and I just started going through them when you screamed. I have a gut feeling the answers are there and we just haven't found them yet."

"Will do," Henry said as he walked away.

Felix and Izzy looked at each other. "You go first," she said.

"I thought you weren't afraid."

"I thought you were a cop."

"Point taken." Felix flipped his flashlight on high beam and started down the stairs. He waved his arms, brushing cobwebs out of the way as he descended. "This is really why you wanted me to go ahead of you, isn't it?"

Izzy smiled. "Perhaps."

They reached the bottom of the stairs and stepped onto a hard packed dirt floor. The space was dark, dank, and musty, as if no one had ventured down there in years. Izzy turned on her phone flashlight and walked over to the foundation wall. Stacked flagstone. "This seems to pre-date the church. The church itself must have been built on top of an older, existing structure. What's that?" She stepped over a few feet and trained her light into a small opening. A skull stared blankly back and she jumped. "Holy hell."

"What is it?" Felix took a look. "Okay, then. I'm calling for the M.E." He pulled his phone out then put it away. "No signal." He moved his flashlight around the space. "What do you think this is?"

"A serial killer's private lair?"

A low groan came from the opposite side of the room. They cautiously walked over to an old door with rusted hinges. "You going to open that?" Izzy asked.

Felix drew in a breath and pulled the heavy door open, the bottom scraping loudly against the dirt floor. More groans and rattling. Felix hit the space with his light. Lying in the middle of the small square room was Chad the contractor, a pile of rusted chains nearby, the dumbwaiter ropes dangling over him. He rushed over to the man. Chad struggled to sit up. "You shouldn't move," Felix said.

Chad shook his head, leaned up on an elbow, and looked at the pair. "How did you find me? I thought I was a goner for sure," he whispered roughly. "Lost my voice from all the yelling. Been banging these chains together, trying to get someone's attention."

"Henry found a hidden staircase and we followed it," Izzy said. "But it looked like it hadn't been used for decades. How did you end up down here?"

"I was going through those change orders and decided to take a look at one of the rooms Henry wanted to demo."

Izzy stood. "Let's leave him here, Detective."

Chad raised a hand, groaning with the movement. "Sorry. Sorry. One of the rooms *you* wanted to demo. Got a call and leaned against the wall while I was talking. Next thing I know, the wall's moving. Lost my balance and fell down that shaft." He pointed toward the opening in the ceiling and the dumbwaiter ropes. "I tried to grab hold of those ropes but couldn't get a grip." He stopped to catch his breath. "Then I woke up here, flat on the floor, in the dark, no cell signal. Luckily, I had just stuffed a pile of Halloween candy and a bottle of water in my pocket right before I went to check the area out. It's kept me going." Chad rubbed his leg. "I think my ankle might be broken."

"You guys have been down here a while. I thought I should probably overcome my fears and check on you," Henry said as he carefully entered the small room. "Plus, occupational nosiness. Oh, hey, you found Chad." He grinned at Izzy. "Guess you didn't kill this one after all."

"Funny."

The three leaned over to help Chad to his feet and up the stairs.

They reached the top and led the project manager to a chair. "You were right," Henry said to Izzy. "There was an old project notebook in a box stuffed under the plan table." He handed her the book.

"How long have you had these?" Izzy asked Chad.

"The pastor dropped off that box of notebooks earlier in the week," he said. "I was going to bring them to the next construction meeting."

Izzy opened it to the bookmark Henry had placed. "This building was constructed on top of the original church graveyard. Apparently, they dug up the bodies and interred them into the walls, catacomb style, before construction began. That explains the bones we found and the stories about bodies being buried in the walls, but not the dumbwaiter." She scanned through several more pages. "Henry, look at this."

He leaned over her shoulder. "Wow."

She glanced up at the detective. "There are references here to this location being on the underground railroad. This is historically significant. And likely explains the dumbwaiter *and* the hidden staircase," Izzy observed. She gently closed the old project book. "Nothing supernatural about any of this."

"Except we're treading into *Poltergeist* territory now, what with this church being built on top of a cemetery," Felix said. He checked his phone. "Signal's back. Excuse me, I'm going to call for an ambulance for our friend here."

As the detective walked away, a thin, reedy moan followed by the sound of rattling chains echoed up the stairwell, along with a blast of cold air. Izzy slammed the door shut. She and Henry stared at each other. "I'm going to pretend I didn't hear that," Izzy said. "What I do hear is a cup of spicy hot chocolate calling me from the food truck outside. Join me?"

"Wouldn't miss it, boss."

EF YOU DON'T WATCH OUT

BY C.L. SHORE

Maggie stood in the kitchen, trying to stand straight and still. It was hard, very hard, especially since her best friend Betsy was making faces at her from across the kitchen. Mother knelt in front of her, pinning up her skirt, her mouth full of pins.

"I wish Miss Clark would let our Girl Scout troop have navy blue uniforms instead of this dusty brown color," Maggie said.

"Khaki," Mother said. "This color is called khaki. Often used for uniforms."

"I don't care, it's not as pretty as blue." Maggie never could understand how Mother spoke so well with a mouthful of pins. Plenty of practice, she reckoned, after sewing most of the clothes for her children, plus herself, and the occasional shirt for her father, Dr. Thomas O'Brien.

Mother sat back on her heels and motioned for Maggie to twirl around. "Looks straight. I'll hem it tonight and you'll be set for the parade next week. Your neckerchief and badges will add some bright color."

"You do a fine job with sewing," Betsy said from her perch near the window. "My mother took me to the dressmaker, but my dress doesn't look near so nice."

Mrs. O'Brien stood without tripping on her skirts, another talent Maggie admired. "Thank you, Betsy. Maggie, change into your Saturday clothes. We'll have lunch as soon as your father comes back from house calls. Someone out in the country broke out in a rash, hope it isn't the start of smallpox again." She sighed.

Maggie twirled several times in her dress. "Before you start with lunch can you measure Betsy and me against the door frame? We haven't done that for over a year!"

Mrs. O'Brien smiled. She knew the two girls had been referred to as "the almost twins" for years at school. They both had dark brown hair, although Maggie had more of a reddish cast to her locks. They both had turned-up noses and freckles. And they'd always been within an inch of each other in height. Now they were twelve, and each girl had grown over the summer months.

"Betsy, you first," Mrs. O'Brien said, grabbing a pencil from the kitchen table. She lined the girl up against the door frame and made a mark level with the crown of her head.

"You next, Maggie." Her daughter took the place vacated by her friend. "Well, I never!" Mrs. O'Brien said. "You're only a half-inch apart!" The two girls giggled and ran upstairs.

Maggie took off the Girl Scout uniform and put on her old school dress. "I don't care what Mother says," she complained to her friend. "Miss Clark is ridiculous for not choosing navy blue. She's just so . . ." Maggie made a face with scrunched up eyes and protruding tongue.

Betsy laughed. "You'd better watch out, Maggie. We're in the month of October. And you know what Mr. Riley said in his poem. If you mock your elders, the goblins might get you!"

"Hmmm. Well, I know a lot of people like Mr. Riley's poems. That's why we're having this big parade next week. But he writes funny. Didn't he learn to spell in grade school?"

"Course he did. My mother says it's dialect. To let us know how the people in his poems talked. Like Little Orphant Annie."

The steady rhythm of horse hooves increased in volume outside Maggie's window. "Papa's home!" She opened her window to wave.

A rock shot from somewhere out of Maggie's view. It whizzed past the horse carriage and hit the dining room window frame with a thud. Blaze, their stallion, whinnied but didn't startle.

"Lousy papist!" someone shouted from behind the O'Brien's shed. Maggie didn't know what a papist was, but her father would. Or she could look it up in their family's heavy dictionary.

Her father stepped out of the covered carriage and saw Maggie leaning out of her second-story window. "Maggie! Get your head inside and close that window!" Maggie obeyed as he ran toward their shed. She sat on the edge of her bed.

"Someone hit our house with a rock. Father is checking into it." Maggie looked down before turning toward Betsy. "Stay for lunch? You know my mother won't mind."

"I think it would be fine. My mother went out to the country today to visit someone. And Sam is helping our cousins move their hay to the barn."

At the mention of Sam's name, Maggie's heart did a little flip-flop. Betsy's older brother was almost fifteen and he was very handsome. Maggie secretly hoped that they'd get married someday. He didn't seem to notice Maggie much, though.

"Maggie!" Her mother called up the stairs. "Come down for lunch! Betsy's welcome, too."

Maggie's father and her younger brother, Tad, were already seated. The table was loaded with hot food. Cornbread right out of the oven, sausage, applesauce and stew warmed over from the previous night. Mrs. O'Brien always gave Daisy, her hired girl, Saturday afternoon and evening off. Next week would be different, though, due to Riley Days. Daisy would work Saturday but have Sunday off.

Father didn't bring up the rock incident. Maybe he'd already told Mother, Maggie thought. He held the newspaper in front of him. There was an ad on the back page, featuring a young woman with black, bobbed hair.

"Maybe I'll get my hair bobbed," Maggie announced. "What do you think, Mother? I've seen some high school girls who've done it."

"Maybe when you're in high school we'll think about it," Mrs. O'Brien said.

"You can't do it unless I do," Betsy said. "Otherwise, people won't think we're the almost twins anymore."

Mrs. O'Brien pulled the paper down from her husband's face. "Do we need to worry about smallpox again?"

Dr. O'Brien set the paper aside. "No. Although chicken pox could start going around. The youngest child in that family had chicken pox. Just as contagious, but not as deadly."

"That's a relief. With the Riley Days parade next week and all of the people coming in town, we don't need smallpox on top of that."

"I'm more worried about a repeat of the shenanigans from a few years ago." Dr. O'Brien set down his fork. "We don't need that experience again."

Betsy and Maggie exchanged glances.

"Well, I'm excited about the parade next week," Tad announced. "My class is going to march and plant a tree in the park."

"Well, so are the Girl Scouts, Mister Smarty-Pants."

Mrs. O'Brien directed a look at Maggie and the rest of the meal was quiet. Afterward, Betsy left for home, and Maggie began her Saturday chore, sweeping the front porch. A few crispy leaves were on the surface this week. Given the amount of orange and yellow color in the sweet gum tree, there could be quite a few next week. But sweeping would have to wait until after the Riley Days parade. So many people would be in Greenfield! It would be quite an event. Seven days to wait. Maggie hoped they'd go by quickly.

MAGGIE WINKED at Betsy across the classroom. She could hardly wait for school to end. First, they'd have their weekly Girl Scout meeting and find out about the parade instructions for Saturday morning. Then, she and Betsy would go with Sam and his friend Fred out into the country to see a haunted house. At least, Sam said it was haunted. Maggie told her parents that the Girl Scout meeting was likely to go extra late. Betsy's parents didn't seem to care how late she and Sam stayed out, as long as they were together. It might be dark by the time they got home; the days were getting noticeably shorter.

The Girl Scout meeting seemed to last forever. Miss Clark walked around the group of girls, barking instructions. All twenty-four troop members were to meet in the lot behind Betsy's father's Main Street Mercantile by eight-thirty in the morning, uniforms pressed and neckerchiefs neatly tied.

The girls sprinted to Betsy's house where Sam and Fred were waiting with bicycles. "You can ride on the handlebars," Sam said. "C'mon Maggie."

Maggie sat atop the handlebars and Sam took off, heading west. Fred and Betsy followed. Maggie could hear Betsy's giggles. She found the arrangement with Sam kind of romantic. Yes, she would like to marry that boy. Maggie hoped the ride went on for a long time.

She was disappointed. After about ten minutes, Sam pulled into an overgrown country lane. Maggie almost fell off the bike as it slowed but managed to land on her feet. Fred and Betsy were close behind. The bicycles were left lying on their sides in the tall, dry grass.

Clouds gathered in the west, hiding the setting sun. Sam led the others around a bend in the lane. The second story of a faded white house was visible above a hedge of overgrown bushes. As they continued to walk, Maggie could see the structure from its side, featuring a long, covered porch. It was a big house, she realized, once you could see its length. A screen door was off one of its hinges on the porch. A couple of shutters hung precariously.

"This place is Dark Star Manor," Sam whispered. "Some people say a crazy doctor ran a hospital here and buried smallpox patients out back. The house is supposed to be haunted."

"I don't believe in . . ." Maggie started to say in a voice that wasn't a whisper. Sam jumped to her side and covered her mouth, just as Betsy pointed behind the house and let out a muffled "Oh!" White, cone-shaped objects were bobbing in the tall corn and underbrush behind the house. Because the ground's surface was hidden by vegetation, the figures appeared to be floating. They were getting bigger, which meant they were getting closer, Maggie figured.

Sam's hand dropped from Maggie's mouth. "Run!" he yelled as he turned and sprinted. Maggie saw the white objects pause, then move forward. She ran with the others, back toward the road, back toward the bicycles hiding in the tall grass. Sam and Fred picked up the bikes as the girls tried to mount the handlebars, clumsy with fright. Maggie turned and saw a white apparition waddling down the lane. The boys took off with the girls riding in front of them, and the waddling object appeared to stop.

Maggie could hear Sam breathing hard behind her. The road was bumpy and she gripped the handlebars so she wouldn't fall off. Sam peddled until he passed the crest of a hill, then brought his bicycle to a stop. Fred followed suit. "What the heck was going on there!" Fred wanted to know. "Did you know something strange was happening at that house? Were you trying to trick us?"

"Are you joking?" Sam answered. "I had no idea!"

Maggie moved close to Betsy. "Goblins?" she whispered.

Betsy nodded. "Maybe." Her face appeared to be as white as a sheet.

Sam must have overheard. "A lot scarier than goblins," he said, shaking his head.

Maggie spoke louder. "We need to get home. I think it's going to rain."

They parted near the mercantile on Main Street. It started to drizzle as Maggie walked up the stairs to her front porch. Daisy saw her from the parlor as the door closed.

"Land sakes, child! You look a soggy fright! Get up to your room right away and change before you track mud all over!"

Maggie put on her Saturday clothes before dinner. Her mother didn't notice. She and Father were engaged in a terse conversation about a doctor friend testifying something. Maggie was distracted by her own thoughts. As she got ready for bed, she saw Daisy talking with her gentleman friend near the back alley from her bedroom window. They looked worried, too.

MAGGIE WOKE up early on Saturday. Mother had wanted her to stay in the house after school Friday, and she did not object. She finally looked up the word "papist." So, the man throwing the rock was angry with Father for being Catholic? That didn't make sense to her.

The day dawned bright and sunny. Shadows were still long, though, when Miss Clark gathered the girls together and lined them up. Maggie was disappointed that she and Betsy would be split up in different lines, and on opposite ends of their lines, to boot. She would be on the north side of the street and Betsy on the south. They agreed to find each other at the park before the ceremonies.

Noisy crowds lined Main Street. The marching band just ahead of the Girl Scouts was almost drowned out. Maggie caught her mother's eye briefly as the troop passed. Her two aunts and their families were there, too. The troop arrived at Riley Park, and the lines disintegrated into several knots of tightly packed scouts. Maggie looked for Betsy in vain. Too many girls wearing the same thing, plus the hats. The hats made her search difficult.

One of the younger scouts approached Miss Clark. "Found this, Miss," she said. She held a scout hat in her hands.

"Carelessness!" Miss Clark huffed. "Thank you. I'll keep it until our next meeting."

Troop members clustered around their leader, preparing for the planting. Maggie hoped no one noticed she was leaving. She made several loops around the park, always widening the circle, looking for Betsy. So many people! She never caught sight of her friend. She finally gave up and went home.

Her house bustled with activity with the aunts and their families running all over the parlor and kitchen. Maggie waved to her mother and ran up to her room to change out of her uniform. She could see

Daisy and her beau outside the shed from her window. The boyfriend shook his finger and stamped his foot.

Maggie put on her best school dress before going downstairs where lunch was waiting. Her aunts were teasing her father about not owning a Model T.

"Well," Father said, "Mr. Ford is lowering the price to $300. I might buy one for family outings. But I'll still use the carriage for house calls. So much better on the rough country roads."

From the parlor window, Maggie saw Sam approach the front door. Daisy intercepted him and they exchanged a few words before Sam left and ran to the neighbor's porch. Maggie thought Sam looked concerned. Worries about Betsy gathered at the back of her brain like a threatening storm. Even though she was very tired, Maggie tossed and turned before she fell asleep that night.

A GRAY SKY greeted Maggie when she awoke. She could hear people stirring downstairs. The aunts had left the previous afternoon, but it was Sunday and her father's turn to pick up the priest at the train station and get him to church for Mass.

Insistent knocking interrupted the rhythm of the murmuring voices. Maggie put on her duster and crouched at the head of the stairs.

Father strode to the heavy front door and threw it open. Betsy's father practically fell into the entryway. Sam followed him in. Maggie dashed to her room and quickly ran a brush through her hair before returning to her perch.

"Terrence!" Father said. "What is happening! How can I help?"

"I don't know, don't know. Betsy didn't come home yesterday and now this . . ." he held out a piece of paper with many crease marks across it.

"Oh my!" Father scanned the sheet. Mother ran to his side, putting a hand on his shoulder. He lowered the paper and looked at his friend. "What does this mean?"

"I think it means someone wanted to kidnap Maggie. But they got Betsy instead."

Maggie felt her heart thud before it started beating a mile a minute.

"Terrence, Thomas, come into the dining room. I'll pour everyone some coffee." Maggie could hear the shakiness in her mother's voice.

As the adults moved out of the entryway, Maggie waved at Sam. She padded her way down the stairs in stockinged feet and diverted him to the parlor.

"What's happening Sam? What did the letter say?"

Sam's usually ruddy complexion was pale. "The letter said something like 'We got the wrong girl.' Someone wanted to kidnap you, Maggie. But I guess they thought Betsy was you!"

"Oh, no! Was that all it said?"

"No—they said they would release Betsy if Father delivered you. Out to that house we rode to on Thursday."

"What should I do?"

"I don't know. Nothing. You can't go out there. But we can't leave Betsy there either." Sam shook his head, looked down at the floor. "I'll go out there. I'll dress . . . like you! Can I borrow some of your clothes?"

"I don't think they would fit. But—wait—I have a dress of my aunt's that she left for me yesterday. To grow into. Let's go upstairs. Try it on over your clothes."

Sam could get into the dress, but the back waist was unbuttoned.

"Don't try to talk me out of this idea, there's no time. I'll be back." Maggie bounded down the back stairway to her mother's sewing cabinet and grabbed the large shears. "I've been thinking of bobbing my hair anyway. We'll cut some off and make a switch for you." She gathered her hair together at the nape of her neck, tying it with two ribbons, keeping them about an inch apart. "Cut between the ribbons. Do it! No time to waste."

Sam had sweat on his upper lip. He grabbed the shears with shaking hands and did as Maggie commanded. The dull edge of the scissor's blade pressed against her neck. It took Sam effort to saw through her thick hair. Maggie gulped as her head felt lighter and she saw her shorn locks dangling from Sam's hand. She pulled her cloak from its peg and put it over Sam's head and shoulders. With pins and the ribbon, she was able to arrange the tail of hair so it fell over Sam's right shoulder. "I don't know if I can ride my bike in a skirt," Sam said.

"Father has the carriage ready for his trip to the train station. We'll take it." They slunk down the back stairs and Maggie grabbed Daisy's work cap and her own coat. Let's go." This was one time she was grateful that Father hadn't bought a Model T. She could drive with Blaze providing the power. She sat in front, with Sam in the back seat of her father's two-seat carriage.

Sam was silent until they reached the crest of the hill where they'd stopped Thursday night after making their get-away from the white, pointy-headed creatures. He directed Maggie to stop and ran toward a scarecrow in the field. After some effort, he pulled up the stake that anchored it and took the crude mannequin down. "This is going to have to be our parent," he said.

Maggie knew her father kept an older coat and hat in the back of the carriage, in case the weather changed when he was making house calls.

"I always knew you were smart," she said.

After they crested the hill, Maggie slowed Blaze to a walk. The day was gray and misty, although Maggie doubted it would rain. She felt herself shiver when they turned onto the lane leading to Dark Star Manor. "Stop a minute," Sam said. He was trying to put Maggie's father's extra coat and hat on the scarecrow. It took him a few minutes to succeed. "I hope it's misty enough that this scarecrow will fool them. Those criminals need to believe there's a parent here."

"True. I think they will believe it. And if they're wearing those get-ups, they won't be seeing well anyway." Sam situated the well-dressed scarecrow in the front passenger seat as best as he could. Scarecrows weren't designed to sit, and Sam struggled to keep it from sliding out.

Maggie had Blaze walk about a hundred feet further down the lane, until the carriage was directly across from the house. She could see pointed white hoods bobbing among the hedges and cornstalks west of the mansion. There were five of them, and they all appeared to be looking through the mist toward the carriage. A deep voice boomed, "Send us the doctor's girl!"

Sam placed a hand on the back of the scarecrow's neck and leaned it forward slightly out of the carriage door. He used his deepest voice and Maggie said a silent prayer that it wouldn't crack. "Send Betsy back across the field. They'll pass halfway. I won't send Maggie until I can see Betsy."

The white hoods moved together and two appeared to lean toward each other. The duo moved toward the house, and one opened the door. A few seconds later, Betsy appeared in her scout uniform, minus the hat. She began walking at the edge of the cornfield, escorted by one of the hooded kidnappers. Maggie thought her friend was limping.

Sam moved the scarecrow back into the passenger seat as best he could. He slipped past Maggie and stood on the side of the carriage away from direct view of the mansion.

"Now I'm glad you have my hair showing. Let me fix the hood. Take smallish steps." Maggie made a few adjustments to Sam's ensemble.

Sam nodded and stepped behind the carriage in front of the scarecrow, and then took small deliberate steps toward the approaching figures of Betsy and her escort.

Maggie was worried. She'd pictured Betsy approaching the carriage alone. She prayed again, for Sam's safety and wisdom as she peeked around the scarecrow.

Sam was within ten feet of Betsy and the hooded figure. Suddenly he ran toward the duo, pushed the hooded figure into the cornfield and picked up Betsy. The hooded figures watching at a distance began to run toward them.

Sam yelled, "Put father in the back seat." It took Maggie a second to realize he was talking about the scarecrow. Maggie managed to move it just as Sam and Betsy crashed into the carriage. Sam pushed Betsy in, before climbing over her and sitting almost on the scarecrow.

"Gi'dap, Blaze!" Maggie yelled. Blaze whinnied and cantered down the lane, away from the pointed heads, and away from the road they'd taken from town. Maggie hoped the lane wasn't a dead end.

"Easy, now," called Sam from the back. "Betsy is hurting. Try to avoid bumps."

Avoid bumps? Impossible. Maggie could see the top story of a small frame house peeking above the corn ahead. Maybe they could hide there. "Is anyone following us?" she asked Sam.

Sam had Betsy cradled in his lap; he craned his neck to get a view out the back window. "Not as far as I can tell. It will take a couple minutes to round up their horses or car. Don't know if they can use either wearing those white get-ups."

The house appeared to be neat and tidy and there was a fair-sized barn in the back. Maggie reined Blaze in and directed him to turn into the lane curving behind the house. She climbed down, feeling as if her legs were made of lead as she ran toward the home's back door. She pounded on it with her fist, yelling "Help! Help us!"

A blue-eyed woman peered at her from the door's small window. She cautiously opened the door about two inches. "Goodness, child. You gave me a fright! I saw this carriage and I thought the doctor was coming back!"

The doctor! "I'm the doctor's daughter! Some bad people are trying to hurt my friends and me. They kidnapped my friend, who is in the carriage now. She's in pain. Could we please hide in your barn?"

"Yes, the barn it will have to be. We've got chicken pox in this house. Circle your horse around and pull through. The big wagon is out in the hayfield now, you should have room."

Maggie ran back to the carriage. "Hang on Betsy. C'mon, Blaze." He followed her commands and circled back to the north entrance to the shed. Plenty of room to pull in down the middle. Blaze halted, and Maggie got out of the cab and gathered up some hay to throw in front of him. *I know father will pay for it.*

She stepped back up into the carriage. "Betsy, how are you? What happened?" Betsy's skin was as pale as white marble.

"My stomach hurts. They kept me in the basement! I had some bad smelling water to drink and nothing to eat." She closed her eyes. "I just want to go home."

"I know, I know," Maggie said. "Betsy, I feel so bad. They wanted me, but I guess they got us mixed up. Did they take you from the parade? I couldn't find you afterwards."

"Yes." Betsy struggled to speak. "Yes, they did." She closed her eyes.

Maggie looked at Sam. His eyes told the story, he was worried, too.

"Children! Children!" The woman from the house stood in the doorway of the shed. "I'm not coming closer due to the pox. Two men on horseback just left. They forced their way into the house, said they were looking for you. I told them I didn't know anything and we had the pox. When they saw my youngest, they left in a hurry. My husband is riding our workhorse into town to get your father. Hopefully, he'll be out here soon."

"He'll probably come with Betsy and Sam's father," Maggie said. "He was at our house when we left."

"Shouldn't be too long. Our workhorse is slow. But your folks will probably bring a car back, I reckon. Be patient. And quiet. I'm going to close the door to the shed."

"Thanks, ma'am," Maggie said.

Betsy let out a long breath. Maggie was encouraged to see a subtle smile on her lips. "It's not far to town," Betsy said. "And Father's car is fast."

"You're right, Sis. Be strong. Father will be here within the hour."

Sam was likely right about that. "You know, Sam . . . I think you can take off your costume now," Maggie said.

Betsy's smile became just a little wider. "Yes, up close, you don't look very believable as a girl."

Sam shed the borrowed clothes. "And that is a good thing." Once the cloak was off, the pinned switch of Maggie's hair was evident and odd-looking.

"What is that?" Betsy leaned forward gingerly. "It feels like real hair."

"It is real hair," Maggie affirmed. "Mine."

Betsy's eyes became round before they closed. "Oh, Maggie. I'm so sorry."

"Don't be. I was determined to get my hair bobbed one way or the other." She squeezed her friend's hand.

Betsy laughed a little at that before putting a hand on her stomach. "Oooh. It hurts when I laugh."

"Just lie still, Sis. Dad will be here soon."

"All right. First, I need to tell Maggie a secret, though." She beckoned to her friend, who leaned close to her. Betsy whispered a few words before falling back on the straw.

Sam caught Maggie's eye. "Don't let her fall asleep," he said. Maggie nodded. They continued talking in low tones about the parade, about school, anything they could think of, to keep Betsy distracted.

Blaze gave a soft whinny just a second before Maggie heard her father's voice outside the shed's door. "Father!" She stood and ran to the door as it opened from the outside.

Betsy's father entered first. "Where's my girl?" he said, searching the shed, trying to force his eyes to adjust to the dimness. "Betsy!"

"I'm here, Father. I'm here."

He located his daughter on the straw and ran to her, kneeling at her side.

"You're alive, you're alive . . . ," he kept repeating.

"She said they made her drink some bad-smelling water," Sam said to Dr. O'Brien, who had one arm around Maggie. "And she said her stomach hurts. When she laughs, especially."

Dr. O'Brien gave his daughter a quick squeeze before stepping into the cab of the carriage. He tossed out the scarecrow before returning with a small bag.

"This is my emergency bag, the one I always keep in the carriage, just in case." He took out his stethoscope and listened to Betsy's lungs and stomach. Then he pressed the back of his hand to her forehead.

"I don't think she has a fever. Her chest and belly sound normal enough. But we need to get her home."

The two fathers conferred. Mr. Sullivan felt calm enough to drive.

Betsy would be moved to her family's automobile, and Sam would ride home with them. Maggie would go home with her father in the carriage. Dr. O'Brien would call on the Sullivans later and examine Betsy more completely.

Maggie helped her father put the scarecrow and Sam's costume, with her hair still attached, into the back of the carriage. They climbed in the front seat and directed Blaze out of the shed. Then, Betsy's father drove inside, close to where Betsy was laying on the straw. He and Sam then assisted her into the back seat of the automobile where she could recline. They drove off; Maggie and her father followed in the carriage.

"Where did you go?" he wanted to know. "We were all scared out of our minds when we discovered that you and Sam had gone!"

Maggie hung her head. "I'm sorry, Father. But we had to do something to help Betsy. We couldn't wait. We got her back. And neither Sam nor I got hurt."

Her father nodded his head. "Those are all things to be thankful for. But you look strange. Why are you wearing that silly hat?"

"It's Daisy's. I'll tell you soon, I promise. When we get home."

They were passing the old mansion where she and Sam had rescued Betsy. "That's where they had Betsy." Maggie cast a few side-long glances to the north, trying to scan the yard and fields for any white figures. There were none, as far as she could tell without turning her head.

Her father nodded. Blaze knew the way and Father didn't speak again until they reached their home. "Let's go inside and let your mother know you're fine. Then, I'm going to Betsy's house to examine her, and take my medicines along."

Mother looked frantic, wide-eyed with her hair falling out of its bun. "Maggie!" She wrapped her daughter in a crushing embrace. "I'm so glad you're back, safe."

Father got his leather bag out of his office closet toward the back of the house. "I'm going to the Sullivan's. Back soon. I want to look at Betsy again."

Mother planted a kiss on his cheek before turning to Maggie. "Get yourself upstairs, young lady. Clean up a little bit." She sighed and a tear came to her eye. "I'm so glad you're home."

Maggie trudged up the wide staircase. She removed her cap and looked at her reflection in the mirror. What a fright she looked! She had to laugh. Her hair did look sawed-off, but there was plenty to work with for a bob. She put on her Sunday dress and arranged Daisy's work cap back on her head, tucking in the hair that stuck out. She made her bed and sat on its edge.

She didn't want to go back downstairs until Father returned. He'd be more matter-of-fact about her haircut than Mother. She reviewed the morning's events, going over them several times.

She heard Blaze whinny as Father returned. He got the horse and carriage returned to the shed before walking into the house. Maggie saw him greet Mother in the downstairs hallway, kissing her on the lips.

She walked down the stairs, making her footfalls loud enough that they would be heard.

"Maggie! Come into the dining room," Father said. "Mother, get Tad, too. I think we need to have a family discussion."

"Take off that silly hat!" Mother insisted.

Maggie obeyed. Mother gasped so loudly that the cat jumped off the sofa in the next room and ran for her hiding place in the kitchen. "What did you do?"

"Well, we needed Sam to look like me . . . I'll explain."

"Fine," Father said. "Let's sit down at the table. And Maggie, you need something to eat." Tad had two ginger cookies in hand. Mother disappeared into the kitchen and returned with a glass of milk and a plate of apple muffins, setting them in front of her daughter.

Maggie downed half the milk and one muffin in short order. Then Father said, "Maggie, tell us what happened once you left the house. Then I'll share some things with you all."

Maggie told about her haircut, Sam's costume, their successful trip to the house to exchange one prisoner for another, and how they'd managed to elude the culprits. Father sat back and shook his head.

"Well, I can't say I'm not proud. But please don't ever, ever do anything like that again."

Maggie found herself crying. Hard. But she didn't feel sad. Maybe she was crazy?

Mother came to sit beside her, giving her a squeeze. "My brave girl," she said.

Father leaned forward. "Well, I learned something when I went back to take another look at Betsy. Once I got to the Sullivan place and opened my bag, I could tell someone had tampered with my medicines."

Mother sat back, a worried look on her face.

"I didn't do it!" Tad said.

"I know that, son," Father said. "Give me a minute. The vial that had been opened contained a medicine that can make people sleepy. It can also give them a stomach ache, an unfortunate side effect. I think someone took some of that medicine, mixed it with water, and gave it to Betsy once she was captured."

"Who . . . ?" Mother began.

Father's mouth hardened into a straight line. "Daisy is not welcome back in this house. If by chance, she does return, do not let her in."

Tad and Maggie exchanged glances. Maggie thought Tad's eyes could pop out of his head.

"Children, I need to tell you some things I'd been trying to protect you from. I wanted your childhood to be carefree and safe." He took a deep breath. "Remember that group of people in white hoods who paraded down Main Street a couple of years ago?"

Maggie nodded. She was only nine at the time but had a hazy memory of white-robed figures marching down Main Street. There appeared to be hundreds of them.

"That group calls themselves the Ku Klux Klan. While they claim to be in favor of the family and America, they hate several groups of people in this country, including Catholics. And right now, in Indiana, their leader is in jail for murder. A physician friend of mine will testify at the trial next month. Maybe someone in the Klan thought that kidnapping the Catholic doctor's daughter was a good idea. Maybe they hoped they'd get some ransom, maybe they just wanted to do something hateful." He sighed and pushed back his chair. "I need to let someone know what's been going on. I'll go downtown and make some inquiries. In the meantime, keep all doors locked. No one comes in until I get back, understood? And if any adult male develops chickenpox in the next few days, I'm going to be suspicious."

Everyone nodded, including Mother. Father paused before opening the door.

"I understand a visitor will be arriving later. Sent by Mrs. Sullivan." He winked at his daughter.

Maggie's mind had been struggling to merge the morning's events with the information Father had provided. She'd almost forgotten Betsy's whispered secret back in the barn.

She nodded. "Betsy told me she would ask her mother to send her hair stylist. To properly bob my hair."

THE MANY WIVES OF AXEL FLYNN

BY STEPHEN M. TERRELL

Makayla bent down to look into the aged face of her great-grandmother. The old woman shifted a bit in her rocking chair. She slowly awoke, revealing eyes that were once a dazzling green, now dulled by nearly 90 years.

"Oh, Makayla, dear," Keana said, her voice catching a bit as she awoke. "My, I must have dozed off. That happens a lot these days. It's so good to see you."

"I've got someone for you to meet," Makayla said. "This is Tom Wilkey. He's the young man I've told you about. Tom, this is my Gramma K—Keana Fitzgerald."

A tall fair-skinned man in his mid-20s stepped forward, delicately holding out his hand. "Good to meet you, Mrs. Fitzgerald."

"Call me Keana." She shook Tom's outstretched hand with surprising strength. "I'm old, but I'm not feeble. You can actually shake my hand. It won't break."

Tom grinned in surprise. "Will do, uh, Keana."

"Gram, I wanted you to meet Tom because we're getting married."

Keena's eyes sparkled. She looked toward Tom. "You didn't get my great granddaughter knocked up, did you?"

"Gram!" Makala blurted, her face turning pink. "I'm not pregnant."

Keana winked mischievously. "You young people didn't invent sex. Back in my day, people said that when a couple got married, the first baby could come any time. The rest took nine months."

Makayla and Tom laughed through their embarrassment.

"That's the thing about being almost 90. You don't have time to beat around the bush."

The conversation digressed into how Makala's first year as a teacher was going and plans for a summer wedding the following year.

"I hope I'm still around," Keana said.

"Oh, you'll be there," Makala said.

"So why are you two dressed in that get up?"

"We're on our way to a Halloween Party. We're dressed up from the musical Hamilton. I'm Eliza and Tom is Hamilton."

"Watch for that Burr fellow," Keana said, then her brows furrowed. "Be careful. I don't much like Halloween. Too much bad stuff happens."

Makayla waved her hand, deflecting Keana's concerns. "Oh Gram, it's just some fun. A party. You went to parties when you were young, didn't you?"

Keana nodded. "Yes, child. Me and my twin sister, your great aunt Moira, rest her soul, we went to lots of parties. But we stopped going to Halloween parties."

"Why's that, Gram?"

"Pull those up," Keana said, pointing an arthritic finger at two nearby chairs. "I have a story to tell."

I HAVEN'T SPOKEN about this in seventy years. This goes back to the fall of 1951 when Moira and I were college freshmen.

We grew up in Franklin. It was just a little farm town back then. Moira and me both had bright red hair and green eyes. Everybody knew us, but they couldn't tell us apart, so they just called us the Irish twins.

We both wanted to be teachers. After high school, off we went to Ball State. It was just a little teachers college back then, but it seemed so big to us. We were so young, so naive. Or maybe we were just stupid.

We made some friends and started getting invited to parties. I think the fact that we were twins and redheads made us a bit of an item on campus.

Halloween came along. One of the girls down the hall got invited to a fraternity party, and told us to come along. Moira and me hadn't been to a Halloween party since we were 10 or 11. It was kids' stuff where we grew up, but we thought it would be fun.

We dressed like the Bobbsey Twins. Grown up Bobbsey Twins, that is. It was a big party. Lots of boys there. And beer. We'd never tasted beer before, but we drank it because everyone else was.

As the night went on, this one boy started paying a lot of attention to us. He wasn't being pushy or anything, just fun. His name was Denny. I think his last name was Conrad, but I'm not sure after all these years. He was tall and handsome, a real charmer to small-town girls.

He was a senior engineering student at Purdue, so the fact he was paying attention to two freshmen turned our heads. His younger brother was a member of the fraternity that was holding the party. He said there weren't any girls at Purdue, so he came to Ball State on weekends. We danced, and flirted, and he sneaked a kiss or two from both of us.

Women's dorms had hours. I guess it was to protect our honor, or something like that. On weekends, freshmen had to be back at midnight. Looking back, it all seems so silly. Denny encouraged us not to leave. We already knew how to sneak back in the dorm after hours, so we stayed.

Denny told us a couple of scary Halloween stories and kept bringing us beer. It was two o'clock or so when the party started winding down.

"You want to see something really spooky?" he asked. "I grew up not far from here. There's this cemetery out in the country. It's where most of my family is buried. There's an old story about ghosts that sometimes appear during the night. Wanna go see?" When we hesitated, he added, "You're not scared, are you?"

Moira and me were probably more drunk than we thought, and we had a bit of a wild side. We shouldn't have gone, but he was cute, and we were having a good time. And after all, a dare is a dare. So, we said sure.

Denny had this big black Packard. We all sat in the front seat. There was plenty of room, but Moira squeezed right up against Denny, and I slid in next to her. Denny drove. It wasn't ten minutes until we were on this two-lane blacktop heading out into the country.

"What's this big bad scary ghost thing all about?" Moira asked.

"You'll find out," Denny said. I saw him put his hand on Moira's knee and slide it up a bit. Moira didn't slap his hand or move away from him.

Denny drove for half an hour or so. We went through some little crossroads town, then turned down a gravel country road. We were way out in the country, not a light to be seen. I was starting to get a bit uneasy.

Denny slowed the car and started looking. "It's right around here someplace."

"What?" I asked.

"Stone Creek Cemetery. It's near a creek and some woods. There's an iron arch over the entrance, but it's hard to see."

"There!" Moira shouted, pointing a finger.

"Damn, those green eyes of yours must see in the dark. That's it." Denny turned onto a gravel path. "The tombstone we're looking for is just up here at the top of the hill."

Denny drove slowly, gravel crunching underneath his tires. After a short distance, he stopped and turned off the car. "We're here."

Moira gave a nervous giggle. We all slid out the driver's side door. I had never been in a cemetery after dark, and as far as I knew, neither had Moira. I could feel a chill creep up my spine and the fine hair on my arms pricking to attention.

There was not another light in sight. Not a farmhouse, not a barn.

Nothing. Other than the popping of the cooling engine, we were in complete silence. Summer insects and birds were long gone. The cemetery was cradled by mostly-bare trees with few leaves left for the wind to rustle. A gnarled ancient oak stood in solitary silhouette; its giant branches raised like misshaped hands beseeching heaven. I thought I heard the faint gurgle of the nearby creek carried on the wind, but before I could be certain, the sound faded into nothingness like a shadow in fog.

Heavy clouds danced in front of the full moon, casting it in shades of garnet and rust. Around us, tombstones stood at attention like so many soldiers standing rank and file, their height measuring in death the place each person occupied in life. Decay was carried in the air—drying leaves, stands of corn shocks, and fields filled with the last of drying soybeans awaiting harvest.

Someplace distant, an owl hooted. I felt myself jump inside my skin.

"Spooky, isn't it?" Denny finally said, a smile crossing his face.

Moira and I nodded.

"I've got a flashlight. I'll show you my great uncle's tombstone."

Denny's flashlight swept across headstones as he led us in a winding route to the top of a small hill. The light stopped on an obelisk of gray granite, one of the taller headstones. Carved into the stone, untouched by age, was a single name: FLYNN.

"Here it is. This is my great uncle's tombstone." We studied it for a moment. "Come around to the other side," Denny said. "That's where the story starts."

We followed him, stepping between the grave markers. Denny moved the light onto the engraving on the monument.

AXEL FLYNN

1867—1922

Truth lies with him and God

Underneath the inscription, carved into the stone, was a nearly full-sized axe.

"My dad said they put the axe on the tombstone because it was what everybody called him, but no one knows for sure."

We stood there looking for a long time. It was me who finally spoke up. "What a strange epitaph. What does it mean?"

Denny ignored my question. He moved a few steps to his right and shined the light on a plain sandstone grave marker. The name was weather-worn but still legible.

AIMEE O'CONNOR FLYNN
1865—1893
Beloved wife of Axel Flynn

"That was his first wife," Denny said. "She was a beauty with long red hair and green eyes, just like you two."

"But she died so young," Moira said.

"Lots of people died young back then," I said.

"A couple of years after Aimee died, Axel went on a trip and came back with his second wife." Denny shined the light on another, nearly identical stone.

JUDE MURPHY FLYNN
1869—1899
Beloved wife of Axel Flynn

"Jude was his second wife?" I asked.

Denny nodded. He swung his flashlight over three more markers lined up in a row.

Oona Reilly Flynn
1877—1905

Nora Byrne Flynn
1887—1911

Erin O'Neill Flynn
1893—1918

"THESE WERE HIS WIVES, TOO," Denny said. "All five of them. All of them Irish. All with red hair. All with green eyes."

I felt a chill. Maybe it was the coldness of the night setting in, but I didn't think so. I looked toward Moira and could see she was feeling the same eerie coldness.

"Oh my God!" Moira said. "Five of them. And they were so young. What happened?"

Denny smirked a bit. "Five wives, all young Irish redheads, and all died after only four or five years with old Uncle Ax."

"Did anybody look into this?" I asked.

"Uncle Ax's brother, Cormack, was the doctor around here. He signed the death certificates on all of them. They died of typhoid or tuberculosis or some fever. At least that's what Ax's brother put on the death certificates. People had suspicions, but nobody could prove anything."

"That's terrible," Moira said.

Denny clicked off his flashlight. He walked over between Moira and me and put his arms around our waists and pulled us close. He spoke with his voice just above a whisper.

"The ghosts of Ax's five wives haunt this cemetery." Moira and I rolled our eyes, but Denny continued, his voice deadly serious. "They rise from their graves looking for girls with red hair and green eyes to take away with them."

Denny pulled us even tighter, his hand sliding under our breasts. He spoke, separating each word. "Looking . . . for . . . girls . . . just . . . like . . . you."

The lonely tremolo of a screech owl carried on a frigid gust of wind. I felt a chill start at the back of my head and slowly crawl down my spine and into my soul. I tried to fight back my fright with reason. There were no such things as ghosts. But I sensed my faith in reason deserting me.

"Of course, you girls are lucky. I'm here to protect you. Fortunately, I share my uncle's preference for redheads with green eyes." Denny's hand moved down, trying to slide inside the waistband of my underwear. "If you're nice to me, I can keep you safe."

Next to me, Moira gasped.

I grabbed Denny's hand, twisted it and shoved. He lost his balance and fell away from Moira, awkwardly twisting. He landed hard, his shoulder crashing against a tombstone.

Even in the dark, I could see that Moira's face was pale. The buttons of her blouse were undone. I put a protective arm around her and could feel her shaking.

"Bitches!" Denny hissed.

"I want to go home," Moira said, her voice trembling.

"Moira's right," I said, my voice filled with rage. "You need to take us home. Now."

Denny got up, brushing dirt and grass from his pants. "I guess you aren't women yet," he said. "I'll take you home. First, I gotta take a piss. Turn around while I take a leak."

Growing up around farm boys, Moira and I had seen boys pee lots of times, but we turned as he walked toward some trees.

"What a creep," Moira said.

I nodded. "Just brought us out here hoping to get in our pants. Well, lesson learned."

It was then that we heard the car start and gravel being thrown by the Packard's spinning wheels.

Moira and I both yelled. We ran toward the sound only to see red taillights swerving out of the cemetery and onto the country road.

"You bastard!" Moira yelled. I had never heard her swear before.

The car was gone. We were left in the dark and cold and stillness of the cemetery. We stood there for several minutes, staring into the blackness in anger and disbelief.

After a moment, Moira spoke up, her voice quivering. "Keana, what are we going to do?"

As we stood there, a banshee-like scream cut through the stillness —shrill, piercing and not quite human. There was a long silence, then another scream. Moira and I clutched on to each other.

"What was that?" Moira asked.

"Maybe an animal," I responded. "What else could it be?"

"That didn't sound like any animal I've ever heard," Moira said. "It sounded like someone getting their skin ripped off."

"It was an animal," I said, trying to reassure myself. But I wasn't convinced.

Something moved. I didn't quite see it. It was more an awareness that something unseen had crossed behind us. I could tell that Moira sensed it, too.

We turned back and faced the headstones. There was nothing there, yet something seemed changed, different.

"Did you see something, Moira?"

"I'm not sure. You think maybe Denny is sneaking back to scare us?"

"He's not had time to get back here on foot, and we would have heard his car."

"Maybe he was right about the ghosts. Maybe there are ghosts here."

"Don't be a ninny, Moira. You know there aren't ghosts." My voice betrayed that I wasn't as confident as my words. "We're way out in the country. There are woods all around us, and a creek back over there someplace, so there's got to be lots of animals. They make all sorts of sounds."

Moira held me tighter. "I'm cold, Keana. And scared. What are we going to do?"

"Well, we're gonna castrate that son of a bitch when we find him."

Moira snickered. "I'll hold him down and you snip them off."

We pulled each other closer and laughed, driven more by nerves and cold than humor. Soon we were shaking with laughter that rolled into tears.

Then we heard a scream again.

Our laughter stopped. Once more, it seemed something unseen moved around us.

We stood perfectly still, our breathing shallow, listening to our hearts pounding inside our chests. We waited. Long silent minutes passed.

"Moira, we don't know where we are. We don't know how far we are from some farmhouse. There are no lights around anyplace, and the clouds have covered the moon. I think we need to find a spot where we are protected from the wind, huddle together to keep warm and wait for it to start getting light."

"You mean spend all night here in the cemetery? Couldn't we just leave here and find someplace else?"

I looked at the tiny luminous dial on my watch. "It's after three o'clock. It starts getting light an hour or so before sunrise. That's only a couple of hours from now. If we start tromping around, we could twist an ankle or break a leg. It's not too cold tonight and we're dressed pretty warm. We won't freeze. I think it's best if we just stay put until it gets light enough we can see where we're going."

Moira hesitated, then nodded.

"Let's get up against that big headstone," I said. "It will give us a windbreak."

We trudged up to Axel Flynn's monument, and sat down on the base, leaning against the cold smoothness of the side of the stone engraved with only the name FLYNN. We held each other close for warmth. To take our mind off the situation, we sang camping songs from our scouting days. There were no more screams. Exhaustion and the unfamiliar effects of alcohol gradually overcame our fears, and we dozed.

A mechanical rumble woke me. The sun wasn't up yet, but deep oranges and purples from the not-yet-risen sun painted the morning sky.

Moira and I kept tight against each other all through the night, but now that I was stirring, I felt cold and stiff. I stood, stretched, and scanned the landscape looking for the source of the sound.

A battered rust-colored pickup truck chugged into the cemetery, its dim headlights barely lighting the ground before it. The truck rattled over several bumps. Then there was a backfire, the truck stopped, and the driver's door opened.

"Moira, wake up. Someone's here."

Moira stirred, rubbing her eyes.

"Wake up. There's someone here. We can get him to help."

The truck door slammed shut. An old man wearing worn coveralls, shit-kicker boots, and a battered cap stood next to the truck, looking toward where we stood. He spit a reddish-brown spray onto the gravel at his feet. His voice was as harsh and thick as his tobacco spittle.

"What the hell you doing up there? You ain't supposed to be here!"

"Sir, can you help us? We got left here last night. We need help." All the fears and cold of the night burst in a stream of tears and sobs.

Moira put her arms around me. She, too, was crying.

The man swore to himself, hitched up his coveralls, and walked toward us, limping heavily on his left leg. His skin was weathered and deeply creased. His right eye was milky and stared off at an odd angle. There was a scar down one cheek and two fingers were missing off one hand.

He stopped just a few feet from us, looking us over with his good eye. "You twins, ain't ya?"

"We are. I'm Keana Sullivan and this is my sister Moira."

"You been up here all night?"

"We got here about three, I guess."

"Out here on some Halloween dare, I suppose. Damn kids always coming out here on Halloween." The man spit out another stream of tobacco. "I look after the cemetery. Halloween nights, I keep watch until about one to chase off kids coming out here. But you're older than I usually get. Guess you showed up after I went back home."

"We're sorry, sir," Moira said, her voice still catching amid her sobs. "We came out here with a boy. Then he just dumped us. Drove off in his car and left us here."

The caretaker shook his head as he reached into a pocket on his coveralls and brought out a pack of Red Man. He pulled out a pocket knife with his deformed hand, smoothly flipped open the blade and cut off a plug of tobacco, inserting it into his cheek. He carefully returned the knife and tobacco pack to his pockets.

He spoke with his cheek bulging, but his words were surprisingly clear. "He just up and left you?"

We both nodded in response. "It was awful," Moira said. "We were scared and cold, then we heard these horrible screams during the night. I never heard anything like it."

The caretaker rubbed his gray-bristled cheek puffed full of tobacco. "Them screams most likely was a fox."

"A fox?" I said. "You sure? It was awful."

"Them foxes can make awful sounds at night. Sounds just like a woman's scream, only worse. Don't hear 'em often this time of year, but once in a while you do."

"Thank God you came when you did," Moira said. "We need help, Mister . . ."

"Casey Gant. Just call me Casey. Me and the misses got us a farm just a piece down the road," he said, pointing with his good hand. "I'm the caretaker of sorts for the cemetery. Don't get paid nothing, but I look after the place. Keep the fences mended, grass mowed. So, what were you doin' out here?"

I dried my tears on my sleeve. "We just came out to see some gravestone. Denny, the boy that left us, he told us a ghost story, then started trying to, well, do stuff. When we didn't do what he wanted, he just took off."

"Good you stood up to him. Girls like you need to stand up to men like that." After a pause, he added, "They ain't no good." Casey looked off as if seeing something in the distance. I turned toward his gaze, but there was nothing there.

Casey took a deep breath and spit a stream of tobacco on the grass. "You shouldn't have come out here."

"We're sorry," I said.

"Bet he was showing you ol' Axel Flynn's stone—that and his five wives."

My mouth dropped open. "Yes. You know the story?"

"Oh, hell, everybody around here knows that story. When I was a young man, Ax was still around. Him and his brother, Doc Flynn. Ax was a mean old cuss. Guess he deserved what he got."

"Denny, the boy that brought us out here, he told us that all of his wives had red hair and green eyes, like me and Moira. He tried to scare us. Said the ghosts of those wives come out at night looking for redheads like us to take back with them."

Casey spit again, a long reddish-brown string falling back onto the leg of his coveralls. With the back of a calloused hand, he wiped it away. "Well, he may have scared you, but he got the story back-asswards. All those wives were redheads with green eyes. They were all pretty, too, just like the two of you. But he got the ghost part all wrong."

"You mean, there really are ghosts?" Moira asked.

"They's people around here who swear they seen the ghosts of those women. I seen things around this cemetery that I can't rightly explain. I ain't ready to say it's ghosts. But then again, I ain't sayin' it ain't."

"You said he got the ghost part wrong," I said. "What did he get wrong?"

"Hell's bells, girl. Does it make any sense to you that those wives would be coming after the spirits of girls like themselves? If they was looking for revenge, it wouldn't be on girls like you, would it? Ax is the one that killed 'em. He's the one they'd want to get revenge on. Leastwise, that's the story."

Moira and I exchanged glances. Casey was right. In the cold light of morning, it didn't seem that ghosts of the wives would be after us.

"That boy didn't mention Ax's sixth wife, did he?"

We both shook our heads.

"Old Ax didn't stop at five. After Erin was dead, he went off to Chicago and got himself a sixth wife. Fiona Kelly was her name. Just like the rest, she was a redhead with green eyes that could see right through you. My, she was a looker. Them others was pretty—well I didn't meet the first two, but I met the others. They was pretty, but this Fiona, she was special. Just a tiny thing, mind you. She had hair like fire and huge eyes, and a smile that was so big and bright that you couldn't help but smile back. And she sang everyplace she went. It was so sad."

"Sad?" Moira asked.

"Everybody 'round here could see what was happening. Ax was poisoning off these girls, and his brother, Doc Flynn, was covering up for him, sayin' they died of fever or consumption or some such shit."

"People knew?" I asked .

"Damnation, girl. Just cause we ain't educated 'round here don't mean we're stupid." Casey rounded a ball of tobacco juice in his cheek, then spit a wad down at his feet. "Some people around here started talking to Fiona, warning her about what happened to the other wives. We told her to take off while she still could. We even offered to pay for a train ticket to help her get away."

"Didn't she believe you?"

"Fiona was lost," Casey said. "She started telling people about dreams she had. Ax's wives came to her in dreams, telling her Ax killed them, and she needed to do something or he would kill her. But her family was dead or back in Ireland, and she didn't have no place to go. We all figured sooner or later, we'd find her dead."

"Most days, Ax stopped by the post office to get his mail, and he'd hang around the seed store playing checkers. Late one summer, people started noticing that Ax wasn't around. He just stopped showing up. Nobody seen him or Fiona for several weeks. Finally, a couple neighbors stopped by his farm. It didn't look like anybody had been there in weeks. They found Ax, or what was left of him, in the barn. He was hacked up pretty good with an axe blade left in his skull."

Our hands went to our mouths.

"What about Fiona? Did they find her?"

Casey shook his head. "Nope. Never did. Her clothes was gone. Everybody figured she got him before he got her, then took off. The Sheriff looked for her a little bit, but not too hard. Sometimes justice takes its own path and everyone is willing to accept it."

Casey shifted his weight. "You seen that axe on the monument there behind you?"

We nodded.

"Tombstone maker was having a little joke." Casey circled to the other side of Flynn's tombstone. "He put that axe on there as a reminder about how Ax got what was coming to him. The epitaph, too." Casey looked down at the stone. "Either of you girls hurt?"

No," I said. "We're tired and cold, but we're fine."

Casey's weathered face betrayed puzzlement. "Come here and take a look at this."

We walked to the other side of the stone and looked at the engraving of the axe. The blade carved in the stone was covered in red.

Casey removed his cap, and scratched at a tangle of thinning white hair. "I ain't never seen nothing like that."

"There's more," Moira said. She pointed to a trail of dark-red splotches leading across the grass from the tombstone toward the woods.

"Damnit!" Casey said. "Probably a deer that some hunter shot but didn't kill. Always hate to see that. You don't get a kill shot on an animal, you need to track it down and put it out of its suffering. If you don't do that, you shouldn't hunt. You girls stay here while I track it down."

"We're going with you," Moira said. "We're not staying here alone."

Casey looked like he would argue, but he didn't. He had us wait while he went to his truck and retrieved a shotgun, carrying it with the barrel broken over the crook of his arm. "Let's see what we got."

As the sun started to creep over the eastern horizon, we walked slowly through the grass and dried leaves, following a thin trail of dark red splotches around the tombstones. The drops seemed heavier the further we went. The blood led into the surrounding woods, where a lightly traveled footpath moved downhill toward the sound of rushing water.

"Fishermen use this path to get down to Stone Creek," he explained. "Animals follow it, too. Whatever it is, there's more blood as we go."

We followed the path around a bend. We saw a black car wedged between several bushes with the front smashed against a rugged hackberry tree. The nameplate on the trunk said PACKARD.

"It's Denny's car," I said.

"Denny? That boy you were with last night?"

Moira and I nodded.

"Stay here," Casey said. Moira and I didn't argue.

Casey made his way through the brush to the driver's door. "Oh, Jesus," he said. A few minutes later, he pushed his way through the brush back to where Moira and I stood.

"If that's his car, he didn't get far. Maybe he was circling back to scare you and lost control. Almost got to the creek. There's another blood trail leading from the car. He must have hit his head pretty good. Maybe that's where the blood came from. Let's see if we can find him."

We searched through the woods and along the creek for half an hour, shouting Denny's name. Casey waded across the creek on some rocks and searched on the other side, but he couldn't find a trace of Denny, not even footprints.

"We better call the Sheriff. He'll get some people out here to hunt for this boy."

We walked back to Casey's truck. The inside of the cab smelled of oil and manure, but we were thankful to be leaving the cemetery.

About a mile down the road, Casey pulled into a rutted driveway. Chickens scattered out of the way as Casey drove up to a simple white farmhouse.

We were met at the door by a tiny elderly woman who lacked an inch or so of being five feet tall. Her threadbare pink housecoat hung nearly to the floor. Long white hair cascaded over her shoulders and halfway down her back. She greeted us with a large smile and held the door open with long slender fingers. She seemed unsurprised, like Casey regularly brought young women home with him from the cemetery.

"This is my wife, Anne," Casey said to us, then turned to his wife. "Some boy dumped these girls at the cemetery last night."

"Oh my," Anne said. "You dears come in here and sit down. You must be cold and hungry." A faint accent of some kind hung at the edge of her words, but not enough to be identified.

"Well, the boy got his comeuppance," Casey said. "He wrecked his car. I gotta call the Sheriff. Can you fix these girls some breakfast?"

Moira and I sat at the kitchen table. Casey's wife brought blankets and draped them over us, then went about fixing a breakfast of coffee, biscuits with gravy, ham, eggs and potatoes. After Casey called the sheriff, he sat with us while Anne cooked, softly singing something about the blood of Jesus. Never had food smelled so good.

Within an hour, the Sheriff and a dozen farmers congregated in front of the house, some with hounds baying and pulling at long tethers. They headed out to search the woods, fields, and along the creek.

While they were gone, Anne doted on us. She spoke only a few words, offering us tea and showing us to two overstuffed chairs near a woodstove in the living room. With full stomachs and little sleep, I dozed. When I awoke from a brief nap, I saw Anne gently singing to Moira as she slept.

Casey and a deputy returned to the house in mid-afternoon. The deputy, tall and lanky, didn't look much older than us. The sheriff sent him to drive us back to our dorms at Ball State.

"Have you found anything?" I asked.

"No sign of him," the deputy said. "Sheriff figures that he hit his head when he crashed. He must have got himself confused. Wandered up in the cemetery leaving that blood trail. Then he made his way back to his car and somehow stumbled into the creek. Current is pretty strong there. Hate to say it, but the sheriff thinks his body will turn up downstream in a few days."

"You ask me, it was them girls," Casey said.

"Us?" Moira and I shouted, nearly in unison.

"No, not you. Ax's wives. I think they did it."

The deputy laughed. "Casey, you been lookin' after that cemetery too long."

"Well, how'd you explain the blood on that tombstone axe? And all that blood in the car? That weren't no head bump caused that."

"We'll know when we find the body," the deputy said. He realized his indiscretion. "I'm sorry ladies. I shouldn't have said that. I guess I better get you girls back to school."

Casey walked out the door, heading back to join the search at the cemetery. The deputy walked out with Moira. I started to leave, but turned. Anne was walking out of the room, carrying our dirty tea cups, singing softly to herself.

"You sing beautifully, Fiona. Thank you for looking after us."

Casey's wife stopped in mid-step. She hesitated, then turned to face me.

"Your white hair is beautiful," I said. "People's hair color changes. And you can change your name. But you can't change that tiny size of yours, or the way you love to sing, or the color of your eyes."

The elderly woman looked back at me through emerald eyes and gave a small nod. "Anne is my middle name," she said quietly. A long silence passed before she spoke again. "You know, Casey saved my life. He's gruff sometimes, but he is the kindest man you will ever meet. You're not going to say anything, are you?"

"Of course not."

Fiona's face brightened into a beautiful full smile. "You and your sister take care of each other." Then she turned and walked into the kitchen.

They never found Denny. I kept checking the newspaper for some fisherman to snag a body caught on a sunken log, but nothing like that happened. A year or two later, the Army Corp of Engineers dammed up that creek for a new reservoir. By the time Moira and I graduated, a lake covered the whole area, and with it, the graves of Axel Flynn and his wives.

KEANA LOOKED up from her near trance. "I'm tired now, child," she said. "Don't mind an old woman and her stories. My memory probably isn't very good, so who knows how much of that happened. But that's the way I remember it. Now you and your boyfriend go ahead and go to that party, and have a good time."

Makayla got up and gave her Gramma K a kiss on the cheek. As she leaned back, she could hear Keana's rhythmic breathing. The old woman was asleep.

THE MYSTERY OF THE MIRROR
BY SHARI HELD

I watch them, the young Americans with trendy $200 haircuts and designer clothes straight from the front pages of Vogue. I listen to their carefree laughter and idle chatter regularly punctuated with a giggle or an OMG! They haven't a care in the world. Their charmed lives lie ahead of them. Dinner and dancing with handsome men who drive fancy sports cars. Trips to Europe and exotic islands. They take it all for granted. Like their lives are unfolding in a script of their own making.

I was like them once. I never thought tragedy could befall me. Not me. After all, I was the blond, cornflower-eyed youngest daughter of a wealthy entrepreneur. His beloved golden girl.

Ah, look at the time! I'd better get to the kitchen. The cinnamon buns will be coming out of the oven soon. They smell so heavenly I can almost taste them.

"FIONA, you've got the best dad," Ginny said. "I can't believe I'm in Cork, Ireland to celebrate Halloween—er, I mean Samhain. Your dad really knows how to throw a birthday party!"

"It's pronounced sow, like the pig, followed by when," Anne said. "Samhain."

"Whatever," Ginny replied.

"I agree," Fiona said. "This is my best birthday present ever. It's a big change from having cider and doughnuts around a campfire back home in Indiana. So, yeah, he's not bad for an old guy. I got lucky, I guess."

The girls traipsed down to the lobby of Byrne House. It was traditional with dark wood, framed paintings on practically every inch of wall space, a huge fireplace, and the family coat of arms prominently on display.

Ginny sighed. "I keep thinking we'll see someone who looks like that hunky Jamie Fraser on *Outlander*. Maybe he'll be in a kilt—and nothing else."

"For Christ's sake, Ginny," Anne said. "Jamie Fraser was a Scot. Scots wear kilts. We're in Ireland. Home of the Celts." Anne rolled her eyes. "With your botched sense of history, I wonder how you ever passed Mr. Gillespie's history class."

"Make that debauched!" Fiona said.

"You guys can quit picking on me any time now," Ginny said.

"Hi, Dad," Fiona called out as he entered the lobby.

"Hi, Sweetie. Girls. Sorry. I was pulled into a conference call at the last minute. But I should be free most of the time now."

The girls' smiles took a downward dive. He laughed and held up his hands. "Don't worry. That doesn't mean I'm going to get in your hair. I'll be on the links every chance I get. You girls are old enough and smart enough to stay out of trouble. And no beer. The legal drinking age in Ireland is eighteen, and I happen to know none of you are eighteen yet. Remember, I'm only an iPhone call away."

"We'll be fine, Dad," Fiona said. "Today we're shopping at the English Market. And we've already signed up for a tour of area castles."

"Yes, Mr. Murphy, don't worry about us," Anne said. "This place is a history lover's playground."

"Plus, some castles have their own ghosts, like the White Lady at

Fort Charles," Ginny said. "When her father shot her betrothed, she threw herself into the ocean because she couldn't bear to live another day without him. Isn't that romantic?"

Anne snorted. "Kind of stupid, if you ask me."

"Well, no one did," Ginny said, sounding miffed. "I'd just love to see a ghost."

"The grand finale on Samhain Eve is the Dragon of Shandon Festival with a parade featuring a dragon and 500 other creatures from the Otherworld," Fiona said.

Mr. Murphy laughed and shook his head. "Sounds like you have everything under control. But save a day to come out to Old Head with me. They have a fantastic spa and a first-class restaurant I think you'll like. My treat."

Fiona smiled. "Sounds wonderful. We could all use a little pampering."

"Yes, thank you. That will be great," the other two girls echoed.

～

CALL ME AN EAVESDROPPER. *You wouldn't be wrong. I love hearing the cheery banter of the young ones. Those three are so casual, taking their youth and beauty for granted. Anne, with her long brunette hair and exotic feline eyes. Fiona, a classic Irish beauty with red hair and green eyes. And Ginny, a blue-eyed, dimpled blonde. A golden girl. Just like I was.*

Mr. Murphy is a good father. Gives them their freedom but makes sure they understand the rules. That's very important. Especially around Samhain.

～

THE GIRLS MADE their way upstairs. Their bedroom suite was outfitted in shades of pale yellow and baby blue. The rooms smelled like furniture polish with a faint odor of decaying roses.

"That was the best ever," Ginny said, looking at her companions for agreement. "I don't know about you two, but I could have knocked around in the English Market all day."

"We didn't have all day if we wanted to catch Blarney Castle," Anne said. "Admit it, Miss Shopaholic, you enjoyed it, too."

Ginny dropped her bags on the floor and plopped down on the king-size bed. "Yes, I did—especially the part about the ghost of the witch who's entrapped there during the day and comes out at night."

"Ghosts and witches aside," Fiona said, "now we can tell everyone back home we kissed the Blarney Stone."

"What's on the agenda for tomorrow?" Anne asked.

"We're going with Dad for our spa visit. He made our reservations, so we're all set."

"Great!" Ginny said. "We'll be all mani-pedi-ed and looking good for the Samhain parade. Maybe we'll meet some guys there. They can protect us from all the evil spirits from the Otherworld."

"Are boys, mani-pedis, and supernatural phenomenon all you think about?" Anne asked. "I hate to tell you, but you're in danger of becoming a teenage stereotype."

"You take that back!"

Ginny threw a pillow at Anne and soon all three girls were engaged in a vigorous pillow fight. They were laughing so hard they flopped on the floor next to the fireplace to catch their breath. Before long, all three were fast asleep.

Ah, look at the three darlings, now. Maybe they'd enjoy a lullaby. As a child I enjoyed hearing my mother sing Too Ra Loo Ra Loo Ral to me. Especially when I was snuggled up safe and sound in my bed with the covers tucked under my chin. Sleep well.

THE SHRILL RINGER on the alarm went off way too early the next morning. The girls scrambled to get ready. Before they knew it, they were at the spa.

"And what color will you be havin', miss?" the manicurist asked as she motioned Fiona to take a seat in the pedicure chair.

"Ruby Slippers, please." Fiona sank into the chair and placed her feet in the tub of warm, floral-scented water.

"Ah, to match your 'air." She nodded to Ginny and Anne. "Go ahead and pick out a color. Set yourselves down and start soakin'. I'll be with you in a bit."

"So, are you stayin' in one o' our suites, then?" the manicurist asked Fiona.

"No. We're just here for the pampering while my dad's playing golf. We're actually staying at a B&B in Cork."

"Lots o' nice spots in Cork," she said, beaming and nodding her head like Fiona had given her a correct answer to a tricky question. "Have you been to the English Market?"

"Yes," Anne said. "We also saw Blarney Castle. The history here is so awesome. I couldn't believe—"

"What we're really here for is to celebrate Samhain," Ginny said. She looked at Fiona. "And your birthday, of course. I'm so hoping to see a ghost or two tomorrow night."

"Ireland is home t' many ghosts. And Cork is full o' them. Some proprietors exploit it. Others try to erase it from the books." She put the last brushstroke of Ruby Slippers on Fiona's pinky toe, then turned toward Anne and motioned her to take her feet out of the water. "So, what B&B will you be stayin' at?"

"Byrne House," Fiona said. "Have you heard of it?"

"Aye," she said, looking solemn. "There be plenty o' ghosts in that house, I wager. You know what Byrne means, don't you?"

All three girls shook their heads.

"It means 'raven.' Ravens are considered ill omens by most. Sometimes, especially during Samhain, ravens have been known to connect the real world to the Otherworld where the spirits live." The old woman shook her head and crossed herself before continuing.

"Most spirits are benign. Just hangin' around and watchin' folks, mayhap livin' their lives through others. It's the evil ones you 'ave to watch out for."

At that point, another manicurist took over. "Be careful," the old woman said over her shoulder as she gathered her smock and towels. "And mind the rules."

No one said anything for a minute. Then Ginny piped up. "Well, that was creepy, wasn't it? Maybe we should explore our B&B. I didn't want to say anything, but I've felt like someone has been watching us at times."

"You're so susceptible," Fiona said. "That woman was just feeding us a line of bull—what she thought tourists would want to hear. She's probably on her way home laughing at the gullible Americans she met at the spa!"

"I'm going to Google Byrne House and see what I find," Anne said, picking up her iPhone. "She knew her stuff," she said minutes later. "Byrne does mean raven. And ravens don't have such a great reputation."

"They do eat dead stuff at the side of the road," Ginny said.

"Nothing here about ghosts, though," Anne said. "I agree with Fiona. The old woman was just giving us a piece of the local lore. Probably hoping for a bigger tip!"

AFTER BEING PAMPERED at the spa, the girls ate lunch and shopped before entering the pub. There, each scored a "pint of the black stuff," otherwise known as Guinness. Later, they'd cajoled Fiona's dad, who was celebrating his best golf score ever, into ordering a bottle of wine with dinner. Of course, they'd helped him with it.

"No ratting me out to your parents when we get back home," he told them on their ride back to Byrne House.

Ginny and Anne nodded off and Fiona and her dad talked about his project.

"This is a big deal," he said. "The company has never opened an international office before. And to have it be here in Ireland, the land of our ancestors, makes it very special to me."

"I'm so proud of you. And, so glad you brought us here." Fiona leaned over and kissed him on the cheek as their car pulled up in front of Byrne House.

THE GIRLS RALLIED when they got back to their suite, but neither Anne nor Ginny was in the mood to stay up and talk.

"I'm heading to bed," Anne said. "Who knew pampering could take so much out of you?"

"I think it was the combination of beer and wine," Fiona said.

"But you had just as much as we did and you're not ready to hit the sack," Ginny countered.

"Guess I can handle my booze better. I think I'll stay up a bit and read."

"Knock yourself out," Ginny said. "Come on, Anne. I get the bathroom first!"

AH, here they are again. My sweet girls. Back from their adventure. I've been wondering about them. Did they enjoy the outing? Were they pampered at the spa? Did they catch the eye of any young gentlemen? Byrne House is so lonely without their cheery chatter. If only I could have gone with them.

FIONA TURNED the sconces down low, changed into her jammies, and snuggled into an upholstered chair in front of the fireplace. She could swear she smelled roses as she sank into the soft cushions. Her foot nudged something on the floor by the lamp table, and she bent over to see what it was.

A book. She scooped it up and held it in her hands. The book,

Byrne's Laws, was cracked and smelled musty. As she placed it on the lamp table and reached for a *People* magazine, the book fell open to a chapter titled "Rules for Samhain." Fiona scanned through pages on how to set the table, what to serve, and who to invite for Samhain. Evidently you didn't want to issue an open invitation to the spirits, you shouldn't invite fairies, and witch balls could trap an evil spirit. But what really caught Fiona's attention was the section entitled "The Mystery of the Mirror." It read:

> The Raven Mirror is the only remnant remaining from the fire that demolished most of the original Byrne House. It has a sordid history. Legend has it that between midnight and three o'clock on Samhain if you leave an offering of a glass of wine in front of the Raven Mirror you can call forth spirits from the Otherworld. Check the mirror closely and you will find an old Gaelic spell used for inviting the dead to cross over through the veil. Most people think it is all a bunch of foolishness. But be careful. Here's the mystery. You won't know if you'll be welcoming a benign spirit or one intent on mischief or harm. According to the stories, both have happened at Byrne House. And no one who had boasted they were going to utter the spell and invite a spirit over has ever revealed what happened. Not one word. Some of the old stories claim they were never the same. If you decide to try to see for yourself, be very careful. It's one invitation you may live to regret.

A yellowed sheet of notepaper slid out of the book. Fiona put the book aside and began reading the note, which was in tiny, but legible, writing. It was dated October 1920 and evidently authored by a young woman. It, too, referred to the Raven Mirror.

> Father translated the spell, (see below) but he doesn't want me to go near the mirror. Not even to offer up a glass of wine, much less chant the spell. Do I dare do it alone? Yes! Wouldn't it just be the bee's knees to share a glass of wine with a ghost.

Fiona finished reading the note and stashed it in her pocket. Bee's knees! What a hoot! She wondered about the girl who had written it. Had she used the ancient spell? If she did, what had happened to her? And were these the rules the old lady in the spa referred to? She pulled on her robe, grabbed her iPhone, and headed to the third floor.

There it was. She turned on the lamp on the table underneath it. The ornate, ancient mirror, featuring a carved raven, must have been magnificent in its time. Fiona touched it with her finger and traced the letters carved into the bottom of its frame. Then she read the translation from the yellowed page:

Let the veil be lifted between our worlds.

I invite you, in the spirit of goodwill, to show yourself this Samhain.

Come drink with me and enjoy the pleasures of this world once more.

Wow! Wouldn't it be cool to reenact the spell? Wait 'til she told Anne and Ginny. She started back to the suite. But something stopped her from charging in and waking them up. Ginny would be totally into it, but she'd gab the entire time and spoil the mood. Fiona could just hear her now: "How long do you think it will take? Do you think we'll get a really cute guy ghost? What if they prefer white wine?"

And Anne, who didn't care for anything out of the ordinary, would complain about being forced into the stupid scheme. If a ghost did appear—Fiona was keeping an open mind about it—Anne would probably bombard it with question after question on how things were done in its time, boring it back to the Otherworld.

No, she wasn't going to tell either of her friends what she'd found. This was her secret. Her birthday present to herself. She hid the copy of *Byrne's Laws* under the chair and slipped the note back into her pocket.

∾

THE NEXT DAY the girls stayed close to the B&B, taking in Fitzgerald Park, Cork Public Museum, and the historic City Gaol. They were meeting Fiona's dad in Cork's Victorian Quarter for an early Samhain Eve dinner. Then the girls would watch the Dragon of Shandon parade.

"I can't wait!" Ginny exclaimed. "I'm wearing my leggings and booties with my poncho over my warmest sweater. It's going to get down to 42 degrees tonight."

"We'd better hustle if we're going to meet Dad on time."

"We're almost ready," Ginny said. "How about you?"

Fiona just smiled. It wouldn't be long before they'd return to the B&B and she'd summon a spirit. "Heading out now," she replied, opening the door.

"GOD, THAT WAS FUN," Ginny said as she kicked off her shoes. "Kind of like Mardi Gras."

"Have you been to Mardi Gras?" Anne asked, sinking down on the bed.

"No, but I've seen pictures and videos. Streets full of people having fun and making noise. Same idea. They probably even have a Voodoo dragon leading the Mardi Gras parade!"

"I bet lots of people we know have been or will go to Mardi Gras," Fiona said. "But I'm pretty sure we'll be the only ones who can say we've celebrated Samhain at the Dragon of Shandon parade. I didn't know what to expect, but it was something else."

"I just loved getting caught up in the spirit of it," Anne said. "The whole thing about lifting the veil to the Otherworld. For a while there, I really wouldn't have been surprised if I'd seen a ghost or two."

"Well, I declare," Ginny said in an exaggerated Southern drawl. "I just might make a believer of you yet!"

"Don't count on it!"

They changed for bed and tried to stay up, but called it quits around two o'clock.

Fiona came so close to mentioning the ritual she planned to perform later, but every time she almost gave in to the urge, she reminded herself that it was for her. Her birthday present to herself. Something she'd always have that no one else had experienced. Besides, if it turned out to be a dud, no one would ever know.

THERE SHE IS, my beautiful Fiona. So daring to take on this mystery all on her own. Honestly, I didn't think she had it in her. But I'm so glad she decided to go through with it. She's smart, that one. And level-headed. She'll be able to handle an experience outside of her own worldview. Something that will make her appreciate her Irish heritage even more.

As SOON AS she heard the chorus of light snores coming from her two friends, Fiona grabbed a glass and the bottle of wine she'd lifted from her dad's room earlier, slipped on her robe, and headed up to the third floor, using the flashlight on her iPhone to guide her.

Slowly Fiona approached the mirror at the end of the hall with the same sinking feeling in the pit of her stomach that she'd had watching those scary movies every Halloween. At least her knees weren't knocking like they did then. She stopped and looked up at the mirror. It seemed very different at two in the morning. Even a bit sinister. She imagined she heard the raven caw.

Fiona shook her head. Nonsense! There was no reason to be afraid. Nothing was going to happen. How many times would she have the opportunity to invite a ghost to come over to the other side using an ancient spell? If she chickened out now, she'd regret it the rest of her life.

She put the wine and glass on the table, placing the corkscrew beside them. She wasn't going to risk her dad's wrath by opening the bottle if it wasn't necessary. She pulled the note out of her pocket, recited the spell, then slipped the note back in her pocket and took a step back.

The atmosphere in the hall changed immediately. Fiona felt she was getting smaller like Alice and that the whole world around her was all fogged up. She couldn't see anything, but her sense of smell was working overtime. A dank, peaty smell enveloped her. It was so heavy she felt she would suffocate. What was happening?

Fiona heard a noise like the wind swishing through the trees. The fog cleared and the odor dissipated. She looked into the mirror and saw a young woman. A pretty blonde with bright blue eyes. The girl was reaching out to her and saying something Fiona couldn't quite hear. Fiona "touched" the reflection of the girl's hand on the mirror. But Fiona's hand didn't stop there. She watched as it disappeared through the glass as easily as if it had entered a pool of water. She could see her hand in the mirror like it was no longer part of her body. Then she felt the girl grasp it—but nothing happened. It was like time stood still.

She must be asking me to pull her out.

Without thinking, Fiona stepped closer to the mirror.

Suddenly, the girl's grip on her hand got stronger. She pulled Fiona inside the mirror, shoving her aside. Then the girl jumped through the mirror to the other side. Fiona pulled herself up and watched in horror as the girl bowed her head and began chanting.

"You who welcomed a spirit from the Otherworld, are now bound to take your guest's place as she will take yours. Here you will remain until someone chooses to set you free."

Fiona banged on the mirror and called out, but the girl did nothing, just stood there, head bent to her chest. Finally, the girl raised her head and stared into Fiona's eyes.

Fiona gasped. It was her own face staring back at her. Tears were in the girl's eyes.

"I'm sorry. But I've been trapped behind the veil since 1920. You can't blame me for wanting to get out. To live again. When you found my note in the book, I knew you were my best chance to escape."

"No," Fiona wailed, as she pounded on the mirror. "You can't leave me here. What about my father? My friends? My life?"

A sympathetic look flashed over the girl's face. "He's *my* father now. They're *my* friends. And it's *my* life. Someone else will find the note I left and rescue you. Just like you rescued me."

"What are you doing out here?" Ginny and Anne were walking toward the figure they thought was Fiona. "We woke up and you weren't in the room."

"Oh, I couldn't sleep and I thought I'd come up here and leave an offering. Isn't that what you're supposed to do on Samhain?"

"Yeah, well you're never going to attract a ghost with an unopened bottle of wine," Ginny said. "You don't have to be Irish to know that. Here, give it to me. Let's go back to our suite and get 'rat-arsed,' as they say here. This place is really giving me the creeps."

FIONA WATCHED AS THEY LEFT, a tear slowly trickling down her face. No one would ever know that the girl walking with them wasn't her. The only hope she had was that someone else would find the note, go through with the spell, and invite her to be their guest on Samhain's Eve. It had taken one hundred years before the other girl—she didn't even know her name—had been rescued. Everyone she knew would be dead by then. Tears were rolling down both cheeks now. She reached into her pocket for a tissue. And pulled out the note.

It was with her. In the Otherworld. No one would be coming to her rescue. Not in one hundred years. Not ever. She thought back to what the old woman at the spa had told them.

You had it all wrong, lady. It's not just the evil ones you have to watch out for.

SHATTERED

BY JANET E. WILLIAMS

Memory is like a broken vase. When it shatters, fragments large and small scatter across the floor. You sweep up the pieces and one by one you carefully fit them back together like a jigsaw puzzle. If you're lucky, when you finish you have something resembling the vessel it used to be. Most of the time, the cracks and missing pieces render it useless.

That's what Halloween 1965 was like for me. The fragments of the night my older sister vanished have been reassembled in my 60-year-old brain into something not quite whole or clear, with cracks and missing pieces that left me uncertain of what was real. It didn't help that the police, my parents and counselors told me I couldn't possibly have witnessed what I told them I saw.

I thought about that night as I stood in front of the old Bower house on Halloween more than half a century later. The mansion, three stories of mottled red brick with a turret and a lancet window at the very top, was always dark and imposing. It was scary to an eight-year-old in bright daylight and terrifying in the dark of night.

On this night, the Bower house stood empty, windows boarded up and brickwork crumbling. The portico's columns looked barely capable of holding up the roof. The wrought iron fence that surrounded the property was corroded by decades of rust and the gate hung on a single twisted hinge. The yard was cluttered with stray plastic bags snagged in the overgrown weeds and mounds of brown leaves piled up against the fragments of the fence that remained.

I hadn't ventured down this dead-end street in Irvington since that policeman—he told me to call him Officer Dave—walked me to the door of this house to help me remember what happened. I remembered. I told him how my sister, Katie, six years older than me, and her friend, Mary Sue, were supposed to walk me door-to-door as I went trick-or-treating but about halfway through the evening, they took me to the street where the Bower house was located. Mary Sue whispered something to Katie, who then turned to me and told me that I was a big girl now and I could trick-or-treat on the last couple of streets by myself. She said she would meet me at the end of the block in an hour to take me home but I refused to leave.

"Just come on," Mary Sue said as she took Katie's arm to lead her to the door of the Bower house.

"Go Annie," Katie said. "You'll be okay."

She turned and went with Mary Sue, who rapped loudly on the massive door. When no one answered she pushed it open. I stayed on the sidewalk by the gate, my plastic Batgirl mask sliding over my eyes. I had been too scared to either leave or follow, but not too scared to be really angry at my sister for ruining my evening.

"Katie, don't," I hollered. When I started crying that I was scared, she turned back and removed the charm bracelet that dangled from her wrist. She had filled it with charms of the places she wanted to travel to and always wore it. Pressing it into my hand she whispered that her bracelet brought her luck and would keep me safe. Before I could say anything, Mary Sue returned for her and pulled at her sleeve, and then together they went up the sidewalk and entered the house. The door drifted shut.

I waited, my plastic pumpkin only partially filled, and shivered as a light breeze picked up. What had started as a relatively warm late October day gradually turned colder as the sky darkened.

"Katie!" I yelled. "I'm leaving and I'm gonna tell Mom." But I didn't leave. Not right away. I thought about approaching the house but remained at the gate, fingering the bracelet. I was angry and impatient and after a few more minutes I dropped the bracelet into my pocket and left. Katie would be in big trouble abandoning me to go Halloweening on my own. I didn't care. I was one pissed-off kid and I went from house to house for more than an hour. I thought about returning to the block where the Bower house stood as Katie told me to, but instead I went home alone. My plastic pumpkin was filled to the brim with all kinds of candy that I vowed never to share with my sister.

I expected Katie to be there, getting reamed out by Mom and Dad for leaving me to wander the streets of Irvington on my own. But she wasn't. When I walked in alone, they were surprised and then angry when I told them that Katie abandoned me at the Bower house.

Mom called Mary Sue's mother and when she learned she hadn't returned either, Dad said he would go and talk to Old Man Bower himself, maybe apologize for the girls bothering him. Bower was a crank and scared us kids because he yelled at us for even playing in front of his house. Our roller skating with the metal of the wheels scraping against the concrete street especially annoyed him. I knew he wouldn't dare yell at my dad.

I'm not all that clear about what happened next because Mom sent me and my little brother, Ben, who was home sick that Halloween, to bed.

I awoke the next morning to a house filled with police and some neighbors. Mom should have been fixing breakfast and getting us ready for school. Instead, Mrs. Gibson, the new lady who had moved in across the street, had her arm around my mom as they sat at the kitchen table. Mom had been crying. Dad was with one of the policemen. He jabbed a finger at the officer, demanding they go and search the Bower house immediately.

"Tell them what you told us, Annie," Mom said as she rose and took my hand. She led me into the living room with one of the policemen, the one who told me to call him Officer Dave.

He was the cute cop, the one all the girls, including Katie, swooned over. I didn't get it, but he seemed nice enough as he sat on the sofa next to me and leaned in, putting his hand on my back and in a low, soft voice asking me to describe everything I remembered from the night before. I told them about Katie and Mary Sue walking me along a couple of Irvington streets and picking out some of my candy for themselves before turning into the dead end where the Bower house stood.

"Th-they left me on the street," I stammered, trying to hold back tears.

"So, they went and left you alone?"

I nodded as I broke down crying.

"Did you see anyone answer the door? Did you hear anyone?" Officer Dave asked. I shook my head no.

"What about cars? Did you see any strange cars parked in the area?"

I told him no, that I only saw a police car at the end of the street where Bower lived. He pressed me for a few minutes about whether there were other trick-or-treaters in the neighborhood or anyone else walking by. I tried really hard to remember, but my answer was still no. But seriously, how would I have known what to look for? All I saw or all I remembered seeing was my sister and her friend entering the house and then vanishing forever.

When I started crying Mom pulled me away from Officer Dave and put her arm around me. Gently, she told me they needed my help and to remember anything that I saw no matter what. I sniffed and Mom wiped away my tears. Her hands felt cold, almost like ice. She would die shortly before I graduated from high school, a tumor in her breast from a lump she never bothered to get checked.

"Then get a search warrant if that's what it takes!" That voice belonged to Dad and he was yelling at a man in a suit who looked like he was in charge of all the policemen in the house. The man shook his head and mumbled something to Dad, who seemed to calm down a little.

The morning was a blur of activity. But at some point before lunchtime Officer Dave ushered my dad and me to his patrol car, putting us both in the back seat. The grill that separated the front from the back made me feel like I was in a cage. I buried my face in Dad's jacket that still carried the scent of the dried leaves we played in only yesterday and for a couple of seconds I felt safe again. Until we got to the Bower house.

As my dad stood by, Officer Dave took my hand in his and had me tell him again what I saw the night before. His grip was firm, almost too tight, and his tone seemed different as he kept repeating after my every statement, "Are you sure?" His demeanor reminded me of how Mrs. McIlvaine, my second-grade teacher, would question us when she knew we had lied. I wanted to yell that I was telling the truth, that Katie and Mary Sue really did go into the house. I didn't yell, but instead told him the same story again.

"Then let's talk to Mr. Bower," he said, walking me to the door. When Dad followed, Officer Dave tried to wave him back. But Dad insisted on going and after a tense moment he relented but cautioned my dad to keep quiet, saying, "He's my uncle. Let me handle him." Together we approached the house.

Old Man Bower scowled as he opened the door, but his expression softened when he saw Officer Dave.

"Davey, come on in," Bower said. He didn't seem so scary in the daylight. Up close, he was feeble and withered, only a little taller than me with hollow cheeks and wisps of white hair sticking out behind his ears. As we stood inside the foyer, a smell that I later realized was cat urine made me want to gag. Old Man Bower steadied himself with a cane and I thought that Katie could have knocked him over with one shove.

After they exchanged a few words, Officer Dave asked me, "Did you see him? Was he at the door last night?" I shook my head no and Old Man Bower assured Officer Dave that no one had entered or broken into his house the previous night.

"That's what I told him," Bower said, nodding at my dad. His voice was scratchy but not nearly as menacing as I expected. "And if they had, you can be sure I would have been the one calling the police. Come on in and see for yourself."

Officer Dave had me wait in the foyer while Bower took him and my dad through the house. Did Katie and Mary Sue really come in here, I asked myself. After what seemed like forever, Officer Dave and Dad returned, thanked Bower for his time, and took me back to the street.

"I'm sorry, there's no sign that anybody but that old man has been in the house," he told Dad. To me, he added, "You must be mistaken. It was dark, hard to see. Maybe you only thought they went inside."

That was how it ended. Everybody assumed I got it wrong and couldn't possibly have seen what I said I witnessed. Over the years there were rumors that the girls had run away with some hippies who were passing through or were kidnapped and murdered by a stranger. But they amounted to nothing and no trace of Katie or Mary Sue was ever found. Mary Sue's parents divorced a couple of years later and even though Mom and Dad stayed together, they were hollow versions of the parents I once had. As for me, Katie's disappearance left an ache inside I could never fill and all I had left of her was an old charm bracelet.

I don't know what brought me back to that house half a century later. Perhaps it was finding that bracelet in an old jewelry box, reminding me of how much I missed her. Or maybe it was the article in the newspaper about this mansion, one of the first built in the neighborhood, describing how it was about to be razed to make way for senior apartments. My sister would have been a senior by now. I couldn't imagine anyone actually living on this site, no matter what kind of building would rise from the rubble.

I've had nightmares about that house that years of therapy couldn't erase. I always regretted that I never stepped beyond the foyer to see for myself that Katie and Mary Sue weren't there. And I never forgave myself for letting her give me her lucky charm bracelet. It might have brought her the luck she needed that night.

The weather this Halloween evening reminded me of that night, mild during the day but overcast and chilly as it began to get dark. I caught the scent of dried leaves as they crunched under my feet when I approached the house. The scent made me think of my father, who died just a couple of years after my mother. Doctors said heart attack but I know it was grief and never knowing what happened to his first-born child.

My whole life I felt my memories of that night were like that shattered vase, reassembled with pieces missing or not even in the right place. On this night, I resolved to muster the courage that failed me half a century ago. I would cross the threshold and confront what I feared might be beyond the door.

I didn't need to actually open the door. It was already open a crack and cautiously I pushed it a little wider and entered. I ventured beyond the foyer to a hallway that led to what appeared to be a living room to the right and a library or office to the left. Old Man Bower had died a few months after that Halloween night and the house, already in decay, continued to decline. The years of neglect showed up in the dust and cobwebs, cracked walls, and floors where the wood was so worn that if I hadn't stepped carefully, I would have fallen through.

The library drew me in with walls and walls of books coated in dust and decay. A table that looked like it had been used as a desk was to the left near windows covered by heavy, dark curtains. I struggled to see in the darkened room and used my cell phone flashlight so I wouldn't stumble over the papers, books and other detritus covering the floor. The stench was awful, something like a mix of the cat urine I smelled that first time through the door and the debris of long-dead animals. I sneezed from the beads of dust floating in the glow of my light.

I spent a lifetime questioning what I saw that night but here, inside this place, I knew I was right. As I held her charm bracelet, I could feel my sister's presence. This was where she vanished.

As I cast the flashlight across the shelves, a reflection bounced back at me. I went closer to examine it and realized it was a latch on one of the bookcases that doubled as a door.

I pulled it open with considerable effort, dust swirling around as the hinges squealed from years of not being moved. Venturing inside, I discovered a short hallway that led to steps to the basement.

I hesitated, fear welling up. But I felt compelled to keep going, almost as if I could hear Katie encouraging me and saying, "Go on, Squirt. Be brave. You can do it."

"For you, Katie," I whispered, stepping cautiously down the steep and creaky staircase.

At the bottom was another door, slightly ajar from the way the house must have settled. Swallowing hard, I opened it and the smell of rot, dirt, and bodily waste choked me, sending me reeling back a couple of steps. The darkness inside was absolute and I paused before flashing my light, unsure of what I would find.

Even with the light I could barely see inside. As my eyes adjusted to the dark, I could make out a cot with crumpled blankets, a small table with a broken chair, and something I couldn't distinguish piled in the corner. It looked at first like a mound of old, tattered clothing.

I went closer to examine the pile and as I slowly cast the light over the debris, I saw a hat lying nearby. It was a policeman's hat, I realized as I flashed my light over it to see more clearly. Inside the lining I could make out faded letters—D . . . A . . . V—and I couldn't make out the rest.

"Dave? Officer Dave?" I whispered.

With my phone, I snapped a couple of pictures of the mound of tattered clothing and that's when I saw it—something resembling a hand extended from an arm wrapped around what looked like a body.

Oh God, no. I couldn't breathe as the images came into focus and I realized that it wasn't one but two skeletons huddled together.

I dropped my phone and the bracelet and backed away, stumbling over some debris and falling backwards. My head slammed hard against the floor and woozy, I tried to push myself up. I couldn't and dropped to the floor, sliding into blackness thinking of Officer Dave, Katie, and how no one would know I finally found her.

"C'MON, just hold onto your sleeve so I can get this over your coat."

Someone was tugging at my arm but who was it? That voice. It was a voice I hadn't heard in decades.

"Mom?" I said, but my own voice sounded high and a little squeaky.

"Don't you Mom me. You're not going trick-or-treating without a coat under your costume."

It was Mom and, where was I? I must have really hit my head hard. I looked around and, heavens, I was in our old family kitchen. I recognized the scuffed yellow linoleum floor, the Formica table and metal chairs, and the burnt orange refrigerator and stove.

I had to be hallucinating or maybe I perished in that basement of death.

"Stop fidgeting," she snapped as she finished with the sleeve. I caught a whiff of Lily of the Valley, a cologne she used to wear.

Not dead because I was pretty sure dead people don't have a sense of smell.

"Get moving, Squirt!"

Katie? Nobody's called me Squirt since that Halloween night. Katie dashed into the kitchen, putting on her coat.

Mom slipped the mask over my face, handed me my pumpkin-shaped bucket for candy, and Katie dragged me to the door. The plastic on my face was hot and sticky and the slits that passed for eyes made it hard to see.

"Now don't you give your sister a hard time tonight," Mom said to me and then to Katie, "Be sure to bring your sister home by eight."

My little brother, Ben, came to the doorway in the kitchen, crying, "Why can't I go, too? I want to go!" It was coming back to me. Katie got saddled with taking me trick-or-treating that night because Dad worked late, and Mom had to stay home with my brother because he had a fever. Katie wasn't happy about that because she and her best friend, Mary Sue, had to put their plans on hold. Mom made me promise to share my candy with my brother when I returned, and I had grudgingly agreed.

"No!" I said as Katie tried to take my hand.

"There's nothing to be afraid of," Mom said. "Your sister will watch out for you and besides, Officer Dave said he'd be out in his patrol car keeping an eye on everything."

I stiffened when I heard that name but we were out the door before I had a chance to say anything. Katie started off by dragging me from house to house in our neighborhood. I must have seemed a little dazed because she had to walk me to a couple of the houses and ring the doorbell herself.

"What's wrong with you?" she said as we continued walking, turning down a familiar street. This was where Mary Sue lived.

"Why'd you bring her?" Mary Sue asked Katie when she saw me.

"I gotta take her around to a few houses and then we can . . . " Katie looked at me and whispered the rest of whatever she had to say.

That was something else that came back to me, the feeling of wanting to be part of my sister's world but being cut out because I was too young.

Mary Sue joined us as we continued going from house to house up and down the streets of Irvington.

"What's with her?" Mary Sue asked. "She's not saying a word."

"I think she's mad that she has to go with me tonight, when I'm the one who should be mad."

No. I was confused. How did I end up here, walking streets that were familiar yet weirdly out of time—cars with giant grills that looked like teeth ready to snap, vacant lots where newer houses stood, saplings that I knew to be towering maple trees? No, Katie, I wanted to say, I'm not mad. I've lost my mind.

Katie and Mary Sue chattered away like I wasn't even there. That was the Katie I remembered. This felt so real, from the cooling night air to the faces of friends and neighbors I passed as we made our rounds. If this was another one of my nightmares, it was the most realistic one yet. And if I was dead, then I must be in some kind of hell doomed to repeat the worst day of my life.

As we walked, I realized that step-by-step we were heading to the dead-end street where Old Man Bower lived. Stop, I wanted to shout but the words wouldn't come. We turned the corner, Katie and Mary Sue walking ahead, giggling and talking about meeting someone this evening. Katie dangled her bracelet and said something about hoping it would bring her luck. I didn't remember that from before and I was torn between trying to listen more closely and doing something, anything, to make them stop. I couldn't, so I kept plodding on behind them.

"Why are we going down here? There's only Old Man Bower's house down here," I finally said.

They ignored me and kept going until we were standing in front of the Bower house.

"Who is it? Who are you meeting?" I demanded, channeling my grown-up self through this eight-year-old body.

Katie wheeled around and bent down to meet my face and said, "Who says we're meeting anyone?"

"I—I heard you just now."

Katie looked from Mary Sue and back to me.

"Hey, listen, Annie. Mary Sue and I just need to, ah, run a little errand," she said, crouching to look at me at eye level. Then, with a glance at Mary Sue, she added, "It's kind of grown-up stuff."

"No! Let's get out of here." I pulled away.

"We won't be long. You can trick-or-treat on the next block over and I'll meet you on the corner in an hour."

I shook my head.

"C'mon, Kate. Ignore her." Mary Sue tugged at Katie's sleeve and together they started through the wrought iron gate. "And he won't wait forever."

Katie turned back to me. "Look, it'll be fine. Go on. You're always wanting to do stuff on your own." She started up the sidewalk with Mary Sue.

No! This can't be happening again! I was desperate to stop her. I grabbed her arm and her charm bracelet snapped off, falling to the ground. She was so furious with me that she didn't notice. I begged her to stop but she shook me off and continued with Mary Sue. Aside from crying and threatening to tell Mom and Dad, I was powerless. Helpless, I watched them go to the door and enter.

This had to be a nightmare, no matter how different and real it felt. Tears clung to my plastic mask and a cold breeze blew strands of my hair and tickled my ears. The smell of dried leaves and decaying earth overpowered me.

I tried screaming one last time and nothing came out. They disappeared into the house as I agonized about why I couldn't stop them.

This was the point when, in most versions of my nightmares, I woke up in a cold sweat, my face wet with tears. I'd be filled with a deep ache in my soul, heavy with grief and regret.

But that night I didn't wake up. I was still that eight-year-old standing on a lonely street, only this time I was sure of what I had witnessed. I was certain of what lay beyond the door of Old Man Bower's house.

Instead of continuing to trick-or-treat as I did the first time, I picked up her bracelet and I raced toward home. I saw Officer Dave's patrol car parked a couple of blocks away and went to it, but he wasn't there. So, I continued home as fast as I could run. This time I knew where they were and where they would end up, but would it matter?

I tore into the house, the kitchen door slamming behind me. Mom heard the bang and was about to holler at me when she saw that I was sobbing hysterically.

"Oh, honey. What's wrong?" She wrapped her arms around me and I started choking out the words and showed her Katie's bracelet, charms dangling as the world faded to black.

"Nurse, nurse, I think she's coming around."

I tried to say something, but it came out as a groan because my throat was raw and my mouth dry. I tried opening my eyes, but everything appeared as though I was submerged in water. My head pounded and I wanted to puke. I tried to get up but a nurse gently pushed me back down.

"Don't try to move just yet. You've had a nasty head injury," the nurse said.

"She'll be okay, won't she?" That voice was vaguely familiar, but I couldn't quite make it out.

"Bad concussion, but all of her vital signs are looking good. It might take some time, but she should recover," the nurse said to the woman in the room. She patted my arm and left.

"Oh, Squirt, you gave us all a scare," the woman said.

Squirt? Nobody had called me Squirt since . . .

When she finally came into focus, seated at my bedside was a slender woman with short gray hair and glasses. She looked like . . .

"K-Katie?"

"Of course," she said. "Who'd you think it would be?"

I had to be hallucinating. Another nightmare. Or I died in that god-awful basement.

"What the hell were you doing at that old Bower place? And what were you doing with my old charm bracelet?" The voice brought me back to this hospital room and the woman who stroked my hand. "Good thing the work crew found you when they did or you'd be a goner."

"But Katie. How can it be? I saw you, Mary Sue . . . " I stammered, struggling to push myself up and get a closer look at the woman beside me.

"Mary Sue? What made you think of her? I haven't seen or even thought of her in years."

"But the Bower house, the basement. And the bodies, did they find the bodies?" I was nearly incoherent as I rambled about the Bower house.

"Bodies?"

"You and Mary Sue and . . . "

"You really did get a wicked bump," she said. "Otherwise, I can't imagine why you'd want to dredge up that awful night."

"I don't understand. I saw the bodies and found a hat. It was Officer Dave's." My voice was weak, almost a whisper before adding frantically, "Photos. I took photos. Where's my phone?"

"Here. The workers found it in the basement where you fell," Katie said after a moment of rooting through her purse.

Trembling, I opened the photo app and scrolled through dozens until I came to the newest ones. Sure enough, there were dim images of the bodies in the corner.

"See for yourself."

I shoved the phone at her and she studied it for a few seconds before saying, "You mean these?" She turned the screen in my direction. "Aren't these from your granddaughter's first birthday last week?"

"No!" I grabbed the phone and flipped through the photos and nothing. The images from the basement had vanished. My head was spinning.

"You had a serious head injury. It's no wonder you're confused."

I shook my head and told her the bits and pieces of what I remembered about her disappearance, Officer Dave, and the bodies in the basement.

Katie listened and sighed deeply. "If it hadn't been for you that Halloween night, there might have been a couple of bodies. But no, there aren't any bodies now. Just a dilapidated old house."

"And Officer Dave?"

She told me that Officer Dave had been flirting with a lot of the girls at the high school and told Mary Sue to meet him at the Bower house. Old Man Bower let his nephew use an old room in the basement for his "girlfriends." Mary Sue had dragged my sister along with the promise of partying with Officer Dave. But he got angry when he saw Katie with Mary Sue. He was expecting her to be alone. When Katie threatened to tell her parents after realizing that he was planning something more than drinking and smoking pot with a teenage girl, he panicked and locked them in the basement. Who knows what he planned to do with them? The girls were rescued when both sets of parents descended on the house and found the basement room because of what I told them. I could never explain how I knew about the room or Officer Dave.

Later, after Officer Dave was charged with holding the girls against their will, others came forward and told stories of how the town's trusted policeman had taken other girls to the basement. All were too terrified to say anything about what happened to them in that room until he was arrested in my sister's case. He died in prison in the 1970s.

"You saved us, Annie," Katie said, gently squeezing my shoulder. She pressed that old charm bracelet into my hand and added softly, "I think you should keep this."

As I held the bracelet and began to drift off, happier images of a life with Katie and my family began flooding my dreams. My nightmare had finally ended. Today, my memory of Halloween 1965 is still like that broken vase, only the fragments have been reassembled into a new vessel, with the cracks invisible to everyone but me.

HARVEY'S HOUSE OF HORRORS

BY JOAN BRUCE

"Let's do something special for Halloween this year," I suggested to my best friend, Mandy Malone, as we talked on the phone two nights ago.

"What do you have in mind, Candi?" Mandy asked. "Wait, before you answer that question, I'm not passing out candy at my front door this year so don't try to persuade me. The kids in my neighborhood already think I'm a cranky old woman and I want to keep it that way."

"We shouldn't let others think of us as old ladies," I replied. "Yeah, we're in our mid-forties, but we're not ready for the nursing home yet. Remember all the fun we had in our twenties?"

"I remember it all too well," Mandy said. "So, how do you propose we reclaim our youth?"

"Harvey's House of Horrors."

"I thought it closed years ago after Harvey Marcum moved on to that big spooky place below ground."

"It did, but his son, Harvey Junior, reopened it a few days ago and according to one of my clients, it's better than ever. She couldn't stop talking about it today as I did her nails."

Mandy didn't say anything for so long I wondered if she was still there.

"I suppose we could check it out," she finally replied. "I remember Harvey's being a scary place. But you'll need to drive. I don't want some jerk keying my beautiful Jaguar convertible in Harvey's parking lot."

IT WAS JUST after seven on Halloween night when I pulled into Mandy's semi-circular driveway in my Ford F-150 and laid on the horn. A minute later, Mandy ran out of her McMansion and climbed into my truck.

"Why do you blast your horn every time you pick me up?" she asked. "My neighbors are probably peeking through their blinds and wondering if I've suddenly become a NASCAR fan. And if I run into one of them next week, they'll probably accuse me of lowering property values."

"Sorry, I'll bring my limo next time. Hey, you didn't say you were dressing retro for our visit to Harvey's."

"It was a last-minute decision," Mandy said. "I was rummaging through my walk-in closet last night when I ran across my old black motorcycle club jacket."

"And it still fits."

"Yeah, it was Butch's wedding gift to me. He was so proud of it. It has the official 'Indy Bad Boys' emblem embroidered on the back and 'Butch's Babe' stenciled in pink italics underneath."

"That's so sentimental. Wearing your first husband's wedding gift. What about Marvin? Did he buy you clothes, too?"

"No, Marvin bought me expensive jewelry and a five-bedroom house before he died," Mandy said. "Look who's talking? Aren't you wearing your ex-husband's high school football jersey?"

"Yeah, I couldn't decide on what to wear, then I spotted Bobby's jersey sitting on a pile of clean clothes I hadn't put away. Normally, I wear it as a nightshirt."

"Won't he want it back if we run into him tonight?"

"Probably, but I'll tell him it was part of our divorce decree, along with this truck he had to turn over to me. He won't know any better."

HARVEY'S HOUSE OF HORRORS sat just off a narrow gravel road, about a mile south of the Bartonsville town limits. Legend had it that a lumber baron built the now dilapidated three-story structure as a wedding gift for his wife. Once it was completed, his wife refused to live in it. The house was too ostentatious. The man became so upset he chopped up his bride into tiny pieces and buried her remains in the backyard. After the man went to prison, the house stood vacant for several years until Harvey Marcum bought it at a sheriff's auction.

"This place looks like it hasn't changed in twenty years," Mandy said as I steered my truck into Harvey's gravel parking lot.

"You're right, but at least they've added some lights in the lot. Now, we won't fall into a pothole and sprain an ankle."

The young woman at the front door charged us each fifteen dollars. As she handed Mandy back her change, she asked, "Are you a member of the Indy Bad Boys motorcycle club?"

"I was once Butch Muldoon's babe," Mandy said proudly.

"That's so bitchin'," the ticket taker replied.

Our tour of the haunted house was a huge disappointment. Like other haunted places, Harvey's had plastic skulls dangling from the ceiling, fake blood spatter on the walls, and loud, creepy music playing in the background.

"The decorations look like the same ones Harvey used twenty years ago," Mandy said when we finished the tour. "There was a good inch of dust on everything."

I laughed. "My favorite part was the dude holding the hatchet in the middle of his forehead after it came unglued. But the guy lying on the floor with the hunting knife sticking out of his chest and the pool of blood around his body seemed real."

"This place sucks big time," Mandy said. "So much for reclaiming our youth."

Johnny Edwards was sitting at a table at Ralph's Diner enjoying his breakfast when I walked in Saturday morning. Johnny was a disabled Afghanistan war veteran who got around town in a motorized wheelchair. He was also a reporter at WYMN-AM, the town's radio station and he and I have been known to stick our noses into recent murders in town.

"What's up?" I asked after sitting down next to him.

"Hear about the murder last night?"

"What murder? Where?"

"Harvey's House of Horrors."

"You're kidding," I said. "Me and Mandy went there last night trying to reclaim our youth."

"See anything out of the ordinary?"

"No, except maybe this one guy. He was lying on the floor with a hunting knife sticking out of his chest."

"Hmmm?" Johnny said before backing away from the table.

"Where are you going?" I asked.

"Sheriff Melvin Pickle is holding a press conference in a half hour. I'm hoping he'll identify the victim and provide some more details about the murder."

"Let me know what he says."

Saturdays at Tips & Toes were often unpredictable. Sometimes we were swamped, especially if a bunch of bridesmaids showed up early and wanted their nails painted the same color. More often, only a handful of regulars had appointments and the day would drag by.

Today, me and Trudy Castle, the salon's other manicurist, had only a few clients, but each one was anxious to tell us of the murder last night at Harvey's House of Horrors and who did it.

"A Satan worshipper probably did it," one of my regulars said confidently.

"Wouldn't a Satan worshipper be more inclined to like the haunted house and not kill anyone who worked there?"

"Oh . . . I guess maybe you're right, Candi."

Another regular, Rosie Simmons, said she felt sorry for the Marcum sisters after losing their half-brother, Harvey Marcum, Jr., last night.

"How do you know them?" I asked.

"They're renting the house next door to me," Rosie said. "The police were at their place half the night."

"What do you know about them?" I asked.

"Not much," Rosie said. "They've only lived there a few months. But the older one, Martha, seems a little odd."

"In what way?"

"She carries around a hunting knife attached to her belt. How many women do that?"

"None that I know of," I replied.

It was a little after five when Johnny Edwards entered the salon. I was busy working on my last client of the day.

"What's the latest on the murder?" I asked him as I continued painting my customer's nails.

"You're busy," Johnny replied. "Let me grab something to eat at Ralph's and I'll meet you out front when the salon closes at six. Then, we can talk about it."

Johnny was true to his word. He was patiently sitting in his wheelchair when I walked out of work.

"What's going on?" I asked.

"Plenty," Johnny said. "Sheriff Pickle identified the victim as Harvey Marcum, Junior but he refused to divulge any more details about the murder."

"Did he mention if Junior was murdered with a hunting knife?"

"No, he was tight-lipped about the weapon that was used, but I've been busy chasing down leads on my own all day."

"What did you find out?"

"Old Harvey had two daughters when he lived with his first wife in Indianapolis. That was before he divorced her, moved to Bartonsville, married Hilda Jackson, and they had Harvey Junior. Apparently, the half-sisters learned of Junior's plans to reopen the House of Horrors and they wanted in on the action. The sisters felt entitled to any profits from the house's reopening."

"Who told you all that?"

"Believe it or not, your ex-husband. I ran into him earlier today."

"Bobby? How's he involved? Is he dating one of the sisters?"

"I don't know about that," Johnny said. "Bobby did some construction work at Harvey's before it reopened. He said Junior was always arguing with his half-sisters on how to run the place."

"That's not unusual. Growing up, I fought with my half-brother, Randy, all the time. I don't understand why Sheriff Pickle didn't reveal the weapon used to kill Junior."

"Perhaps he's not ready to tip his hand yet to the prime suspect."

"Maybe so, but one of my regulars told me today how Junior's older half-sister always carries a hunting knife on her belt."

"Are you thinking what I'm thinking?" Johnny asked.

"Yeah, we need to check out the sisters."

JOHNNY INSISTED on driving to Harvey's House of Horrors. It was easier for him than climbing inside my jacked-up F-150. I didn't complain. His tricked-out van had all the latest gadgets, including hand gears and seat warmers.

"Think the house is still considered a crime scene and it won't be open?" I asked.

"After what Bobby told me today about the half-sisters, my money is on the place being open."

After parking his van in Harvey's parking lot, Johnny and I approached the house's front door.

"How much did we bet?" Johnny asked after we noticed a bunch of yellow crime scene tape lying on the ground next to the front entrance.

"Hey, weren't you here last night with that biker chick?" the ticket taker asked me. "If you've come back looking for a refund, you're out of luck. We don't give them."

"No, my friend and I want to speak to the Marcum sisters. Are they around?"

"I'm Stephanie Marcum. My older sister, Martha, is inside. She likes to scare our visitors."

"You don't look very busy tonight," Johnny said.

"I know," Stephanie replied. "I thought Junior's death might attract more customers. Aren't people curious to see where his murder took place?"

Johnny and I glanced briefly at each other before I told Stephanie I needed to go inside and speak to Martha.

"Sure, but it'll cost you fifteen dollars," she replied. "We're not running a charity here. Sorry, mister, we aren't handicap accessible, so you'll have to wait outside."

Before entering the house, I instructed Johnny to call the cops if I wasn't back in ten minutes.

The first part of the tour was the same as last night. It wasn't until I was halfway through the place when a woman, dressed like a zombie, jumped out in front of me and shouted, "Want to die?" She waved a large sword in the air.

I let out a loud scream before turning and in a calmer voice asking her, "Are you Martha Marcum?"

"Lady, I'm in costume," she replied, lowering her sword. "You don't ask someone their name when they're in costume."

"Sorry, but I'm just trying to find out more about your half-brother's murder," I said.

Martha had a bewildered look on her face. "In that case, step around the corner so we can talk without anyone hearing us."

I did as Martha asked, including following her into a tiny room off the hallway. Once there, she turned and asked, "Who are you? And, why are you so interested in Junior's murder?"

"I'm Candi DeCarlo," I said, trying to choke back some fake tears. "Harvey and I once dated in high school. He was such a terrific guy. I should have married him back then when I had the chance."

"That's very interesting," Martha said when I finished my story. "Junior spent most of his teen years in reform school. He never went to high school in Bartonsville."

"Oops, my mistake," I said. "I swear that's where I met him. So, can I ask you another question? Why aren't you wearing your hunting knife tonight? I hear you never leave home without it?"

"Who told you that?" Martha asked, her voice rising a few octaves.

"I can't reveal my source," I replied. "It's the code of ethics we manicurists now follow with clients. Hairdressers have the same code. What's said in the salon stays in the salon."

"Lady, you're pissing me off," Martha replied, waving her sword in the air. I took that as my cue to rush past Martha and step into the dark hallway again.

Martha followed me out of the room, but a family of five was standing in the hallway. Martha was forced back into character. "Want to die?" I heard her yelling at the family.

I continued down the hallway before ducking into a room that might have been the house's kitchen in a former life. I found a tiny broom closet off to the side and hid inside it. I then pulled out my cell phone and called Johnny. He didn't answer.

What's up with that?

Time to call Mary Donovan, the night dispatcher at the Bartonsville Police Department and one of my regular clients.

"Bartonsville Police Department. What's your emergency?"

"Mary, it's me, Candi. I need your help."

"What have you done now? Found us another murder victim?"

"No, I'm stuck inside a broom closet at Harvey's House of Horrors. There's a woman chasing after me with a large sword. Hold on a sec. Yeah, I can still hear Martha Marcum dragging her sword along the dark hallway."

"A sword, huh?"

"Yeah, Mary, it's ginormous. I think Martha wants to slice me up into tiny pieces. She suspects I know that she killed her half-brother, Harvey Marcum, Junior."

"That's quite a story, Candi," Mary said. "Are you trying to solve another murder on your own?"

"Maybe."

"I would send some officers out there, but the House of Horrors is outside the town limits. You'll have to call the sheriff's department."

"I don't have their number in my list of contacts. Besides, Martha is likely to find me any second," I said. "Can you call the sheriff's office for me?"

"Relax, Candi. Johnny Edwards called me a few minutes ago. He told me what's happening out there. I've alerted sheriff's deputies. They should be there momentarily."

I REMAINED SCRUNCHED inside the broom closet at least another ten minutes before a Barton County sheriff's deputy wandered into the kitchen and yelled out my name. Once I came out of the closet, the deputy explained that he and his fellow officers had taken Martha and Stephanie Marcum into custody for further questioning.

"Your friend, Johnny Edwards, is waiting for you out front," the deputy added.

I thanked him for rescuing me before running outside as fast as I could.

"Johnny, I'm so happy to see you," I said, leaning down and giving him a huge hug.

"Me, too," he replied. "One of the deputies I know said Martha was holding a machete in her hand and it looked like she wanted to use it on you."

"Sword. But, yeah, she's a truly scary person," I said. "I asked her what happened to her hunting knife. She wasn't wearing it tonight."

"I wouldn't have confronted her that way, but I'm glad you're okay," Johnny said. "But, listen, maybe we should stop trying to solve murders on our own for a while. What do you say?"

"Sounds like a good idea to me."

THE SIMULATOR

BY RAMONA G. HENDERSON

I f I had known how much fun and how much power I would have in death, I would never have wished for such a long life. I love being able to watch anyone I choose, anywhere, any time. And I especially love the ability to simulate anything I wish.

Look at them lined up and leaning against the wall, waiting for the professor to open the door. Eight o'clock classes have turned into a joke, especially on Fridays. Maybe two out of the whole bunch care to be here, hoping to learn something. Most are hating the fact a course in professionalism is required for a nursing degree. Three of them look to be in their pajamas. At least they appear to have run a brush through their hair. Here comes Professor Borman now. The students badmouth her a lot behind her back. I'm not sure why; I find her rather attractive and inspiring.

PROFESSOR KATE BORMAN greets the class. "Good morning everyone." She scans her ID card to unlock the classroom door. The nursing students take their seats, usually in the same spot every Friday, even though they do not have assigned seats.

HERE COMES THE BACK-ROWS BUNCH. I think they sit back here so Professor Borman can't hear them. Jordan seems upset this morning, and I know why. I startled her at the cemetery. I didn't think the portal I chose was so scary. He hadn't been dead long.

JORDAN TAKES a pen and notepad from her book bag. "I hate coming to this classroom; it's creepy the way the lights flicker. I know it must be haunted."

Ted, sitting in the row behind her, bellows a scary sound. "Wooooo, wooooo."

Kyle, sitting next to Ted, starts singing. "Who you gonna call? Who you gonna call?"

Sarah chastises them. "Shut up, you guys, that's not funny. Jordan's been jumpy since we went on that Halloween-special Crown Hill Cemetery Tour last weekend."

"Why wouldn't I be? I'm the one who saw the ghost."

Ted laughs. "There are no such things as ghosts."

"Then what did I see? You tell me, what did I see last Saturday night? He looked like a dead man walking around."

Sarah shakes her head. "I already told you. It was just some man who strayed away from our group. He probably did it on purpose to scare someone."

Kyle leans closer to Jordan and whispers. "You sound nutty."

"I know what I saw. Simone saw it too, but she won't admit to it."

"I didn't see any man by that big tree."

Jordan shoots her a piercing gaze. "Yes, you did. I could tell by the look on your face."

"If you saw someone, he was probably a guy who works there. I didn't see him."

"You guys are all bonkers this morning. If you ask me, you need fall break." Ted plugs in his laptop. "Good thing it starts next week."

Kyle peers at the front of the room. "Shouldn't class be starting?"

"Professor 'Boring' is probably having tech issues again," Simone quips.

Jordan looks up as the lights flicker. "It's this room. It's haunted. That's why there are always issues."

Ted is irritated by Jordan's persistence. "It's new construction, that's all. There are always a lot of quirky things to work out with new construction."

"This whole building is new, and this doesn't happen in any of the other classrooms we use," Jordan protests. "It's because the med school stores their cadavers under this room. Don't you remember when we took a tour of the new building? The storage for cadavers is directly beneath us."

Kyle shakes his head. "You might as well give up, Ted. You're not going to get anywhere with the Twilight Zoners. If you ask me, they all watch too many of those haunting shows on TV."

POOR JORDAN. Her friends will keep telling her she didn't see anything at the cemetery. In three or four days, she'll start doubting it herself, and then she'll forget about it. Well, as much as I enjoy teasing Professor Borman, I better get downstairs. It's showtime with the med students.

There they are in groups of four, ready to get their hands on something sharp and start whittling. It's a fine group of young people, except for Tessa Ramage. My God, who the hell gave her a spot in med school? I'm sure she didn't earn it by any honest means or merit. I wonder who her latest victim is? Wait, I don't need to wonder. I can just hang out with her until I find out. This will be an interesting adventure.

I'm the cadaver at the end. I still can't believe Ramage's group is assigned to me. How can death be so cruel? Wasn't it enough that I had to be subjected to that nasty fiendish gorgon in life? To know her hands touch me in death is too much to bear, but she can't hurt me. I don't feel a thing, certainly not the piercing pain she inflicted me with in life. On the other hand, I can probably make her feel something. This is going to be fun.

~

As Tessa pulls on her nitrile gloves, Neal, one of her lab partners, rolls the tray of instruments toward her. "You're up first this time, Tessa."

Tessa picks up the scalpel. "Okay, Franky, baby, let's go for it."

"Who's Frank? We named him Mac."

"He reminds me of Frankenstein's monster. That's probably what we should have named him."

"OMG, you know who this guy is. I knew something was wrong the first time he was unveiled. The look on your face. It was all you could do to keep from gasping."

"We thought you were just upset to see a dead person the first time," Ling says.

Brian is agitated. "Dr. Morgan said he was a professor who died of a myocardial infarction. Was he one of your professors? Is that how you knew him?"

"Keep it down. Someone will hear you." Tessa holds up her hand to quiet them. "For heaven's sake, I didn't have a personal relationship with the old guy. He was just one of my biology professors in undergrad, that's all."

"If you ask me, that's a personal relationship," Neal whispers. "What the hell's the matter with you, Tessa? You think you can break any rules you want. You think you can walk on water."

From the other side of the table, Brian whispers, "You should have told Dr. Morgan to assign us another cadaver. We are not to work on a cadaver we had a personal relationship with or even knew when they were alive."

"You know, at the end of the term, we will meet the family that donated the body. Thank them and show our appreciation for allowing us to study using the remains of their loved one," Ling reminds her.

"It's no big deal. His family doesn't know me."

~

How sweet of Ling to be considerate of my family. But, in typical Tessa fashion, she's lying to all of them. My family will never forget her name as long as they live. She put my wife through hell and made my entire family worry.

∼

Brian is more irritated. "It's a big deal to us."

"Did you ever consider how this could affect our team?" Neal asks.

Tessa rolls her eyes. "Stop worrying. We need to get started." As she prepares to make an incision, something bumps her from behind. "What the hell, Neal? Are you trying to make me cut myself?"

"What are you talking about?"

"You bumped into me."

"No, I didn't. How could I bump into you? I'm standing more than two feet away from you. You slipped somehow."

Tessa glares at him. "Don't let it happen again."

Neal looks at the other two lab partners, and they shrug.

∼

Where is she? I think I smell her perfume. Yes, I'm certain that's it. How can anything smell so sweet and be so rotten to the core? She's approaching someone. It's that young man who assists Dr. Morgan and Dr. Wiseman. Ben, yes, that's his name, Ben Goodwin. I can tell by her smugness; he is about to be her next victim. God help him. Wait, maybe I don't have to rely on God. I may be in a position where I can help him myself. Perhaps this is why I linger here, to protect Ben from Ramage's wrath. I need to get closer to hear their conversation.

∼

Tessa hurries to catch up to Ben. "Have you thought about what I said?"

"Tessa, you know I can't do that."

"Of course, you can. The old guy always forgets things."

"He's a great teacher, and he's a good man. Maybe he is somewhat absent-minded. That doesn't mean someone like you should take advantage of him."

Tessa is insistent. "It's asking very little from you for the amount of money I'm offering."

"Tessa, what's wrong with you? This is not middle school, and you're not bribing me to poke my finger through someone's cupcake. You're probably smarter than eighty percent of your classmates. Just study for the test like everyone else."

"But I have weekend plans. I won't have time to study."

"There's very little social life for medical students. Haven't you figured that out by now?" Ben peers out the windows at a white sedan that has just pulled up and parked next to the curb.

"Is that your precious Suzanne?" Tessa asks. "It would be a shame if she found out her fiancé was sexually harassing a female under-classman while he's supposed to be assisting her professors." She runs her fingers under the lapel of his white coat.

He steps back from her. "You wouldn't dare."

"You have no idea what I can do to you."

"You little witch."

"You shouldn't keep Suzanne waiting. After all, you may never have lunch with her again after today. Think about it. If Dr. Wiseman leaves his briefcase behind in the simulation lab, and he probably will, just forget to look after him this time. No one will know the difference."

Ben shakes his head. "No, I won't be blackmailed by you. Suzanne has more faith in me than that. She will never believe you." Ben turns and walks away.

She raises her voice. "I wouldn't be so sure about that. Others have believed me. Remember the Me Too Movement, Ben, me too."

Ben walks briskly to the door and flings it open as if escaping the flames of hell.

Tessa laughs and mumbles to herself. "That prick's not going to help me. He'll be sorry." She turns and crosses the foyer to buy something for lunch.

AFTER THEIR CARDIO-PULMONARY SIMULATION, the medical students sit around the conference table debriefing.

Tessa congratulates Ling on her performance, making certain Dr. Wiseman hears her. "You did very well, Ling."

"You all did well. I am very impressed with this group," Dr. Wiseman says. "Does anyone have other comments or questions? No? Well, if there are no more questions, you're dismissed. After what I've seen today, I'll be expecting some high marks on that exam Monday."

The students exit the conference room and make their way to the front doors of the simulation lab. Some linger in the hall, divide into study groups, and head for their reserved study rooms. Tessa spots Dr. Wiseman's briefcase on one of the chairs in the conference room. She casually places her lab coat over it so it can't be seen and walks out with the others.

"Are you studying with us?" Ling asks.

"I can't stay; I'm going out of town this weekend."

"I envy people who don't have to study all the time," Ling says.

Tessa stops walking. "Oh, I left my lab coat in there. You go on; I'll see you Monday morning."

Tessa turns and heads back to the conference room to retrieve her coat. She takes Dr. Wiseman's briefcase and slides it into the large bag she is carrying. Using the back hall, she enters the back door to the simulation lab's observation area. Hearing footsteps, she retreats to the closest entrance to an individual sim lab and ducks behind the bed. It's Ben Goodwin looking around to see if Dr. Wiseman left anything behind. He checks the observation area and the conference room. Not finding anything, he leaves as quickly as he came.

Tessa lets out her breath. *That was close.* She stealthily walks to the back hall and hides in one of the exam rooms. She checks the time on her cell phone to make sure Daphne, the receptionist, hasn't locked the main door. Trying to get out after hours would trigger the alarm, and she doesn't want to come up with an excuse for the campus police.

She rifles through the briefcase until she finds the key to Monday's exam. She hates leaving an electronic trail, but it's too close to five o'clock for her to copy it by hand. She takes her cell phone from her pocket, photographs the questions and answer key, and looks at it with pride.

JUST LOOK AT HER. She thinks she's so clever. Now the question I have to ask myself is, can I do to her in death what I could only think about in life? Why waste time? It will be much easier to do it here. I don't care to follow the conniving little witch to wherever she's headed this weekend. I rather fancy a couple more tours at Crown Hill. I will need a portal. Ah, there, on the other side of the observation window. Should I worry about her being around me in this afterlife? I think not. I've yet to see anyone I knew that has passed on. I'm not sure where I am, but I believe she is headed for a space on a much lower level.

TESSA RETURNS to the conference room and places the briefcase back on the chair where Dr. Wiseman had left it. She makes her way back to the observation room so she can exit through the back hall. The lights flicker, and Tessa stiffens at the sound of footsteps behind her. When she turns, she sees the male mannequin the students had used for the cardio-pulmonary simulation earlier. Tessa gasps. "This is impossible. The patient simulators aren't programmed to walk!" She sees the computer that controls it, and it is not turned on. She backs into a small hall that leads to a door. The Simulator follows her.

Before she can scream for help, it grabs her neck with both hands, backs her into the wall, and lifts her off the floor. As she beats her fists against its chest and kicks her feet, the mannequin strangles the life from her. Her movement stops, and she falls into a limp heap on the floor.

The Simulator watches as a dark cloud swirls and shrouds the soul that's leaving her body and pulls it down until it disappears into the floor. Then the Simulator picks up her lifeless, soulless body and carries her from the lab.

AT FIVE MINUTES TILL FIVE, Ben Goodwin returns to the simulation lab. "Sorry, Daphne, I know you're ready to go, but Dr. Wiseman called me and thinks he left his briefcase in the conference room. I left my ID card hanging on my jacket in the car. Please don't lock the door. It'll only take a few seconds. I checked earlier, and I didn't see it."

Daphne laughs. "No problem, take your time. The only thing I have planned this evening is a tour of Crown Hill Cemetery. I don't know why I let my husband talk me into that. I am not looking forward to it."

Ben is baffled to see the briefcase sitting on one of the chairs in the conference room.

How in the hell did I miss that? I really need to get more sleep. He calls Dr. Wiseman and tells him he has the briefcase and will lock it in the doctor's office. He leaves carrying the briefcase, unaware of the grisly event that had taken place a few minutes before.

ON MONDAY MORNING, everyone is surprised when star pupil, Tessa, doesn't show for the exam.

Ling is concerned. "What do you think happened to Tessa?"

"Who knows and who cares." Neal fastens his backpack. "I'm sure it won't affect her grade. She probably wasn't prepared, so she's going to make up some outlandish excuse that will make Dr. Wiseman feel sorry for her."

Brian nods. "That's for sure. Tessa can wheedle her way out of anything."

Ling sighs. "Sometimes I wish I had that talent."

"Oh, no. Believe me, you do not want to be anything like Tessa." Brian looks at his watch. "I need to get off campus for a while. Why don't we go to that coffee shop down the street?"

"Okay, but no hashing over the exam," Neal says. "The first person who brings it up is buying."

AT FOUR IN THE AFTERNOON, Professor Kate Borman goes to the simulation lab to set up pediatric simulations for the nursing students scheduled for eight o'clock the following morning.

Professor Borman checks the equipment in simulation room A. Then she checks simulation room B. "We're going to need the teenage mannequin for this room. The case is a 15-year-old asthmatic female with bacterial pneumonia."

Jeff Culley, the lab technician, quickly gets up from his seat. "That one is on a gurney in the back hall. I'll get it and change them out for you, Professor Borman."

"That would be great. I'll start programming the computer."

Two minutes later, Jeff returns, pushing the gurney with the teenage mannequin. He slides the male mannequin onto the empty gurney Professor Borman has placed next to the bed and moves it to the far side of the room. Jeff starts to put the teenage mannequin on the bed. He pulls off the sheet, jumps back, and gasps so loudly, Professor Borman lifts her head to see what has happened. "It's a body," Jeff yells. "It's somebody. I mean it's a real body."

Professor Borman hurries into the simulation room.

"Dear God, who is this?" Professor Borman asks.

Jeff appears dazed. "I think she's a medical student, one of the first years, but I can't think of her name. I believe she was in one of the last simulations on Friday afternoon."

"I'm calling the campus police." Professor Borman feels the pockets of her jacket for her cell phone. "Jeff, tape a sign on that outside door saying this lab is closed. We don't want anyone walking in here."

Professor Borman shoves her cell phone back into her pocket. "Detective Vance is coming. He wants us to keep the sim lab closed to everyone. I'll go talk to Daphne and have her put a sign on the front door. We are not to touch anything."

Jeff points to the body's left foot. "Look, there's an ID card clipped to her little toe."

Professor Borman steps close to the body and reads the card. "It says Tessa L. Ramage."

DETECTIVE JOHN VANCE from the campus police arrives within two minutes. He calls Homicide, and they arrive fifteen minutes later. Detective Sergeant Brad Hastings is the lead detective, assisted by Detective Kevin Wiley. Hastings immediately has the hallway leading to the simulation lab taped off. He questions Professor Borman, and then he turns his attention to Jeff.

"You're in charge of this simulation lab?" Hastings asks.

"I'm the lead technician, and I was the only technician working here last Friday afternoon."

"You saw the victim here on Friday?"

"Yes, she's a first-year medical student. She participated in a cardio-pulmonary simulation led by Dr. Wiseman at three-thirty."

Hastings has Jeff explain how the simulations work and what is involved. Then he asks him to provide a list of everyone present in the lab on Friday, including those assigned to experiences earlier in the day.

Detective Vance looks startled.

"Is something the matter, John?" Hastings asks.

"I could swear that mannequin opened its eyes." Vance continues to gaze at the simulation room on the opposite side of the window.

Jeff shakes his head. "Oh, no, that's not possible. It's not programmed. You see, I have to hook it up and program it with this computer. It can't breathe, cough, open its eyes, or anything without being programmed."

"It sure looked like the eyelids moved." Vance continues to watch the mannequin.

"It's easy to let your imagination get the best of you in here. It happened to me a lot when I first started working with these things."

"JOHN, get a couple of officers to help you gather the people we need to interview. I'll speak to the receptionist first."

Detective Vance nods to Hastings. "We'll have them here as soon as we can."

Hastings asks Daphne Horne to take a seat in the conference room.

"Mrs. Horne, were you the last one to leave the lab Friday evening?"

"Well, there were two of us. Ben Goodwin, Dr. Wiseman's assistant, was here. He came back to the lab around five minutes till five. I was getting ready to lock the door."

"You say he came back?"

"Yes, he had received a call from Dr. Wiseman because he thought he left his briefcase in the conference room. Ben said he had checked the room earlier and didn't see it, but when he looked the second time, it was there."

Hastings cocks his head to one side. "That seems odd."

"Yes, but some people left after Dr. Wiseman. I suppose one of them could have moved it."

Hastings nods. "Did you hear or see anything unusual after everyone left?"

"No, it was quiet. The only thing was that the temperature seemed to keep getting cooler. It was icy cold when I arrived this morning. I had to call Environmental Services and have them fix the heat. It was much colder in here than outside."

"Is that the maintenance department?"

"Yes, you know how it is, they always have to change the names of things. Anyway, we can't control the temperature. They have to do it. I may have to call them again. It still seems too cold in here." She tucks her hands under the pashmina wrapped around her.

Hastings looks at his notes. "How long was Mr. Goodwin in the conference room?"

"A minute or two. Ben didn't want to hold me up. He came right back."

"You said he assists Dr. Wiseman. Does he have access to the lab?" Hastings asks.

"Yes, but he said he left his ID card in his car. There wasn't any need for him to go get it when I was still here."

"Did anyone use the lab over the weekend?"

"No. The lab was closed all weekend." Daphne shows him some forms. "We keep these on two clipboards on the front desk for students to sign. Every student has to sign when they enter the main door and sign out when they leave."

"Do the students reserve the rooms they use ahead of time?"

"Usually, but not always. If students need to practice and an exam room is open, they can drop in and sign for it. The simulations with the mannequins are planned and supervised with a professor that watches from the observation room."

"I see. Thank you, Mrs. Horne. Here is my card. If you think of anything else, please call."

Hastings interviews Ben Goodwin in the conference room while Detective Wiley goes to interview Dr. Wiseman.

"I'm Detective Sergeant Hastings, I understand you and Mrs. Horne were the last to leave this lab area on Friday. Is that correct?"

"Yes, sir. I left once and came back because Dr. Wiseman called me and asked me to retrieve his briefcase. He thought he left it in this conference room. This is where the last group of students had their debriefing after the cardio-pulmonary simulation."

"You found the briefcase?"

"Yes, it was right there." Ben points to one of the chairs. "The weird thing is, I checked this room after the debriefing, and I swear it wasn't there."

"You think someone moved it?"

"Yes, and now I think I know who it was. I think it was Tessa Ramage."

"Why do you think that?"

Ben takes a deep breath. "I might as well tell you this. It will probably make me look bad, but I want to be honest with you."

Hastings leans in. "Go on."

"I don't believe Tessa was the top-notch student everyone thought she was. Oh, she had the brains, but she didn't apply herself. She seemed to prefer taking the easy way out. She approached me a couple of times and tried to bribe me to gain access to the exam questions for the test the first years had this morning."

"That would be the exam she didn't show up for today?"

"Yes. Tessa approached me on Friday as I was about to leave the building to have lunch with my fiancée. I told her she needed to study like everyone else. I told her I wouldn't be bribed. Then she threatened to blackmail me."

"What did she have on you?"

"Nothing, but she threatened to make false accusations against me. She said she could accuse me of sexual harassment, and people would believe her. She said she could break up my engagement."

"What did you do?"

"I called her bluff, and she said she knew people would believe her because they'd believed her before. Well, that scared the hell out of me. I got out the door as fast as I could."

"I think I'm getting the picture. The key to that exam was in the briefcase Dr. Wiseman left behind?"

"Yes, I think I didn't see it because she had taken it to copy those answers. Then she put it back on that chair where I found it. Dr.

Wiseman has the habit of writing his exams in Word and programming them in the exam website on Saturdays."

"The medical students take the exams on computers?"

"Yes, usually in the large computer lab on this floor."

"Her extortion attempt makes you a suspect. Did anyone else hear that conversation between the two of you?" Hastings writes something on his notepad.

"I don't think anyone was close enough, but I told my fiancée and the two friends that had lunch with us. I thought it was better to let them know I was being threatened than to wait until Tessa started her lies."

"Where were you between four-fifteen and the time you returned to the lab on Friday?"

"I was in the medical library, getting some research articles. I left there and walked to my car. As soon as I got in my car, Dr. Wiseman called me, and I returned to look for his briefcase."

"Can anyone verify you were in the library?"

"The medical librarian and two medical students."

Hastings hands Ben a tablet. "Write down their names and the names of the people you met for lunch on Friday. Did Miss Ramage mention where she was planning to go over the weekend?"

"Not to me."

Hastings slides his card across the table. "Call if you think of anything else."

DETECTIVE WILEY RETURNS to the conference room. "Dr. Wiseman is shook-up. I think he's shocked that something like this could happen on campus. The president of the University called him while I was there. Sounds like they're trying to figure out how to handle the press."

Hastings drums his fingers on the table. "Did Dr. Wiseman have anything to offer?"

"He said she was one of his better first-year students. As far as he knows, she didn't have any enemies. But he doesn't know anything about her personal life."

The evidence bag with Tessa's cell phone is on the table. The phone rings. Wiley quickly pulls on a pair of gloves. Hastings presses the phone through the bag to answer the call and puts it on speaker. Wiley takes the phone from the evidence bag.

A male voice on the other end starts ranting furiously before Wiley has a chance to say anything. "Where were you Saturday, you conniving little bitch? I've been leaving voicemails. Why haven't you returned my calls? Look, I'm not playing these games with you. I was there with the money. I'm going out of town on business. If you're expecting to set up another meeting, it'll have to be after the thirtieth." The call ends.

"I got the number." Hastings flips his notebook around so Wiley can see it.

Wiley looks at it closely. "That's a Chicago area code. I'm guessing she was blackmailing him."

"Sounds like a man with a motive. We'll need all of Ramage's phone records."

Vance taps on the door. "I've got everyone you asked to speak to waiting in the lounge outside. Two officers are with them. They've been instructed not to use cell phones or speak to one another."

"We'll start with her lab partners," Hastings says. "Send in Neal Phillips."

Neal enters and takes a seat.

"What can you tell us about Tessa Ramage, Mr. Phillips?" Wiley asks.

"Tessa was a piece of work. I mean, I'm sorry she was killed, but she was not a nice person. She looked good on the outside, and she was smart, but for some reason, she never seemed to want to apply herself."

"You mean she took the easy way out?" Wiley asks.

"Yes, short cuts that benefitted her, even if they hurt others."

"Can you give an example of what you're talking about?"

"If she was late or she missed an exam, she always seemed to be able to come up with some excuse good enough to fool the professors. It really ticked us off when she didn't tell the rest of us that she recognized our cadaver."

Wiley and Hastings look at one another. Wiley focuses his gaze on Neal. "I'm not sure I understand what you're saying."

"A few weeks ago, we were assigned a cadaver to study. It turns out the guy was one of her biology profs in undergrad. She should have told us and informed Dr. Morgan so he could assign a different cadaver to our group, but she didn't. Why, I don't know. It would certainly bother me to work on the cadaver of a person I knew when they were living. But that was typical of Tessa's style. She didn't play by the rules and didn't care."

Hastings is curious. "If she didn't tell you, how did you know?"

"She slipped and referred to him as Franky. Med students name their cadavers, and ours is named Mac. I assume the guy's name was Francis or Frank. I don't know any more than that."

"Have you told Dr. Morgan?" Wiley asks.

"No, we just found out about it on Friday morning. Now, we're afraid he'll think we kept it from him all semester. We were sure Contessa Tessa would throw us under the bus. She would have most likely lied and said we all knew about it. That's just the way she is. I mean was."

Ling Wu also told them she was upset about the cadaver situation, and Tessa didn't think rules applied to her.

"Did she ever mention a boyfriend?" Hastings asks.

"No."

"Do you know where she was planning to go over the weekend?"

"No, I assumed it was Chicago. She'd gone there before, and she went to college there. I think she still had friends there."

"Is there anything else that might be important, or you thought was unusual about Miss Ramage's behavior?"

"She always seemed to have money for anything she wanted. Most of us have to put off buying things we want, but if she decided she wanted something, she just bought it. I don't know how that was possible. I don't believe she was from a wealthy family. Although she did act superior to the rest of us. Other students called her Contessa Tessa behind her back."

Brian Riker's interview yields the same results. "Tessa, from a wealthy family? Oh, no. Believe me, if she was, she would have bragged about it and rubbed our noses in it every day."

TWO DAYS LATER, the detectives return to the simulation lab. They look around, hoping to pick up something they've missed. Campus Detective John Vance joins them. They sit in the observation room and hash over the case again. Frustration shows on Detective Sergeant Hastings' face. "We've found lots of fingerprints; all belonging to students, faculty, and lab techs. Everyone that could be considered a suspect has an airtight alibi. Even that married guy in Chicago she was blackmailing and no evidence he hired anyone."

"It's hard to believe she had tried to blackmail that biology professor, Frank Garner, when she was in college and then cut on him as a cadaver," Vance says. "What kind of a person does that?"

Wiley sighs. "We know Frank Garner certainly had motive, but we can rule him out. What about the man those nursing students, Jordan Adler and Simone Delong, saw in the cemetery the weekend before last?"

Vance laughed. "Great description. Dark suit and tie, zombie looking. I'm sure that was just some guy trying to scare them and not connected to this case. Simone wouldn't even admit to seeing him until this murder happened. The students are all scared now."

Hastings scrutinizes his notes as if something new might appear. "The test answers were on her cell phone, so we know Ramage stayed in the lab so she could get that exam key. She was strangled, and her neck broken. Bruising on the outside of both hands and wrists indicates she was beating him with her fists. That's strange. Why not scratch his face or poke his eyes? There was no tissue under her fingernails, only a slight amount of fiber consistent with the hospital gown on the mannequin she worked with Friday. We can't pinpoint any evidence of someone else being in the lab. There were no fingerprints on the body or her ID card."

Wiley looks around. "He could have grabbed gloves right here in the lab."

Hastings continues. "The security cameras malfunctioned for an hour around the time she was killed. Outdoor cameras didn't reveal anyone who shouldn't be coming or going from the building on Friday. All we came up with were those scuff marks on the bottom of the wall made by her shoes. Someone lifted her while strangling her. That took a guy with a lot of strength. Who killed Tessa Ramage? And what happened to her shoes?"

Vance shrugs. "It's looking like this one is headed for the cold case files."

Wiley looks at Vance. "Speaking of cold, can't you people do anything about the heat in here? I've been in morgues that weren't as cold as this place. How do the students stand it?"

"I told you Monday, it's not usually like this. Something is wrong with the heating system," Vance says.

You Detectives are a fine bunch of fellows. I wish I could tell you that your search for answers is futile. Tessa has been shepherded into the depths of hell where she belongs.

A loud noise in the hall leading to the front entrance sends the detectives bolting from their seats.

"What the hell was that?" Wiley asks.

They rush toward the sound and discover a pair of shoes in the hall.

"My God, those fit the description of the shoes Ramage was wearing." Hastings draws his gun. "You two check the back halls. I'll look out front."

∽

HAVE FUN, *fellows. Now, I'm going to take an afternoon stroll through Crown Hill Cemetery. It's such a lovely autumn day.*

THE CURSE OF THE BENJAMIN MANSION

BY ROSS CARLEY AND KAREN PHILLIPS

"You're firing me?" Trish pulled the phone from her ear and glared at the screen as if Will, the owner of The Porter Coffee Shop, could see her expression.

"I'm sorry, Trish. This pandemic is killing me."

She tuned him out and took a deep breath, tried to calm herself. She knew this was true. "Marion County might go back into Stage Three," he continued. "If that happens, we'll have to close again."

"How'm I supposed to pay my bills?"

"I'm sorry, Trish, I really am," he said. "But it's either cut staff or go out of business. When things return to normal, I'll hire you back. I promise."

"You mean, *if* things return to normal," Trish scoffed. She knew it was bad.

"Once a vaccine is available, I'*m* sure things will get better. I'll give you a great reference. Good luck, Trish."

She immediately sent a text to her girlfriend Dominique who worked for a catering company.

"Lost my job. Help?"

A few minutes later, Dominique responded.

"Tiny said yes. Need to be at the Benjamin Estate at 5 p.m. tomorrow. I'll pick you up."

"Thanks. I owe you!"

"What are BFFs for?"

"I've always wanted to see the inside. I wonder if the stories are true about the ghost nurse."

"Guess we'll find out."

Trish Googled the estate on her phone and found a website with photos and information. No photos of ghosts, but detailed accounts attributed to a curse piqued her curiosity.

The Benjamin Mansion was built in the 1870s by Cyrus Benjamin, who had made his fortune during the Civil War in foundries and railroads.

Cyrus died in a freak accident before the completion of his dream home. He fell from construction scaffolding and was impaled on a pitchfork lashed to a landscaper's wagon three stories below.

During World War I, the City of Indianapolis purchased the property for use as a hospital and rehabilitation center for wounded veterans. One nurse fell madly in love with a soldier who committed suicide on her watch. Riddled with guilt, the nurse killed herself soon after. Accounts of a ghost in a white nurse's uniform pacing the widow's walk circulated. Stories of the ghost and the curse of the Benjamin Mansion were passed down through generations.

In the mid-1950s the Hoosier Children's Foundation purchased and renovated the mansion as its headquarters. At least one person a year associated with the Foundation perished in an improbable accident or medical incident. The legend of the curse lived on.

Dominique and Trish drove through the black metal entry gates and parked next to an orange van with Tiny's Catering painted in bold letters. Two men wearing face masks and gloves were unloading trays of food from the back.

One of the men was dark skinned and built like a football player. "That must be Tiny," Trish said.

"Yep. Did I tell you he used to play for the Colts?"

Trish shook her head.

"He got injured and now he's doing this. He always loved to cook."

"Can't believe anyone is throwing a big party during Covid," Trish said.

Dominique turned to face her friend. "It's a job. Right?"

"Yeah, sorry. That relief check from the Feds didn't last long. And who knows if we'll get another one. Forget I said anything."

Before getting out of the car the women took a minute to secure their long hair into ponytails, then put on their face masks.

Dominique waved at the men. "Tiny! Jason! I want you to meet Trish."

Trish wasn't listening. She stood transfixed, lost in time, as she stared at the widow's walk atop the four-story Victorian building.

The setting sun cast the front of the edifice in a golden glow, but dark clouds to the north and a cool breeze presaged an impending storm.

Dominique waved a hand in front of her friend's face. "Earth to Trish."

"Sorry. Ever since I was a kid I've been curious about this place."

Tiny took a red bandana from a back pocket and wiped sweat from his brow. His brown eyes settled on Trish. "You don't really believe that hogwash, do you?"

Trish shook her head. "No. All I care about is getting up to the widow's walk."

Tiny raised his eyebrows. "Not on my watch, you won't. You can check it out on your own time."

Trish felt her cheeks redden. "Okay. I understand."

Jason wiggled his fingers in front of Trish's face in an effort to lighten the tension. "Hey, are you afraid of ghosts?"

Dominique grinned. "She's afraid of any guy named Jason. Ever since she saw the movie *Friday the 13th*. So, watch it, buddy."

Trish couldn't help but smile at her friend's teasing.

"Hey, I get that all the time, but I'm a good Jason," he said, his blue eyes twinkling with amusement. "Anyway, according to legend . . . "

"Yes, I've heard it," Trish interrupted. "A nurse appears at night and walks back and forth, back and forth, waiting for her dead soldier to come back to her."

Trish returned her gaze to the widow's walk when a movement caught her eye. A white face looked out from the circular window of the room directly below. Just then, the wind picked up and she shivered.

"Stop it, Jason," Dominique said. "Can't you see you're scaring her?"

"Just a chill from the storm coming in," Trish said, rubbing her arms for warmth. "And I saw somebody in the window of the fourth-floor room."

"See what you did?" Dominique said. "Now you got her seeing things."

"No, really. I did see someone," Trish said. She looked again at the window, but no-one was there.

Tiny chuckled. "Jason's just messing. Right Jason?" He gave the younger man a friendly slap on the back with a meaty hand. "You want Trish to quit? I need all the help I can get."

Jason bent his tall frame and bowed before Trish. "Please accept my apology, dear lady."

"Apology accepted." She turned to Tiny. "Thank you for giving me the job. Sorry to hear about your worker getting sick."

"Yeah, bummer. Eric got a sore throat," Jason said. "I hope it's just a cold and not COVID-19."

"I told him to stay home," Tiny said. "Better safe than sorry. They're expecting a hundred guests tonight. Keep your masks and gloves on at all times."

Tiny handed a box of gloves to Trish and Dominique and they each took a pair.

"We better get moving before the rain starts," Jason said.

Tiny gave instructions and they transported the food and beverages into the large kitchen. While he and Jason arranged the stainless-steel servers and lit the warming candles, Trish and Dominique went into the dining hall. They opened the double doors to the living room. Beyond, they could see the foyer. The lighting from chandeliers had been turned to the lowest setting. The rooms had been lavishly decorated—fake spider webbing clung to every surface, rubber bats hung suspended in air from the ceiling. In one corner of the living room was a cemetery with headstones and skeleton arms poking out of brown cloth resembling dirt.

Dominique clucked. "My, my. Just look at that. Must have cost a fortune."

"Yeah, they sure didn't shop at Dollar General," Trish said.

"Hey, you two," Tiny called out. "Back to work."

"We're not allowed in there," Jason said.

Trish frowned. "Why not? Haunted in here, too?"

"Because we're not guests, just the hired help," Jason said. "This is only their second party. The last one turned out fine. The curse didn't rear its ugly head. So don't jinx it."

Trish and Dominique shook their heads no.

"The entire mansion is decorated. Each room has a theme. Near the end of the evening, the guests are taken in small groups through the rooms. Each room has some kind of scary experience. It's all very mysterious."

"Reminds me of the Poe story, "Mask of the Red Death"," Dominique said.

"What's the big deal if we just take a peek?" Trish asked.

"Off limits, little lady," Tiny said, his voice booming. "Don't ask questions. Just do your job. Got it?"

Trish studied her feet in embarrassment, then looked up at Tiny and said, "Yes, sir."

When they finished setting up, Trish and Jason hauled the empty containers outside. As they were stacking cartons and boxes into Tiny's van, a black delivery truck emblazoned with Virtual Experiences: We Augment Your Reality pulled into the driveway.

Trish and Jason watched the crew, all dressed in black, set up a protective canopy on the lawn between the mansion and Meridian

Street. They turned on high-lumen lamps and unloaded electronic equipment, including huge video projectors.

Jason tapped Trish's shoulder. "Come on, we better get back," he said.

Trish followed him into the kitchen but glanced back to the activity outside. "What is all that stuff?"

"The big cylinders with lenses sticking out of them are super-beam three-D holographic projectors," he said. "They'll project 3D images like a witch riding a broom, the headless horseman, things like that."

"A bit over-the-top, if you ask me."

"You got that right. Nothing but the best for this crowd."

Distant thunder rumbled.

"Not the best weather for it," Trish said.

Jason grinned. "Money can't buy everything."

AT PRECISELY 6:30 p.m. the mansion caretakers, Mr. and Mrs. Bates, entered the kitchen dressed as Morticia and Gomez Addams, and called a meeting. The catering staff and two employees of the mansion stopped what they were doing and stood at attention.

Mrs. Bates, in a black face mask matching her skin-tight floor-length black dress, motioned to a small cabinet mounted on the wall. "This is where we keep the keys." She opened the door to reveal sets of keys hanging from rows of pegs. She removed one large antique skeleton key and dangled it from the tip of a long black lacquered fingernail. "This particular key is to the fourth-floor room, which leads to the widow's walk. It is only to be used in case of emergency. And I repeat only in case of emergency."

Trish frowned. She really wanted to see the widow's walk. She needed a plan.

Jason winked at Trish, then said, "Just out of curiosity, Mrs. Bates, why is that?"

"Young man," Mrs. Bates said. "I saw that wink. Since you are under my employ, I expect to be taken seriously. To be frank, people have been fatally injured trying to gain access to the widow's walk through that room. It is unsafe. People have died over the years, like a painter who fell to his death. So, please stay away.

"My husband and I have been planning this event for months. It must run smoothly, without a hitch. That is, if you want to cater more events in the future." She then gave a pointed look at Tiny who nodded his assent.

Mr. Bates cleared his throat. "What my wife is trying to say is that the room is under renovation. Until construction is finished, the room is simply, and unequivocally, off-limits to staff and guests. Is that clear?" He looked at each and every person with a stern expression until everyone nodded their heads. "I hope none of you believed that garbage in the *Indianapolis Star* about the curse. It wouldn't surprise me if they tried to sensationalize the widow's walk to sell more papers."

"Thank you, darling," Mrs. Bates said in her best Morticia drawl. She shut the cabinet door with a bang just as thunder rumbled outside, closer than before.

Trish jumped.

The lights flickered and Trish noticed a look pass between Mr. and Mrs. Bates. She grabbed hold of Dominique's hand.

"Calm down, girl," Dominique said, giving Trish a reassuring squeeze.

"Don't be frightened," Mr. Bates said, "It's common in old houses. Nothing to be concerned about."

TRISH AND DOMINIQUE checked the chafing dishes on tables lined against the wall in the dining hall.

"Dominique, don't you think that was a little weird?"

"The lights flickering?"

"No. The key to the fourth-floor room. Why show us the key if it's off-limits?"

Dominique shrugged. "In case of emergency, like they said."

Trish shook her head. "Still . . . And I really wanted to see the widow's walk."

Jason pushed a cart with coffee urns into the dining hall. "Psst," he said to Trish behind one hand. "We'll sneak up there later. Okay?"

"I better not," she said. "This is my first job with Tiny and I don't want to get fired. And Morticia said people have been fatally injured trying to get to the widow's walk."

"You believe that mumbo-jumbo?" Jason said with a smile. "She was just being melodramatic. After all, it is Halloween."

"THOSE COSTUMES sure didn't come from Walmart," Dominique said. She and Trish were cleaning up in the kitchen with Jason.

"Most of them look custom-made," Jason said.

"I like the swashbuckling pirate. He looks like Johnny Depp in *Pirates of the Caribbean*, sword and all," Trish said.

"You like pirates?" Jason asked. "Shiver me timbers, but you're a fine wench. Argh."

Trish giggled and flicked soapy water at him.

By seven-thirty, the noise level from the living room implied alcohol was freely flowing from the bar. The occasional shriek of laughter could be heard above the music being played through the D.J.'s speakers. Outside the night was pitch dark with occasional bursts of lightning.

"Did you see Nurse Ratched?" Trish asked. "Looks like she just stepped out of *One Flew Over the Cuckoo's Nest*."

"That's one of my favorite movies," Jason said. "The costume, mask, and wig are perfect, and the hypo she's waving around looks real."

"I'm sure it's not," Trish said.

"He's obviously afraid of needles," Dominique said.

"Who isn't?" Jason said. "Hey, and how 'bout the two dressed as Batman? Damn near identical. I'll bet they're pissed. Probably paid a mint, too."

"I expect their wives are upset," Trish said. "It's almost as bad as two socialites showing up at a cocktail party wearing the same gown."

"Who's the guy named Arnie people are talking about?" Dominique asked. "When I walk up with a tray of hors d'oeuvres, several times people have been talking about him."

"Is someone dressed up like Arnold Schwarzenegger?" Trish asked.

Jason lowered his voice. "Shhh. They're probably talking about the Bates' son, Arnold. I heard he got Covid back in March when the pandemic first started. He recovered but hasn't been the same since."

Trish leaned in. "That's awful," she whispered.

"Poor guy," Dominique said. "What do you mean he's not the same?"

"Something about neurological damage. Got addicted to opioids and the rehab facility he was in won't take him back. Supposedly he's living here in the mansion."

Just then, Tiny entered the kitchen carrying another empty chafing dish. "The natives are getting restless. Let's put out the desserts."

They loaded trays with delectables ranging from Indiana home-made pumpkin pie to petit fours, cannoli, and chocolate mousse served in crystal parfait glasses, and delivered them to the dining hall.

Back in the kitchen Tiny wiped sweat from his brow. "Good work, everyone. Take a 15-minute break outside and help yourself to some of these leftovers." He hooked a thumb to a tray of lady finger sandwiches. "And maintain social distancing. I don't want any complaints about not adhering to guidelines."

They all nodded.

"When you get back, I want Dominique at the bar." He looked at Jason and Trish. "You two look for empties, check for any broken glassware, make sure everything is neat and tidy. When this is over, I want as little mess to clean up as possible."

They pulled off their gloves, exchanged aprons for jackets, and each grabbed a few sandwiches and a bottle of water before exiting the kitchen's back door. Outside the air was chilly and thick with mist. They took off their face masks and breathed deeply.

Trish exhaled, her breath forming a cloud of steam. "Wow. The fresh air feels great."

The trio munched on sandwiches as they passed through the porte-cochere and out to the front lawn. Trees were festooned with orange lights and ghosts floated on wires strung between them.

Near the corner of the mansion, amidst bales of hay, two scarecrows were dressed as "American Gothic," with one carrying a pitchfork.

"Check it out," Jason said, pointing his bottle of water to the other corner of the mansion.

Dominique grinned. "It's Edvard Munch's painting, "The Scream"."

They went to the visual effects crew tent and viewed the holograms projected above, and on, the mansion. A technician was hunched over one of the projectors.

"That's really cool," Trish said, pointing. "Look at the witch riding her broomstick and the ghost nurse on the widow's walk. She's waving to us. Looks like she's trying to get our attention."

"Awesome," Jason said. He turned to the technician. "You guys really captured the history of this place, ghost nurse and all."

"That's weird," the tech said, with a perplexed expression.

"What do you mean?" Jason asked.

"That's what's weird," the technician said. "We didn't program any nurse and we aren't projecting her image. Here, let me show you."

He turned off the projector and the witch vanished.

The nurse froze mid-wave. She stared down at them as if trying to communicate a silent message. After a moment, she hurried to the turret and disappeared.

"That was odd," Trish said. "It's like the ghost was trying to tell us something."

"I thought the same thing," Dominique said. "Now I'm getting spooked."

"Is she from one of the other projectors?" Jason asked the tech guy.

The man shook his head and pointed to the sky. "One is doing the headless horseman there." He moved his finger. "And the other is projecting that ghost pirate ship over there. See? No nurse."

RETURNING to the kitchen from their break, they donned fresh face masks and gloves. Dominique took a bucket of ice to the bar in the dining hall. Trish and Jason collected trash and brought empties to the kitchen. Tiny stayed busy monitoring supplies and regularly checking in with Mr. and Mrs. Bates.

Trish glanced around to make sure she and Jason were alone. She grabbed his arm and squealed, eyes wide with excitement. "I changed my mind about going up to the widow's walk. I have to see if that's really the ghost nurse up there. This is too good a chance to pass up."

Jason frowned. "Look, Trish, my bad. I shouldn't have suggested we take a look later. Tiny won't like it. And the Bates told us not to."

"Fine, chicken. Just kidding." She held up her cellphone. "In five minutes, I'll even set my timer. Cover for me?"

Jason sighed. "Okay, but don't make me regret this."

Trish grabbed the skeleton key from the cabinet, gave Jason a thumbs up, then left the kitchen without a backwards glance.

Jason watched her disappear, a look of concern on his face, then smacked his forehead. "Oh, hell," he muttered. "I better make sure she doesn't get hurt." He grabbed a trash bag as a ruse in case Tiny wanted to know what he was doing and hurried to the stairwell.

TINY APPROACHED the bar where Dominique was handing a flute of effervescent liquid to a werewolf.

"You seen Trish or Jason?" he asked.

"No. I've been crazy busy. These people are thirsty. Who knew werewolves liked champagne?"

Tiny scowled. "I'm serious. If you see those two, tell them to report to me ASAP."

At that moment, a bolt of lightning lit up the room, a clap of thunder resounded, and the lights went out.

Someone screamed.

Trish was almost to the fourth-floor room below the widow's walk when the power failed. Undaunted, she set her phone to flashlight mode, and continued up the stairs. As she rounded the corner, someone climbed the staircase behind her with a heavy tread, breathing hard. She hoped it wasn't Tiny or she'd be in big trouble.

She reached the fourth-floor landing and removed the key when she noticed the door was ajar. She entered the room and shut the door. A powerful stench overwhelmed her. Her flashlight revealed a dirty sleeping bag and several blankets. Empty food containers were piled against one wall and an overflowing chemical toilet sat in the opposite corner.

What the hell? Dominique wouldn't believe her without evidence. She was taking a video with her cellphone when the door suddenly slammed open, knocking her, and the phone, to the floor.

Nurse Ratched lurched into the room carrying a body over one shoulder, unaware of anyone else in the room. Trish scrambled to her knees, searching the filthy floor for her phone. She located it just as the nurse ripped the costume mask away, revealing a man's face. Trish gasped. With a grunt the man dropped his burden onto the sleeping bag. The head of his victim lolled to the side towards Trish and she bit her lip to keep from screaming. Mrs. Bates stared at her, silently begging for help, when the man jammed the hypo needle into her neck.

Realization hit Trish—the man had to be Arnie—and she screamed.

Arnie whipped around and moaned when he saw Trish. "No!" he said.

With her back against the wall, Trish kept her eyes on Arnie as she inched her way to the door. Footsteps echoed on the staircase. Just as Arnie pulled out the hypo from his mother's neck and came toward Trish, Jason exploded into the room.

Arnie, eyes wide with madness, threw back his head and yelled in frustration. He shook his head, shuddered, and stumbled to the door leading to the widow's walk.

When Jason saw Mrs. Bates' crumpled form he turned to Trish. "We need to get help," he said. "But first, give me the key."

Trish, in shock, simply nodded and handed it to him.

Jason locked the door. "He's not going anywhere now." He pulled Trish with him down the staircase. "Come on."

Trish clung to his arm and found her voice. "Maybe Mrs. Bates is still alive. We should call 911. I didn't do anything to stop him, Jason. I feel terrible."

Jason stopped. "Don't beat yourself up, Trish. There was nothing you could do."

He punched in the numbers while Trish used her cell phone to light their way.

"It's so sad," she said. "His parents must've kept him in that room like a prisoner."

"Yeah. It's no wonder he wanted revenge."

A woman answered and Jason explained the emergency, gave her the address, then disconnected.

Down in the main floor candles had been lit and most guests were using their phones as flashlights. Trish and Jason went to the kitchen and returned the skeleton key. They threw their gloves into the trash and joined the growing throng of people outside on the lawn escaping from the darkened mansion.

"So much for social distancing," Trish thought, noting the party goers grouped in tight clusters.

Dominique ran up to Trish and wrapped her in a bear hug. "Girl, where have you been? Are you okay? You look like you've seen a ghost."

Trish was about to answer when several people shouted as they looked up and pointed at the widow's walk.

Dominique gasped, "My God."

The sky had partially cleared and the full moon intermittently bathed the scene in eerie blue light. Arnie was not alone. With him was the World War I nurse, her arms stretched out as if to embrace her long-lost lover. Arnie backed slowly away from the apparition, one step at a time, wielding the hypo in the air as a weapon.

Arnie backed himself to the corner, but the nurse kept coming. In a desperate move, he tried to push her away, but his hands went right through her semi-transparent body. She kept coming. He lost his balance, arms flailing, and fell over the edge, emitting a blood-curdling scream.

The crowd gave a collective cry of horror as Arnie landed solidly on the pitchfork held by the "American Gothic" scarecrow. His body hung limp as a rag doll—the prongs sticking out of his bloody back—a macabre version never envisioned by the artist, Grant Wood.

A large man pushed through the crowd like a linebacker intent on getting to the end zone.

"Here comes Tiny," Dominique said.

"I've been looking all over for you two," he said, concern in his eyes.

Trish was about to respond when emergency vehicles with flashing lights and sirens arrived as well as several TV news vans. Police began to take charge of the scene. They instructed everyone to stay put and not enter the house, or leave the premises, until they were given the okay.

The police escorted Mr. Bates away as paramedics shoved two body bags on stretchers into the waiting ambulances.

Lights blazed as reporters spoke into their microphones and asked, "What really pushed Arnold Bates over the edge? Was it the ghost nurse? Could it have been the after-effects of his having had COVID-19? Or a madman whose mind was twisted by his addiction to opioids?"

The next day Trish saw in the news that Mr. Bates had confessed to providing Arnie's costume and letting him out of the tower room for the party. "I just wanted my son to have a little bit of fun," he said. He claimed he'd no idea Arnie planned to kill Mrs. Bates.

"Yeah, right," Trish thought. She wondered if he was really telling the truth. Or did the whole horrible event have something to do with the curse of the Benjamin Mansion?

And so the legend lived on.

UNDOCUMENTED

BY ELIZABETH A. SANMIGUEL

"I won! I won!"

Olivia jumped up and down, spread her arms and turned around, showing off her spider costume. Estéban rolled his eyes at his baby sister's antics and smiled. She'd been looking forward to the Autumn Festival in Irvington for almost half a year, which was a huge chunk of her five years of life. Their mother had worked for a month on the outfit, and the extra two sets of arms under her actual arms that moved when she moved made Estéban smile.

The annual festival was held outside in late October. Streets on the main drag of Irvington, a small, historic area of Indianapolis, were closed off, allowing the throngs of people to wander around the shops and vendor booths without fear of being run over.

"Can we go get ice cream at Wyliepalooza with my gift certificate? I think there's enough for both of us." She hopped and Estéban smiled as three pairs of hands came together, pleading.

At 16, Estéban was too cool to admit ice cream was a draw. Their mother had left him in charge of Olivia. Getting a sweet treat was for her. His enjoyment was incidental. Anyway, that was his story and he was sticking to it. They walked towards what Estéban thought of as a run-down building but all the gringos in the area probably thought of as vintage. Still, they had really good ice cream.

They each got a cone and headed back outside into the activity and the chilly evening air. Estéban shivered and started to rethink the wisdom of ice cream. Maybe he should have gotten the hot fudge sundae.

Many kids passed by them in their mostly store-bought Halloween costumes. His mother had been gathering scraps from her work as a seamstress for most of the year. Olivia's outfit was much more elaborate than the store ones. Estéban's sociology teacher had mentioned the phrase "Necessity is the mother of invention." Olivia had needed a costume, and Mamá's creativity made something wonderful out of scraps.

"E! Dude!" Estéban heard his best friend Sean call out.

They both went to Howe High School and had become friends over their mutual love of manga, the beautifully drawn Japanese comics. Sean was a blue-eyed blonde with an interest in world cultures. He loved Estéban's mother's cooking. Actually, as an only child, he loved Estéban's family and was pretty much an honorary member.

Sean came over every Saturday evening for dinner. Because he ate so much, he always brought a bag of enough groceries for Estéban's mother to cook a meal for the entire family.

Sean was also interested in Latin culture, and Estéban had spent a good deal of time explaining differences to him. They had had a long conversation about how Halloween and Day of the Dead were different. Sean was bummed there was no candy or dressing up involved.

"It's mainly for prayer and remembrance of the dead," Estéban had told him.

"Oh, there are a lot of cultures where that is a thing. Still, candy would be nice," Sean said. This evening, though, Sean was focused on the Far East.

"Hey, you see the latest issue?" Sean had his phone out and was showing him images from a series they both liked. Estéban didn't have a smartphone and would have otherwise had to wait until he got home to read it. After looking at Sean's phone for what only seemed like a few minutes, he sensed a void. Looking up at the mass of humanity, he did not see his sister. Estéban's chest tightened. Crap, he'd lost his sister.

"Man, do you see Olivia anywhere?"

Sean looked up and shrugged at the mass of people in front of them and shook his head no. They looked at each other and simultaneously said, "In 10."

Meaning that they would both look and then meet back where they were in 10 minutes. When they met back up both without Olivia Estéban wanted to barf. He didn't want to freak Sean out though and decided to keep looking for her on his own.

"Gotta go." He waved at Sean and took off.

Estéban jumped repeatedly, surveying all the people, and ran around yelling her name. No Olivia. After about 20 minutes of this, he thought he should go home and see if she had made her way back to the house. If she got home before he did, he would be in *so* much trouble. Even if his mother was not at home, one of his other sisters would probably rat him out. His brother wouldn't, but that was because Estéban had *way* more stuff on him than Diego had on Estéban. He wouldn't care, though. He just wanted to find her. He was supposed to take care of her and protect her. If anything happened to her, he would never forgive himself.

He headed north towards the park. They lived in a little house not too far from Ellenberger Park just off of Ritter. He kept scanning the area and calling her name in case she had gotten ahead of him. He looked down into the darkness. At the corner of Pleasant Run and Ritter, there was a huge hill and steep stairs that went down into the area where the tennis courts were.

He had just gotten to the park when he saw Olivia's little shape shooting up the stairs and out. She wasn't supposed to go there after dark or unaccompanied even during the day. At the top, she frantically looked around, saw Estéban, flew towards him, and jumped into his arms. She was crying and the thump of her heart was so strong he felt the pounding on his chest. Her distress was palpable and the planned rebuke died on his lips.

"Olivia, what happened?" She wrapped her legs and all her arms around him. He gently patted her back and waited for her to stop crying. After several minutes, he heard her say, "He hurt her."

"Who? Where?"

"The pretty girl. The one who doesn't speak Spanish," Olivia spoke into Estéban's ear.

Estéban immediately thought of Mina, his friend from school. She and her family were totally American, but she looked Latina. "Mina?"

Olivia nodded.

"Where? Where is she?"

Olivia pointed back towards the park.

"Show me." Still carrying her, he went down the steps.

They went far into the park and Olivia pointed toward a small group of trees. In the dark, the only light was from a streetlight on the pathway above. All Estéban could make out was a lump. He went closer. The lump was a person.

"Hey, you okay?" He put Olivia down and went to the person. He turned her over and a slight beam of light illuminated Mina's face. Unblinking, she stared up. No movement.

"Mina? What happened?" He was asking Mina, but it was Olivia that answered.

"The man hit her. I saw him."

"Mina? Wake up!" Estéban picked Mina up and hugged her to him. Was there a heartbeat? No. Not one he could feel. Breathe! Just a small breath—anything!

Mina. Beautiful. Kind to everyone. She would never be one of the mean girls. Estéban blushed thinking about the last time he talked to her. He meant to ask her out, but instead they'd had a long conversation about manga. He rocked back and forth and put his hand to her head. It was wet. How could it be soft? Crushed. Her eyes never closed and she was so still.

"Should we call for help?" Olivia stood just behind him and put her little hand on his shoulder.

Estéban nodded but then thought again. If Mina had shown any sign of life whatsoever, he would have run and gotten someone, forget the consequences. But there was nothing to be done now.

"No, we have to go. Don't tell anyone what you saw. NO ONE." He looked right in her face. "Not even Mamá."

Olivia's lips curved down. "But Ms. Smith said we should call the police to ask for help." A tear from her left eye escaped down her face.

"Do you want them to take away Mamá, too? Do you want us to live in a cage?"

Olivia shook her head and grabbed her brother tight, almost as if she could stop him from being taken away.

Their father had been deported back to Mexico after a traffic stop. While Estéban and his siblings were all U.S. citizens, their mother was not. If the police came knocking at their door, they would likely deport their mother as well. He had no idea what might happen to them if that happened. But he had heard too many stories of children being kept in cages because their parents were undocumented. He picked up Olivia and headed home.

Their mother thankfully was still not home. She probably had to work late again. Their brother and sisters were watching TV and didn't pay much attention to them. Olivia ran into the room she shared with her two sisters and took off her outfit and changed into pajamas.

Estéban took off his jacket and felt his stomach rise into his throat. Bloodstains covered his jacket. What to do? Burn it? It was his only jacket and it was way too cold now to go without.

He and Diego had been goofing around one time and Diego's nose began bleeding all over his clothes. Mamá had cleaned the clothes and gotten all of the stains out. Cold water was the key. Estéban went to the bathroom and turned on the cold water. He got the brush he used to clean the bathroom and started scrubbing. It worked! The jacket was soaking wet, but no stains, except in the sink. He scrubbed that as well. While he was at it, he figured he would just clean the entire bathroom.

As he was finishing, his mother came in the door. She spoke

almost no English, so the conversation was in Spanish. He always felt like a giant compared to his mother even though he was average height. She was maybe five feet tall in heels and so thin. She smiled.

"What are you doing?" she asked him, looking at the immaculate bathroom. She saw his jacket and tilted her head to the right.

"Olivia won the costume contest. We went to get ice cream with the gift certificate and I got it on my jacket."

"*Olivialita*! Come here!"

Olivia came out of her room, unsure.

"You won!?"

Olivia ran up to her mother and hugged her. She smiled up at her and nodded. "Yes, Mamá. My costume was the best."

"It was great," Estéban said. "Those store-bought ones just couldn't compete. No one else looked like Olivia. You don't mind we went for ice cream? She was so happy to win."

"They got ice cream? No fair. I want ice cream," Diego said. He'd come around the corner in time to hear Estéban lying. Well, partly.

His mother turned to him, "Did you take your little sister to the festival? Did you clean the bathroom? Did you make sure your little sister was safe and get her home safe?" Estéban's stomach knotted. Did she have to say safe so many times?

Diego opened his mouth to reply but closed it again. "No, Mamá," he said, conceding. He turned and went back to the television.

Officer Karen Allison, or just plain Allison as she was known around her beat of Irvington, frowned. She heard the call for a dead body found in Ellenberger Park. Only a block away, she hoofed it over there, went into the park, and headed towards the small group of people near a thicket of trees.

An older lady, maybe in her 70s, dressed in jogging clothes was holding her phone and looking down at something. When she saw Allison, the woman waved at her and pointed down at what looked to be a body. As she got closer, she saw the body looked lifeless. She called in and requested a detective on scene and forensics. Allison looked again and her heart sank. She thought the girl might be her missing person called in just this morning.

"OK, everyone, let's take a few steps back," Allison said.

This was Indiana, so they all took several steps back. Allison had grown up in New York and was always amazed at how willing people out here were to do as they were asked by people in authority.

"Who called in the body?"

The 70-year-old jogger lady held up her hand, almost like they were in a classroom. Allison smiled on the inside. "I will need you to hang around to talk to the detectives."

The woman grimaced. "Can I finish my run? My heart rate has already gone down farther than it should."

"It would be better if you could stay. Feel free to run around here as long as I can see you," Allison said. She looked at the jogger. She was fit. Allison tried to keep in shape and spent a large part of her shift walking around instead of driving in a squad car, but she doubted she was in as good shape as that lady.

She studied onlookers, but mainly wanted to preserve the scene until people above her pay grade showed up. She counted 11 people, nine of whom were adults, one teenager, and a little girl. The boy and girl were farther in the back. He was holding her hand and they both looked miserable. She was about to ask who they were when a second beat officer showed up. Crap, thought Allison, why did Wright have to be on today? His name should have been Wrong. She hoped he would turn into a good cop, but he was still so freaking new.

"I heard the call and drove over. You got here fast," he said.

Allison nodded. "I was just a block away walking around."

"Why do you walk so much instead of staying with your cruiser?"

"Riding around in a car doesn't give you much presence in the community, and people are more likely to be afraid of you instead of looking to you for help."

Wright stared at her for a moment. "Isn't that the point? Scare people straight?"

"Uh, no. Most people are not evildoers. We are here to help," she said.

He started to walk over to the body. "I *already* checked her. She's gone. Waiting for forensics and homicide."

He kept walking toward the body and leaned over. It looked as if he were going to touch her.

"Wright! Stop what you're doing and don't contaminate the scene," she barked. He didn't even have gloves on. He stopped, turned around, and looked at her. Still, she was surprised at the look of anger on his face.

"I wasn't going to touch her. There was no need to yell." Wright said it in a tone much calmer than he looked.

Allison decided to give him the benefit of the doubt. He was probably upset at seeing the young victim so mangled. "Wright, just step away. The detective will have your ass if your trace ends up on her," she said softly.

Wright turned and looked past Allison. The forensics guys were here. He nodded and stepped away. They were going to mark off the scene and do what they needed to do. Not far behind was Detective Blanco.

"Wright, move these people back," Blanco said. He looked at Allison and smiled. "Hey, *chica*."

Allison rolled her eyes and smirked. She didn't take offense because their working relationship was pretty good. Plus, while calling every female, no matter their age, *chica* wasn't professional, she didn't think he was being disrespectful. Blanco, born in the U.S., had been raised in Mexico. After a stint in the army, he had become a police officer and quickly climbed the ranks.

He looked over at the body but he didn't get close. He would be given the go-ahead soon. "She looks Hispanic. You think that's why I got called in?" he said quietly to Allison.

"Don't know. I think she might be a missing person called in this morning." Allison took out her phone and pulled up the picture of a teenage girl with an oval face, delicate features, dark eyes, and a sweet gentle smile who went to Howe High School. She had gone to the festival the night before and never returned home. Blanco looked at the pic, looked at the corpse, then back at the pic. "Shit. Yeah, I think you're right."

"She's a 16-year-old high school student named Mina Eleanor Jones. I know this kid."

"Oh. Troublemaker?"

Allison shook her head, "No. Sweet as pie. I was a guest at the high school. She was the one who showed me around. I think she was on the student council or something like that."

"Hispanic? Jones doesn't sound like it, but you never know."

"No. She looks like it, but nope. Not even a little."

"Student council, huh. Sounds like a good kid then," he said.

He didn't sigh, but she could almost hear it. For troublemakers, the people who killed them were more likely to be outside the home. Good kids who ended up dead often meant the trouble came from someone close to them.

"Could be a hate crime. She looks Hispanic," Allison said. It was a bit twisted, but it was much more satisfying putting away right-wing nut jobs than family members. It didn't make her any less dead, though.

"So, did he mess with my crime scene?" Blanco asked, looking at Wright.

"He was about to. I actually yelled at him to stop him from touching the body without gloves. He did lean over her though. I think maybe he wasn't thinking because the sight upset him."

"You're a kind person. I don't think that's why," he said.

"Rookies," they both said while looking at Wright's back. He had stopped herding people away and seemed on alert. He was looking east at one of the park exits. It went up some stairs. On the stairs were the teenage boy and the little girl she had seen before. The boy had picked her up and was moving at a fast clip up the stairs. The little girl stared back, eyes wide.

"Well, that's great. Poor little girl must be terrified seeing a murder victim," Allison said.

Blanco looked in the direction of the quickly disappearing pair.
"Uh-huh."

ESTÉBAN COULD HAVE KICKED HIMSELF. He had no idea why he was
drawn to where he knew Mina was. He had not slept well at all and
kept worrying that his hair and whatever would be all over Mina. On
TV they found people all the time using like an eyelash or other things
too small to consider.

He had gotten up early and planned to go by himself, only to
realize Olivia was behind him and had followed him from the house.
The cop had moved them farther away. Estéban had no idea what he
might do. He just didn't want his mother deported and his siblings to
end up someplace bad.

When all the other cops got there, he decided to leave. They were
at the top of the stairs and he tried to put Olivia down, only she
wouldn't let go.

"Olivia, I am not carrying you the entire way home. Get down."

She relented and released her grip and dropped. She looked up
at him.

"Why are you crying?" he asked her.

She put her hands to her face and seemed surprised there were
tears.

Estéban kneeled down and hugged Olivia. "I am sad about Mina,
too. Why would anyone want to hurt her—I just don't get it."

"Why would anyone hurt anyone else?" she asked.

Estéban wished he had an answer. He looked down at the ground
and shook his head. "I honestly don't know."

"My teacher said the police were supposed to be helpful. Is that
true?"

"Some police are helpful. Some aren't. Especially, you know, if
your skin is dark."

Estéban hated having this conversation with a five-year-old, but
he supposed she had to learn sometime.

"How can you tell the good ones from the bad?"

"Uh, well, by how they act. It's not really possible to tell a bad or good person from looks."

"But you can tell by how they act?"

"Yeah, but it's hard not to make snap judgments waiting around to see what someone does," he said.

"But what if one of the police officers was the one who hit Mina? They would be one of the bad ones?"

"Well, yeah, of course . . . ," Estéban shut his eyes and cursed inwardly as he understood what she was saying. "Oh man, this sucks."

ESTÉBAN AND OLIVIA returned to their house only to find Sean there with his bag of groceries for Saturday night dinner. Their mother was just letting Sean in and conversing with him in Spanish. Dude had a pretty strong accent but while his comprehension was still lacking, his pronunciation improved every day. Sean and their mother turned as they walked up the steps to the porch.

"Oh cool, you found Olivia, then?" Sean said, thankfully in English.

"*Eh?*" Mamá said.

"Nothing, Mamá," Estéban said.

She took the stuffed grocery bag inside. Olivia followed her.

Sean pulled out his phone. "Wanna finish reading the issue from last night?"

"No, I'm good."

"You finish it on your own?"

"No." Estéban went and sat down on the top stair of the porch. Sean followed.

"E. Dude, what's up?"

"Sean, if I tell you something, you have to promise on your life you won't tell anyone else."

"Yeah, okay."

"No, I mean it. I just don't know what to do, but I gotta tell someone."

"I promise. No one," Sean said.

"Mina's dead."

Sean's already white face drained of any color. "What?"

"They found a body in the park this morning. Did you see the police cars when you drove over?"

Sean nodded. "You said a body. How do you know it's Mina?"

"We found her last night."

Sean sat back. "Last night and they're just getting to her this morning?"

"We didn't let anyone know. She was dead and I can't risk having the police here." He moved his head to indicate the house and his mother.

"You sure she was . . . ?"

"I've seen dead people before. You can't go to a Catholic funeral without them displaying the body. She was gone."

"Okay. Well, what's the problem?" Sean's lips were quivering.

Estéban put a hand on Sean's shoulders. "Olivia saw who did it."

Sean stood up. "Well, then you HAVE to risk it and go to the police."

"It *was* the police."

Sean sat back down. "You mean there's a police conspiracy?"

"You watch way too much TV. No, it was one person who is a part of the police. Olivia saw them at the park this morning."

"We can't let them get away with it, E."

"I'm open to suggestions because I got nothing."

They were both quiet a moment.

"Hey, you said Olivia saw them? You think they might have seen her?"

Estéban put his head in his hands. "No, man. Didn't occur to me."

They were both quiet again.

"Glad I could help?" Sean smiled and then he shrugged and looked down at the ground.

Estéban snorted and then tears welled up. He turned away, not wanting anyone to see him weak.

"We'll figure something out. We'll protect her and get some justice for Mina." Sean punched his right hand into his left palm.

"Yeah, how?" Estéban looked at his feet.

"What about the loophole? Maybe we can use it. Didn't your cousin use it?"

"Yeah, but he got shot. Olivia is tough for a girl, but that's asking a bit much."

"I thought if they were victims of any sort of violence you could get amnesty?"

"Yeah, but the reason no one uses it is 'cause no one wants to be a victim of a violent crime," Estéban said. "Besides, Olivia's not here illegally and she saw what happened. I don't want Mamá deported and for us to end up. . . who knows where."

Olivia came back out again and sat between the two. *"Mamá dice que la comida estára preparánda en unas horas y deben hacer sus tareas de escuela."*

"But I didn't bring my homework with me," Sean said, "and if dinner will be ready in a couple of hours, I don't want to go all the way home and then come back."

Sean tilted his head a bit and looked at Olivia.

"You live like five blocks away and you have a car." Estéban crossed his arms over his chest. "We have homework to do."

"Homework is for Sundays. Besides, we need to figure some shit out. Maybe I can report what happened," Sean said.

Estéban shook his head. "What reason would you have for not calling it in right away?"

"Why are you being so difficult?" Sean asked.

"I'm not. You don't think they're going to ask?"

"Oh, yeah. Hmmmm. Olivia, tell me what you saw last night."

"Dijo 'Chica, mejor que me escuches.' Ella dijo, 'Aléjate de mí, loco!' El la golpeó y la tiró."

"Huh?"

"DIJO CHICA," Olivia said, much louder.

"In English," Estéban said.

"Oh, um, he said, 'Girl, you better listen to me,' and then she said,

'Stay away from me, you freak,' and then he hit her. When I got there, I think he was trying to kiss her or something."

"And you saw him. Do you think he might have seen you?"

"Maybe. I was just standing there and I ran away," she said.

"Dude, she's probably in danger. I have an idea, though," Sean said.

Estéban grimaced and took a deep breath. He hoped it wasn't too crazy an idea. "Oh, yeah? What's that, then?"

Officer Allison was nearing the end of her shift and she was still in the park. The forensics people were on the verge of clearing out, but there were still a lot of people hanging around. At least the TV news people had left. She didn't know how many more ways Blanco could have said that they couldn't give any details until after the family had been notified.

At least the body had been taken away. She looked out at the remaining crowd and was surprised to see the boy and young girl from this morning. They were more in the front now and with another boy. The girl was pointing at where Blanco and Wright were standing. The officers both looked at the trio. The original boy picked up the girl and they walked slowly from the park.

Blanco seemed to finish up with Wright and walked back over to Allison. "You want to go with me for the notification?" he asked. "Since you met her, it might make things easier. Something wrong?"

Allison nodded. "Those kids . . . they were in the park this morning."

Blanco looked over. "Oh yeah. I remember. The little girl looked upset."

"Yeah. It's weird. Why bring her back?"

Blanco shook his head and shrugged.

"Where's Wright going?" she asked.

"Told me he has some sort of appointment and has to leave. Since we're pretty close to done here, I told him to go."

"Um, do you mind if I don't go with you?" she said. "I just thought of something I need to do and my shift is almost over."

SEAN, Estéban, and Olivia got to the top of the stairs at the park and headed slowly back to Sean's house. Both of Sean's parents were gone for the day. They tried to be as conspicuous as possible and hoped the cop would follow them. If he didn't, then he probably didn't know it was Olivia who had seen him and at least she would be safe. Estéban wasn't sure this was the greatest idea, but he had no others, so he thought it was worth a try.

They weren't sure if the cop followed or not, so they hung out at Sean's house, waiting. Problem was, waiting was boring. They put on the television. After an hour, it was getting dark and they all started to wonder if they should head back for dinner.

"Didn't she say a couple of hours?" Sean asked.

"Uh, no I think she meant several. Dinner isn't usually ready until around seven," Estéban said.

"Oh. Maybe I can make some snacks."

"Popcorn?" Olivia asked hopefully.

"Yeah, we probably have some." Sean got up and headed to the kitchen.

The sound of popping corn was interrupted by the sound of the doorbell. Olivia hid behind a recliner.

Sean came out looking at his phone. "It's him. You ready?"

"Not really, but whatever," Estéban's voice was slightly higher in pitch than he would have liked.

Sean went to the door and opened it. "Can I help you?"

"Yeah," said the voice outside. Sean then raised his arms and moved back. Estéban wanted to run when he saw the gun in the man's hand. The man was not in uniform anymore, but they still didn't expect him to pull a gun.

"Where is she?" he said.

"Who?" Sean asked, with way more guts than Estéban ever gave him credit for.

"The little girl. Where is she? I know she came in here with you."

"Dude? What's with the gun? You can leave and we won't tell anyone," Sean said. The man raised the gun and pointed it directly at Sean.

"You just missed her. Her uncle came and took her to the police station to report you for killing Mina. Dude, you could probably get off for it by calling it an accident. You kill us and it's all over." Estéban could not believe the bull coming out of Sean's mouth.

"Really, and how do you think anyone is going to find out?"

"On account of we are all being recorded and the video and audio is being sent over the Internet right now," Sean said.

"Liar! Where is the girl?" He fired the gun. Esteban thought it was either a warning or the guy was a majorly bad shot, since the bullet lodged in the wall just to the right of Sean's head.

"Dude. Not lying. Are you completely nuts? You must be to kill someone as nice as Mina!" Sean yelled.

"She didn't need to be such . . . shut up! I don't need to explain myself to you."

"She's 16 and you're old. Plus, you think people around here didn't hear that shot and decide to call it in?"

"Shots around here are called in all the time and are ignored," he said.

"Maybe by you," Officer Allison said. She was pointing her own gun directly at Wright. "Drop the gun or I'll drop you."

"I'm glad you're here, Allison. Arrest these guys," Wright said.

"Yeah, I heard everything. Drop. Your. Gun. I'm not asking you again."

After a count he dropped the gun. "Hands up."

"You need some help, *chica*?" Blanco said. He came in the door right behind Allison.

"Uh, yeah, search him, cuff him, and Mirandize him. That would be lovely," she said.

Blanco went behind Wright so that Wright was in between Allison and Blanco. He began the search and found two more small guns and a knife on him. Wright's mouth quivered and frowned once the cuffs were on him.

Both Estéban and Sean let out breaths they didn't know they were holding.

"You following me or him?" Allison asked Blanco.

"Him. But only because I realized you were following him as well."

Allison turned to Sean. "Was that true about this being streamed on the Internet?"

"Very, very true. Well, at least it was being streamed to a site only my parents have access to, but I also have it recording. Will that do? Olivia won't have to testify, right?" Sean asked hopefully.

"Olivia?" Blanco asked.

Olivia came out from behind the recliner and went to hide behind Estéban.

"She's five," Estéban said.

"What did she see?" Blanco asked.

They were all quiet for a moment. Olivia pointed at Wright. "*El le dio a Mina y la mató. Yo lo vi anoche.*"

"English," Estéban said.

"He hit Mina. I saw him do it last night," she said.

Blanco and Allison looked at one another.

"She might need to testify. Is she a citizen?" Blanco asked.

"Yes, we are. Can I act as her guardian?" Estéban asked.

"Maybe. We'll see. I think it will be okay, regardless," Blanco said.

Blanco exchanged a look with Allison. "Kids should only be scared by ghost stories, not by real life," he said.

"Man, I can't believe all that crap you said. Even after you knew the gun was loaded. You're loco!" Estéban said.

Sean looked down at his feet. "Yeah, there's a chance I've been binge-watching too much Buffy."

"Buffy?" Allison said.

"Yeah, I'm totally into classic TV." He looked at the wall with the gunshot in it. "Can we get him to pay for the repair?"

"One step at a time, kid."

DE-BONED

BY C. J. NELSON

The apparition of an elderly woman floated above me. She held a large bone and used it to frantically point toward my bedroom window. She did not speak. She looked pale and disheveled. I tried to understand the gesturing of the bone toward the window. I reached to touch her and woke up.

I was lying in my bed, alone, without a presence hanging above me. As a retired science teacher, it was natural for me to seek explanations for things out of the ordinary. There had to be a deeper meaning for what I had just dreamt. It seemed very real. I got up to get a drink of water in hopes I could shake off the vision's effects, but peace of mind didn't come.

I've always been accused of being a worry-wart or an empath who's tuned in to other creatures' needs. I've been told I am an HSP, a highly sensitive person. I connect with other life forms, big and small. I am aware of their feelings. That's for real. Heck, I'd go so far as to help a slug cross the sidewalk or help a worm back into the dirt. It's my nature and I have felt this way my entire life. I could not ignore a person or an animal in distress if I wanted to. The lady in my dream was no exception.

I crawled back under the bed covers and snuggled deep, hoping to return to restful sleep. Thank goodness it finally came. Dawn soon inched its way into my bedroom window and I got up to let my recently rescued dog, Bandit, outside, while also letting out a moth wanting its freedom. I can't help being aware of non-speaking creatures' needs. The ability to understand them comes as natural as breathing for me.

On our morning stroll, I had been throwing a tennis ball for Bandit, and he'd retrieve it for another turn. That morning, we chose a new route to investigate. While walking, I took in all the spider webs and cheesecloth ghosts hanging from trees in the neighborhood not far from my house. Yards were littered with phony headstones. Never having been fond of Halloween, or full moons, or the spooky implications, I was reminded of the dream and the ethereal lady. I could still see her suspended above me, looking confused with the bone she gripped in her hand.

Bandit was taking extra time to find his ball. He tends to take time to explore, but always returns. I must have thrown it further than I intended and got side-tracked in thoughts about the ghostly visitor. I caught an object with my toe and almost tripped over it. I figured I needed to sit and re-group.

Finding a place in the grass, I looked at the object on the sidewalk. It was a bone! And it looked just like the bone gripped by the lady in my dream. Bandit trotted over to it, picked it up, brought it to me, and dropped it at my feet.

"Are you trying to tell me something, boy?" I was wary of picking up a bone my dog apparently dug up, evidenced by the dirt on his whiskers and his front paws.

The dog stared at me with wide eyes, tongue hanging out. He barked and wagged his tail, walked way down the sidewalk and stopped to turn his head. He barked again. Sensing an urgency in the barks, I jumped up to follow him, after picking up the bone and shoving it into my pocket. "Wait up, Bandit. I'm not as fast as you are."

Bandit yipped as if he were chuckling and took off in earnest. I did my best to keep up, speed-walking down alleys and across yards with piles of autumn leaves. We covered several blocks in record time. He kept looking over his shoulder to see if I was behind. Bandit was driven to show me something—I felt it. I was already a little winded, but was determined to stay in sight of my pooch.

EVEN DURING THE DAY, Riverview Cemetery was a place most towns-people avoided. Located off of Cherry Street in Noblesville, Indiana, I would pass it countless times a week in my car. I spied Bandit weaving between the old markers and made my way over the crunchy oak leaves littering the dried, brown October grass. What was I doing, walking through the local graveyard on Halloween? I caught myself looking for Michael Jackson-like zombies in broad daylight. The sun was strong, but not warm. I continued to pick my way around the weather-beaten headstones, some tilted like fallen soldiers. To say this was creepy was an understatement.

Half-way across the property, I noticed an older man, pale and skeletal, who was putting flowers by one of the graves. Bandit saw him and stopped close enough to the man to get his ears scratched. Bandit's whole body wagged.

"Good to see you boy," the elderly gentleman crooned to my dog.

"Good morning," I said, nodding at the man.

"What's good about it?" he grumbled, the good mood evaporating. "Thirty years without Berta. Couldn't even bury her properly because of the high river. Couldn't find her remains."

I patted my leg a few times to get Bandit to return and sit beside me, wondering why the stranger and Bandit were so chummy. I felt the man's total resignation for the closure he still looked for. "Anything I can do to help, Mr. . . . . ?"

"Marx. Abe Marx." He put his hand on his chest and breathed heavily. "I just hope I get to see her soon. I've missed her all these years so much, my heart hurts more than ever."

"I'm Kathy Beaumont. Would you like me to take you to your doctor?" I asked.

"No, honey, it's way too late. My future is already in motion." A wan smile crossed his lips. "Thanks for your offer, though. That's kind of you to ask."

Bandit whined as Mr. Marx shuffled away from me with his cane, wearing a jacket that was two sizes too big. He mumbled something about not feeling well.

I watched as the frail man exited the cemetery. I walked to the spot he left, where the headstone with the yellow mums read, Alberta Marx—Born: December 1931, Died: October 1990. Beside her headstone, was a second marker. It read: Abraham Marx—Born September 1930. Died October 2020. My understanding dawned. He was waiting for death to reunite him with his wife.

Wait. It was October 31st. His marker was already etched. "Something doesn't add up, Bandit. I wish you could tell me what you can sense, boy." Bandit barked once to get my attention and bolted off toward our destination, wherever that was. As I looked up, I realized Abe Marx was nowhere to be seen.

At the far side of the cemetery, the whispering leaves collected in windswept piles where the Riverwalk wound beside part of the grassy knoll. The White River was low after a dry summer and a lot of the bank was exposed, but still intact; the sandy part of the river bed sprouted weeds and tree seedlings along the bare soil. I stepped closer to the river, still behind Bandit. I continued to follow my antsy dog as best I could. He seemed to know where he was headed. A few overhanging leaves holding onto their branches thinly shaded the area where I stopped to catch my breath. It was then I saw her.

A misty figure in the form of an older woman floated above the ground. I rubbed my eyes and looked again. The form was still there. *No way*, I told myself. *I am not seeing this.* It was the woman from my dream, still looking distressed. *Someone had to have hung a sheet from a tree for Halloween,* I reasoned.

I'm pretty sure I fainted after seeing the female spirit . . . again. Who wouldn't? She was the same woman from my dream, which spooked me to my core. I felt Bandit licking my cheek. When I opened my eyes, she was still there, suspended above me with a look of concern. I struggled to sit up—at my age, the trick is to not collide with the solid ground by accident. I managed to get to a standing position. The spirit drifted back a bit.

"Who are you? And why are you here?" I asked. My voice shook with the questions. She couldn't seem to vocalize an answer. She lifted her hands up to the sky. There had to be a way to communicate with her, bizarre as it seemed. I sensed her anxiety had to do with the bone in my pocket and that was the mystery.

Who are you and what do you need from me? I sent the thought out, not expecting a reply. I was not disappointed.

Bandit added to my confusion by yipping non-stop and pawing at my pant leg. Normally deductive reasoning was my tool for solving problems, yet I couldn't wrap my head around what to do. I needed to think, without a dog barking and a spirit hovering. I backed away, my hand gripping the bone, still in my pocket. Somehow, I would figure this out, but not here in this spooky place . . . and maybe not even on Halloween.

The floating apparition gave me a weak smile as she drifted into the trees above the river bank and disappeared. Bandit trotted off in her direction, also vanishing into the trees. I yelled Bandit's name until I was hoarse. I even walked to the tree line where he and the spirit disappeared. I ventured into the trees, hoping to catch sight of him, calling his name. No dog. I wandered the area until my feet ached. Still no Bandit. I was exhausted and worried about my dog.

What had gotten into me? I retraced my steps back through the cemetery and debated whether I should go home and take something to relax. My feet needed a rest as much as my throat. I was confident Bandit would find his way home. Meanwhile, a nap would be refreshing. It would be great to wake up with no barking dog or a visible spirit waiting for me to do something I couldn't put my finger on. I took a number of deep breaths. I wanted to figure out what the frustrated spirit-lady needed. I opted to head home for a long nap. When I got there, I put the bone in a bag and left it on a shelf in the garage. I would take it to the police after I woke up. Now, I was the one in distress.

THE SAME WOMAN hovered over me. Again. *I don't know what you want,* I thought.

"You will."

My eyes shot open during my dream. *I can understand you now.*

"Only because you're dreaming," was her response.

Who are you and why are you letting me see your spirit?

She heaved a sigh. "I'm Alberta Marx. You talked to my husband in the cemetery. He was very ill. I just need to be whole again so I can move on into the light with him. It's the reason I decided to connect with you. I really need your help. And you have the missing piece."

I do? And what do you mean "He was?" I saw him this afternoon. I even spoke with him. Why is his head stone already marked? He looked alive earlier.

"The bone Bandit dug up and brought you belongs to me and I need to have it replaced before the day ends. Bandit belonged to Abe and me. It was why he followed me into the woods. He is safe here with me. I am spending my remaining time with him. Bandit has always been crazy about finding bones. When he found that bone, it probably still had my scent. I told him he had to take it to you. You, being tuned into animals' feelings, would pick up on the urgency of bringing it back. Replacing the bone will make me complete. I'll be able to be with Abe to complete his transition. That means everything to me."

You mean he was . . . ?

"Already passed?" She smiled. "Yes. You could speak with him because he's in a transitional stage before he can cross over. I know it's hard for you to understand until you're in our position. Getting that bone replaced is crucial for me to be able to walk into the light with him. Does any of this make sense? Sort of?"

I get the feeling you two need to be together again. It's hard to comprehend how things work on the 'other side.'

"It will become clear to you when your time comes." Alberta's head glowed, outlined like it was caught in the sun's rays.

This dream was unbelievable. This wasn't really happening to me. My eyes filled with tears for Alberta and Abe Marx.

I still have the bone you are missing.

"I know. I saw the spot where you placed it. It is now within your reach."

Wait a minute. Where are the rest of your bones?

She heaved another sigh and lifted her thin arm to point outside the window. "The rest of my bones are at the same spot where we met earlier today."

The curiosity of the scientist in me made me ask. *Was your death a murder or an accident?*

She took a moment before answering. "My death was nothing as dramatic as a murder. I drowned a long time ago in a flash flood. My canoe flipped and I could not right myself. I was dragged a long way down the river in a swift current. The rest is history. I don't know how the pup found my foot bone, but the rescue workers sure as heck couldn't find my body back then. Will you please help me?"

I nodded. *I'll bring the bone back when I wake up. Will that be soon enough for you?*

The spirit began to evaporate. She nodded. Before she completely vanished, I heard "Thank you, Kathy."

I woke up in a cold sweat, wishing it was a chilly November first and Halloween was over. I touched the solid bed beneath me and looked at the ceiling above. I was home. It was another crazy dream, but the bone I found now rested on my nightstand. I knew Alberta moved it from the garage into the house. The day's events got even stranger.

I donned some warmer clothes and walked out into the late afternoon with the bone in my pocket. I shivered as I navigated the streets and alleys, but logic told me it was more from the spirit's visit than the cool air. I saw groups of masked kids clutching bags of candy.

Halloween had taken on a new meaning, more about the merging of two spirits than collecting sweets.

With just enough light left in the day, I found the place on the river bank where Bandit and I stopped earlier. The hoot of a nearby owl and the crackle of dead leaves provided the perfect sound effects for this spooky evening. Combined, they caused BB-sized goosebumps on my arms. As expected, the misty spirit hung suspended above the same spot where I stood that afternoon. Bandit trotted into view. This would be a Halloween I would never forget.

Alberta held out an empty hand. I sensed her desperation.

"Yeah, I have it," I spoke with a calmer demeanor than I felt. Talking to a spirit was totally mind-blowing. I extended the bag with the bone inside.

Alberta put her hand over her heart. She continued by folding her hands together in a gesture of thanks. She bowed her head and then looked at me.

"Where do you want this?" I asked keeping the bag at arm's length.

I watched with my jaw hanging open as she drifted effortlessly over to a spot on the bank. A long finger pointed out the exact place.

Recovering some of my composure, I approached the place the spirit indicated. A coolness encased me. Where was the comfort of a fireplace and my easy chair?

"Here?" I started to shove the bag and the bone into the earth.

She shook her head vigorously.

"Wrong spot?"

Alberta shook her head again and drifted too close to me.

Startled, I dropped the bag and the bone fell out.

The spirit pointed several times from the bone to a certain spot on the bank.

I got it. The bone without the bag. Yuck. Good thing I stuffed a pair of work gloves into my jacket pockets. I put them on and then I carefully picked up the bone and eased it into the place she indicated, patting loose dirt to cover up what I had done. I noticed a full moon beginning to rise over the horizon. I could have sworn I heard a bat swoosh beside my head.

"Can I do anything else for you?"

Smiling, she shook her head again. Her face relaxed as she began to drift upward.

I looked up. I watched, amazed at the sudden appearance of an ethereal Abe beside Alberta. Clouds parted for them. I saw the total purity of a white sky as they waved to us. The couple joined hands, surrounded by a golden glow. They walked into the beautiful light until they faded from view. I felt honored to be a witness.

The lesson learned? A love between two people can continue beyond this lifetime.

Bandit's tail wagged against my leg. The whole process had taken minutes, but it felt like hours. A shrink would have told me I was blessed with an overactive imagination. I wasted no time in making a hasty retreat.

My mission was complete. "We did it, Bandit! They're free. Let's go home."

TWO COMFORTING thoughts crossed my mind later. The first was, the Marxes were finally reunited, thanks to the return of the bone. The second was, I knew where I would be spending next Halloween—on a sunny beach in the Bahamas, far, far away from Noblesville.

THE WOMAN IN BLACK

BY C.A. PADDOCK

Mary wondered if anyone in the house was awake. She checked her watch. 3:00 a.m. It had been a long night of Halloween partying. Her brother and her husband were both passed out by the bonfire, along with a few other guests. She went to the house to check on those who'd opted for bed earlier in the evening.

Slowly she slid the glass door open and peered inside. The living room was empty and as far as she could see, the kitchen, too. But as she stepped across the threshold into the living room, she saw the woman in black sitting quietly in the same chair in the corner in the exact position she was at the end of the party. She continued to believe the heavily costumed woman was her friend Ann, though there'd been no acknowledgement by the woman the whole evening. Mary could not tell if she was conscious or not.

The musty smell of decay emanating from the chair was even more repulsive than it had been earlier in the evening. "Hey, Ann! You can stop fooling around now. Everyone else is asleep." Mary's lips quivered as she spoke to the woman.

When she did not move, Mary tip-toed over and nudged her shoulder. Suddenly, the woman raised her arms and lifted the black veil to reveal her face. Or what was left of it. Murky yellow eyes surrounded by gray skin stared out at Mary. The tip of her nose dripped with black decay and blood rolled from the side of a red-lipped mouth as she opened it to give way to stained brown canines.

Mary jumped back and tripped over the rug in the middle of the room. The ghoul ripped off its black satin gloves to reveal long sharp nails. It hurled itself out of the chair and onto Mary splayed on the floor. She tried to scream but found she could not. She tried to push the being off, but it pressed her back down, scratching her face with its claws. As the evil spirit bent down to bite her face, Mary felt the cold, slimy decay of its nose. She felt the blood drip onto her cheek and the flicker of a barbed tongue. She ripped her arms from the beast's clutches and flung them up to stop the attack. Her arms free now, she gathered all the strength she could muster and pushed the ghoul off her with such force, it released the same shrill wail she had heard earlier. Mary shut her eyes when she heard the thud of the creature hitting the floor.

MARY AND DAVE ANDERSON'S annual Halloween party was the highlight of their year. As they did every October, the Andersons had adorned their brick ranch home with a surplus of seasonal decorations.

A tall, black and white Frankenstein swayed in the breeze on their lawn with other inflatables, including several gray tombstones and a zombie dog. White metal ghosts and pumpkin landscaping lights guided costumed guests along the sidewalk. A large, nylon cobweb twinkled with orange lights from under the covered porch.

A loud bong resonated through the house as the first visitors arrived. Mary, wearing a white sheet with a gold belt, gold sandals, and gold arm bracelets, answered the door. She greeted Kate and Paul, dressed as Yukon Cornelius and Bumble the Abominable.

"Right on time as usual! Don't you like our new doorbell?" Mary said. "Dave installed it just for the party."

"Your gimmicks get better and better each year, that's for sure," Paul said, trying to maneuver himself into the narrow foyer.

Next were Rick and Sarah as a pair of jeans, dressed all in blue with blue hair and eyebrows and name badges bearing the names "Jean" and "Gene." Following them was Mary's brother, Daniel, dressed as chicken cordon bleu. Mary thought her brother could have come up with something more original than blue pants and shirt with a rubber chicken tied to his stomach.

As guests arrived, Mary ushered them into the living room where her husband, Dave, took their pictures so they could remember each year's party. Before the first hour ended, more friends had arrived: a prince and princess, a caveman, a ladybug, a king and queen, silent movie stars, and a witch. The doorbell gonged one last time for the final two guests. Standing on the porch was a man in his 50s with thinning, slicked-back black hair, obviously dyed, sporting a wrinkled brown suit and a white dress shirt unbuttoned at the top, loosely held together by a wide, red paisley patterned tie from the 1970s. The man held open a briefcase filled with an array of goods and asked Mary if she wanted to buy anything from him. Mary snickered.

She stopped her giggle when she realized that standing behind the man was a woman dressed all in black. Wearing an outfit befitting a mourner, the woman had on a black woven hat securing a double-layered veil obscuring her face. Her hands and arms were contained in black satin gloves that met the elbow-length sleeves on her dress. The dress was faded in spots with hints of white as if it had been hanging in a dusty closet for many years. Black brocade ran down the front of the dress from the high neck to its below-the-knee hem. Black stockings covered her calves and peeked out from the open-toed, black, laced oxfords on her feet. She held a single black rose with drops of red on its leaves.

When Mary held the door open to let them in, the woman in black brushed past her and glided down the hallway. Mary's nose twitched at a musty smell lingering in the air. She asked the sleazy salesman, "Who'd you bring with you this time, Steve? She looks like a real winner."

"I don't know her. She was just walking up to the door when I got here. I asked her if she needed any help since I wasn't sure if she could see through that veil. But she just kept walking. I assume she's one of your friends."

"I can't figure out who it is . . . yet," Mary replied. "But her costume sure gives me the creeps. Come on in, Steve. You're the last one here, so we need to get this party started."

As Mary and Steve entered the living room, Dave came up and took Steve's picture before Steve joined the festivities. Dave turned back to Mary.

"Who is that wearing the black dress and veil?" Dave nodded his head towards the figure sitting in a rocking chair. "She just swept past me and headed to the chair. She wouldn't talk to me or let me take her picture."

"I'm not sure. I bet it's Ann since she wasn't sure she could make it. Maybe her plans changed," Mary replied.

In the meantime, Steve, the sleazy salesman, had opened his brief-case and was enticing guests with goods to buy: an 8-track tape of Barbra Streisand, a cheap gold watch, a gold Elvis medallion with his birth year and death year on it, along with a bootleg vinyl album of his final concert at the now razed Market Square Arena. If someone was not interested in those things, he pulled from his jacket pocket a bottle of MD 20/20 and poured them a drink in a plastic wine glass. "If Mad Dog is good enough for me, it's good enough for you," he proclaimed when he handed them the drugstore wine. If the drink was rejected, he would raise the glass, shout "That's more for me and less for you!" and gulp down the cheap liquid.

"Welcome, monsters and ghouls!" Dave shouted to quiet everyone. "Take your seats. It's time to get this party started. As most of you know, we start off with my famous . . . or should I say infamous . . . Left-Right game. Scoot your chairs in to form a circle. That includes you, Woman in Black."

Those sitting near the woman in the rocking chair paused, moving their chairs to let her join them. When the mysterious woman did not move, they closed the circle.

"Still the silent treatment, huh? We'll get you to open up soon," Dave said. "Let's move on. While Mary is handing out the bags, I'll remind everyone of the rules since there are a few newcomers."

Mary handed each guest a large Halloween bag. Mary and her sister-in-law had enjoyed the morning filling each bag with goodies including black metal cats, ceramic pumpkins, spider-shaped votives, stuffed ravens, and other themed items she had bought as gifts.

Dave continued. "I will read my story and every time I say left or right, you pass your bag to the person on the left of you or the right of you. When the story is done, you keep the bag and the goodies in that bag. Are you ready?" he asked.

Everyone moved to the edge of their seats ready for the designated action words. Dave began to read his story.

"Bill and his friend, Mark, left Bill's house which sat on the right corner of Shawnee and Golf Street to go to the Left Behind Thrift Store. They wanted to find ugly holiday sweaters for a holiday party at their advertising company, The Write Stuff. Bill pulled his car out right onto Golf Street. A few moments later as he turned left onto Highway 31, Mark screamed, 'Bill, watch out for that truck right in front of us!' Mark closed his left eye and squinted his right eye so he could still see what would happen. The truck swerved left just at the right time to avoid a collision."

Dave stopped reading to allow everyone to catch up with the story. Laughter arose as some people got confused, handing their bag to the person on their right when they should have passed it to the left, some people ending up with two bags and others none. Once all was straightened out and each person had only one bag, Dave continued telling the story of Bill and Mark and their adventures at the thrift store over the sound of whooshing and clinking bags. When Dave finished the story, he waited until all the movement stopped and each person was holding one bag.

"You can pull out your treats now," Mary said. Oohs and aahs filled the air as people reached into their bags and brought out their new gifts.

"I must have gotten the booby prize," her brother, Daniel, said. "It looks like you finally cleaned out your old Chevy Cavalier." He began to pull random items from his sack.

"I didn't know cassettes still existed." Daniel held up two scratched tape cases and proceeded to read the labels. "Glen Campbell *All Time Hits* and Pink Floyd *The Wall.* When did you become a Pink Floyd fan, Mary?"

Next, he pulled out a small, yellow ice scraper with red lettering from the Grimm Pontiac dealership in Indiana. "And where did you get this? You've never driven a Pontiac in your life."

Mary couldn't believe what she was seeing. She had no idea where those things came from, but she wasn't going to let her brother know that.

"Oh, wait. What's this?" Daniel lifted up a small, crumpled piece of paper pinched between his fingers, allowing everyone to see a dark brown stain covering most of it. "It sure looks like blood on this Half Price Books receipt. I think Mary must have murdered someone breaking into her car, don't you think?" he said to the group.

"I will never tell about that receipt." Mary played along, assuming her brother had sabotaged the game. "Since you don't like my gifts, give it back and you can have these." Mary pulled out a pair of orange socks with black cat faces on them.

"I think I'll hold onto this receipt, as evidence, you know. Just in case someone turns up dead tonight." Her brother stuffed the piece of paper in the pocket of his blue t-shirt.

Mary seized the bag full of junk and took it to throw away. Frowning, she stepped on the lever to open the trash can. She knew none of the things were hers and they were not from her car. Besides, she would never give her guests white elephant gifts as party favors. She still wondered where they came from.

Next came the trivia game.

"This year's trivia is especially hard. It took us months to put the questions together," Dave said. "As always there is a tie-breaker question at the end in case it's needed. All right. You have ten minutes to answer. Mary, start the timer. And . . . go."

The players flipped over their sheets and a soft murmur interspersed with a few groans began as they read the twenty questions and tiebreaker at the end.

At the five-minute warning, a collective moan came from the crowd.

"You've really outdone yourselves this year, Mary and Dave," Sarah remarked, brushing blue hair from her eyes.

"I really like the tie-breaker question. Mary, are you sure you don't know anything about the blood-soaked receipt your brother found in his treat bag?" Rick asked.

Mary grabbed a copy of the trivia game and read out loud the last question. "Who died in a bookstore in the cult movie, *Mary's Nightmare?*"

"I will never tell," Mary said, tilting her head and grinning, feigning guilt. She motioned for Dave to follow her into the kitchen. "Where did that question come from?"

"I don't know. I proofread it last night and that question wasn't on there."

"We need to keep our eyes open. Something's up, I'm sure," Mary whispered as they walked back into the party.

"Time's up!" Dave said. Mary and Dave began to collect the sheets. As they left the room again to grade the contest answers, Dave hit the remote control to his stereo so his favorite Halloween album, *The Original Monster Mash* by Bobby (Boris) Pickett and the Crypt-Kickers, could entertain the guests while they refilled their drinks and grabbed another treat or two. Mary smiled wondering how many knew the correct answer to the trivia question of who sang the song made famous from the album.

After calculating the trivia sheets and identifying the winner, Dave announced a winner. "For the first time ever, someone has gotten all twenty questions right. Luckily, there was no need for the tie-breaking question this year. That's good because Mary was really worried her secret would come out!" Dave laughed. "The winner of the 2020 trivia contest is Steve, the Sleazy Salesman. Let's give him a hand.

"And while we are at it, the winner of the costume contest this year is . . . " Dave paused for effect. "You know as always it was a really hard decision. But the costume that really gave Mary the heebie jeebies and winner of this year's prize. . . The Woman in Black.

"But before we can give you the prize, you need to reveal to us who you are, Ann," Dave emphasized her name as he spoke to the woman still sitting in the rocking chair. She didn't answer.

"We know it's you, Ann," Mary said. "You're the only one that said you might come but didn't show up." Still, the woman did not move.

"You're no fun," Mary said and walked away. "If you won't play along, we'll award the gift card to someone else."

With her continued silence, she and Dave conferred and gave the card to Yukon Cornelius.

"That concludes our official party for 2020. We want to thank you all for coming this year and making it the best party ever. For those who want to stay, we're going to get the fire pit going. Grab your favorite beverage and meet us out back."

Gradually, the partygoers stood up. Some decided it was time to leave, but about ten people lingered, replacing their costumes with heavy jackets more appropriate for the outside. The woman in black stayed in the rocker.

Mary and the remaining guests headed out to the concrete fire pit and sat down. The fire crackled in the cool night and flickered with green and blue flames made by two chemical packets Mary threw into it before she found her seat. A bottle of cinnamon whiskey made its way around the group, some imbibing in the hot fiery liquid, others passing. Mary became mesmerized watching the flames dance and swirl, so much so that when a high-pitched wail echoed through the neighborhood, she didn't move. In fact, no one moved.

Mary looked around at everyone bundled up in their seats to see if anyone else heard the scream. It seemed they were all asleep.

"Hey, People! Wake up! Did you hear that? Where did that scream come from?" When no one acknowledged her questions, Mary jumped up and went over to her brother. She used the back of her hand to smack her brother on his cheek to wake him up.

"Hey, you big doofus, open your eyes! Are you trying to scare me with another one of your tricks?" she said. He didn't flinch nor did his eyelashes flutter. Mary turned around to look for Dave. She spotted him passed out on a white resin lawn chair on their deck. It appeared she was the only one who had heard the shrill sound.

"What is going on here?" she yelled. She couldn't figure out why no one else had woken up from the scream. She wondered if anyone in the house had heard it. She ran back to the house and opened the sliding glass door. When she stepped into the living room, she saw that the woman in black was still sitting in the rocking chair.

"Did you hear that, Ann?" Mary asked the woman she was convinced was her friend. The woman in black lifted her veil. Mary gasped just before the creature attacked.

"MARY, wake up! Did you hear that? Mary, what was that scream?" Mary heard Dave whisper.

"Huh? What?" Mary opened her eyes trying to figure out where she was. She felt a cold, thick substance running down her cheek. She rubbed her hand across the side of her face to wipe it off. When she looked at her palm, she expected to see blood from the beast, but it was a clear mucus. Still coming out of her nightmare, she rolled over just to double check there was no ghoul in the room. All she saw was their black cat crouching in the corner, his yellow eyes staring at her with contempt.

She shook her head. She couldn't believe that she had been dreaming. It felt so real.

"I think it was Pepper. I was having this nightmare where I was being attacked by an evil spirit. It must have been Pepper in my face, trying to wake me up to feed him. I guess I pushed him off." Mary finally answered, stretching each sentence out while she came out of her mental fog.

"He must have hit the floor hard to have shrieked like that. He could have woken the whole neighborhood."

"Yes. He doesn't look very happy with me right now. I better get up and feed him." Mary slid out of bed, pulled her white robe from a nearby hook and slipped it on, tying its gold belt around her waist. She looked at her nightstand and grabbed the book she had been reading the night before. She turned and shuffled out of the bedroom and down the hallway, Pepper racing past her.

She stopped in the living room to survey her surroundings. Halloween hadn't even happened yet. Half-opened orange storage boxes marked Halloween sat in various staging areas in the large room. A skeleton was a pile of plastic bones heaped on the old chair under the stairs. A black cat candle sat on the console table against the wall and a plastic cauldron rested on the stone hearth. Relieved it was just a dream, Mary continued to the kitchen, being careful not to trip over the boxes.

She paused at the entryway. A pumpkin-appliqued dishcloth hung on the handle of the oven. Unopened bottles of cinnamon whiskey and Mogen David wine were gathered next to the sink. But it was what was on the counter of the island that made her pause. Two cassette tapes and a yellow ice scraper were perched at its end. She moved closer to better examine them. She could see through the clear scratched case the name of the tape: *The Wall* by Pink Floyd. She looked at each of the other whatnots. There was Glen Campbell's *All Time Hits* and she could make out the name, Grimm, in red-faded lettering on the scraper. Mary gasped, dropping her book to the floor.

Bending down to pick up the book, Mary saw that the Half Price Books receipt she was using as a bookmark had fallen out. A coffee stain covered one corner of the purchase slip where she had spilled her drink on the seat of her car after stopping at the used bookstore. She had been too lazy to find a real bookmark. A clumping sound startled her. Mary screamed.

"What's going on?" Dave said, standing in the kitchen in broken-down slippers, his worn flannel plaid robe hanging open to reveal brown pajamas.

"Don't scare me like that, Dave!"

"That must have been some nightmare you had."

"It was. It was about a Halloween party disaster." She grabbed the book and the receipt and stood up.

"My mind must have been on overload—me reading this ghost story last night, us pulling out the decorations, and Pepper waking me up." Mary hesitated before she continued. She wasn't sure if she wanted to relive the dream. But the items on the counter had her puzzled.

"Dave, where did all of this stuff come from? They made it into my nightmare."

"Oh! My colleague Tony gave them to me the other day when he cleaned out his desk before his retirement party. I brought these in last night to go through this morning."

"Well, get them out of my kitchen. And while you are at it, get rid of this book and receipt, too. I'm done reading this story."

Mary threw down the book with its receipt next to the other items. She stared at the title of the book, *The Woman in Black* by Susan Hill, for a moment, thinking.

"We need to cancel the Halloween party this year, Dave," Mary said, turning to the calendar on the wall. She took a marker from the pencil holder under the calendar and crossed out the words "Halloween Party" on October 31.

"There'll be no woman in black for us this year."

MASKS

BY J. PAUL BURROUGHS

Police called to investigate break-in at local costume shop

I SHOULD HAVE EXPECTED trouble would be headed my way that afternoon when I read a small article in *The Indianapolis Times*. But who would have thought the mention of a burglary at a local costume shop would end up so deadly? I mean, it appeared on page seven, below mention of Harry S. Truman's latest campaign speech in Ohio. For that matter, all that was taken were a dozen or so masks. The dough in the till wasn't even touched. But it was the start of things that would get both worse and deadly.

My name's Max Keagan, and at age fifty-four, I'm a retired cop. Not retired by choice, mind you. A year earlier in 1947, I went after some cheap hoods who'd knocked over a pharmacy on the Indianapolis eastside. One of the pair produced a piece and fired at me, hitting me in the hip. I was the better shot getting him dead center in the back. I got praise and all that, but when the docs said that my hip would never be the same, the bigshots at headquarters threw me a little retirement party and then kicked me to the streets. Since then, I've taken a security job for the Strauss building in downtown Indianapolis.

Several October days passed with no further mention of the costume shop robbery. Then on the seventh, all hell broke loose. It was near closing time for the stores that stayed open into evening hours on Thursdays. McKnight's Jewelry was just about to call it a night when three figures stepped in. One was wearing a gorilla head, the second a lion mask, and the third, a cartoon bear head. Each carried a forty-five and what witnesses later described as a doctor's bag. They ordered everyone there to lie down on the floor, and then they proceeded to smash the glass cases and dump some of the finest pieces into their bags before taking off. No one saw them out on the streets, and they got away with an estimated thirty-five grand in jewelry.

The next day's headlines read: **Masked bandits strike local jewelry store.**

The article stated "Police suspect a connection between this and a theft of items from a costume shop earlier in the month."

On Saturday the thirteenth, Dewey supporters for the coming election were holding a fundraiser party in the Claypool Hotel Ballroom. The guests were dressed in costumes, so no one batted an eye when three well-dressed figures entered wearing masks as The Cowardly Lion, the Scarecrow from Oz, and a cutsie dog's head apparently supposed to be Toto. It was only when they whipped out their guns that the crowd realized they were about to be victims of a holdup.

One stupid dope who was running for city council and wanted to look the hero made a rush at the threesome. For his derring-do, he took a couple of slugs in the chest and later died. Again, the three managed to slip out and escape.

The next day, the newspapers were full of the story. And, again, the cops didn't have a clue who the three were.

One of the guests who had been forced to hand over his wallet with three C notes inside was my boss at the department store. The next morning, he called me into his office.

"Max, you were a damned good cop," he told me.

"I still am," I replied. "Can't run far with this hip of mine, but my mind's still at one hundred per cent."

"I'd like to hire you to try and find the Masked Bandits."

"I ain't no darn gumshoe," I grumbled.

"No, you're better. Suppose I sweeten the pot? Say, I offer three thousand dollars if you can find and catch the Masked Bandits?"

Three grand is nothing to sneeze at when you're a retired cop with a lousy pension. I accepted.

The following day I went to work. My first stop was where the whole magilla began—the costume shop. It was located just north of St. Clair Street on Senate. The place had been in business for at least a decade. I climbed up a narrow staircase to the second floor where their costumes were kept and spoke to one of the owners.

I had him make a list of all the masks that were taken. In addition to the six already used in the two heists, there were two clown masks, a Charlie Chaplin face, a Frankenstein, Wolfman, and Dracula pull-over-the-head masks.

I then talked over his recent clientele—especially ones who'd left without making purchases. He recalled a man who'd stopped by early in the month trying to decide what he might wear to a costume party hosted by his boss. The owner's wife recalled a guy who'd told her he was in an amateur theatrical at school and wanted to look like a hard-nosed detective. She showed him some things, quoted a price, and he'd backed out, saying he couldn't afford it. There was a married couple who'd looked over Romeo and Juliet costumes, but left saying they'd have to think things over.

Needless to say, their descriptions of the men were vague and of little help. The first man was tall, and the owners debated whether he had brown or blond hair. The "Romeo" wannabe, who the wife thought was too old to play the role, looked to be in his thirties.

I was about to leave, when a shop girl came from the back.

"What about the one creepy-looking guy who came here on the first?"

"Why do you call him creepy?" I questioned.

"He looked slimy like that guy in Bogart movies."

Okay, in Bogie's films there were a number of creepy-looking characters. I asked her to be more specific.

"Y'know, the guy in *Casablanca* who steals the papers from the Nazis and gets captured at Rick's?"

Jackpot! "You mean, Peter Lorre?"

Her mop of chestnut colored hair bobbed up and down. She said he was hoping to be invited to a party and spent over half an hour looking over costumes before leaving without renting one.

I made a mental note to drop by headquarters and ask to look through the mug books for old times' sake. However, my work schedule for the next three days at the department store was tight, and it would have to be postponed.

You know the old adage about Mohammed having to go to the mountain? Well, something like that took place with me on that third day at the department store. I was cruising the aisles keeping an eye out for light-fingered customers when I spotted a little man who absolutely *did* look like Peter Lorre in *Casablanca*, minus the white coat. I decided to play a hunch.

I walked over to where he was admiring some jewelry in a case. He looked up and smiled.

"Pretty, aren't they?" I asked.

"Yes, they are."

"So how are things with the gorilla and the bear? Or were you the bear?"

His bulging eyes grew large. "I . . . I don't understand."

"Okay, what about the Cowardly Lion and Scarecrow? Surely, you must have been Toto."

His face told me I'd hit the jackpot. He spun around and took off on a dead run. I went after him, but my stupid hip slowed me down.

"Stop!" I called out.

He flung himself into a group of women talking together in the perfume department. I couldn't risk firing my piece, possibly hitting one of them. I tried to follow, but he managed to lose me and exit the building.

Damn.

I went immediately to my boss, told him what had happened, and was directed to take time off to visit police headquarters.

There, I located Captain Daniel Sullivan of homicide who'd been a rookie I'd mentored years ago.

"Captain."

"Good to see you, Max, What brings you here? Trying to relive your glory days?"

"Not sure how glorified they were," I replied. "Got a favor to ask. Could I possibly get a look at the mug books?"

"This couldn't have anything to do with a report I got about some guy being chased through the Strauss building earlier today, could it?"

I'd have loved to fill Sullivan in on my investigation, but that three grand reward my boss offered would only make it to my pocket if I, alone, stopped the masked trio.

"The guy was casing our jewelry department. When I stopped him, he took off. Thought you might have his record handy."

Sullivan looked as though he didn't buy my line, but he agreed to let me check the mug books.

I was halfway through the third book when I recognized the face staring up at me. His name was Leon "Bug-eyed" Buzinski. Age 35, he'd done time for petty theft, breaking and entering, and assault and battery. His last address was a duplex on North Dearborn near Brookside Park.

I wrote it down and thanked Sullivan for his help.

"Max, you don't plan on going off half-cocked against the guy you chased out of the store, are you?"

I patted my hip. "Not on your life, with this baby giving me hell."

I DROVE over to the near eastside to the duplex and spoke to his land-
lady who told me Buzinski was at work at a gas station at Emerson
and Tenth owned by his brother. A ten-minute drive brought me to
the garage. An angry customer was standing by a pump raging that
he'd been waiting five minutes for service.

"Look! There's no closed sign, and I've hit my horn, but still, no
one's come out. They think I'm gonna pump my own gas, they got
another think coming."

"Let me check," I volunteered. I walked to the front and tried the
door to the office. It was locked. I tried the first entrance to a bay, but
couldn't raise it. I tried the second, and after much effort, opened it.

"Hello? Anyone here?"

No answer. I went inside and looked around. It seemed odd that it
was abandoned. Where was the brother who owned the place?"

"Help you, Mister?"

I turned around to see a guy in his forties dressed in a mechanic
uniform.

"You the owner?"

He nodded. "Pat Buzinksi."

"I'm trying to locate your brother."

"The little rat oughta been here. He agreed to watch the place
while I was away picking up some parts for that Buick I'm working
on. I come back, the place is open for any guy off the streets to hit the
cash register, and no sign of Leon. What gives?"

He looked around and tried the door to the john.

"What the . . . ? It's locked!"

He went into his office, took out a key from a desk and unlocked
the door. As he swung it open, a body fell forward to the cement floor.

Leon Buzinski's body. His throat had been cut.

THE VEINS in Captain Sullivan's forehead were bulging. "Lemme
guess. You just decided to stop for a fill up and accidentally end up at
a murder scene. Right?"

"I didn't kill him. You can ask the customer who was waiting for service."

"Spill it, Max. What ain't you telling me?"

I coulda lied, but I knew Sullivan wouldn't believe it. I filled him in.

"You come after those three on your own without department backup? Max, these goons are killers! What were you thinking?"

"I'm sure the other two decided they couldn't let him live and lead the law to them, once they heard he'd been recognized."

"Max, I want you to promise me, you'll let the police handle this investigation," Sullivan instructed.

"You have my word; I will not investigate the murder of Leon Buzinski."

"And what about the robberies?"

I said nothing and walked away.

I RETURNED to the department store the following day and worked my normal shift. The store closed at six. I saw all the customers out and waited until the clerks departed. I did a final walk through. At seven, I set the alarm and stepped out the rear exit into the night.

And then the world came down on me like a pile of bricks. I sensed movement from behind, but before I could act, something came hard against the back of my head.

I reached out to get a hold on the wall to prevent hitting the concrete, but something long and hard like a baseball bat struck the back of my lower legs and I dropped into a heap.

My attackers weren't happy with just laying me out. The toe of a shoe rammed into my side and pain erupted.

"Let's get this done," a voice said in a cold, quiet tone. "Waste him now."

I was about to pray for my soul to end up in the right place, when a cry came from the street at the end of the alley.

"Hey! What are you doing?"

I heard the sound of feet shifting on wet payment, and the quiet voice lost its quiet.

"Crap! It's a cop! Forget this guy and get out of here!"

The sound of running feet was the last thing I heard as the darkness swallowed me up.

~

"FELLA? CAN YOU HEAR ME?"

Before I opened my eyes, a tidal wave of pain swept over my body. I heard a groan and realized it had come from me.

"Just lie still. I'll call for an ambulance."

"No!" Jeez, my voice sounded like a bullfrog. "Just help me up."

"I don't think you should be moved. I'm a cop, and my captain would have my badge if I did so."

I again ordered him to help me up in language hardly appropriate for dealing with a street cop. He gave in and helped me to my feet. He flicked on a flashlight and gave me a once over.

"You've got one hellava bump on the back of your head, mister. Let me drive you to the emergency room."

"Just get me to my car." He slipped an arm under my shoulder and along my back. In doing so, the beam of his flashlight dipped to the ground. I saw something and jerked to a stop. "Look down there! We need to get that ball bat they used on me."

"I can come by later and get it. Keep moving to your car."

"No!" came that bullfrog sound from my lips. "It's evidence in a murder case."

"You're not dead."

"Just get it, and pick it up with a handkerchief from the top of the bat. There may be prints. Then, drive me down to your headquarters."

~

"DAMN, Keagan, you look like you've been through a cement mixer!" Sullivan exclaimed when I staggered into his office. "I thought I told you to drop looking into the Masked Bandits."

"But you didn't tell them to drop looking for me," I replied.

"You're damned lucky Officer Gilcrest was walking his beat or you'd be lying on a cold slab in the morgue."

"Why is my body saying otherwise?"

"Well, your pains may have bought us a name of another member of the gang. The bat you brought in is down in fingerprinting."

AGAINST MY WISHES, I was driven to the hospital and checked for a possible concussion. It seems that when my fourth grade teacher called me "a hard head," she was absolutely right. My head had a bump the size of a goose egg, but there'd been no other damage.

When I was released, Captain Sullivan was waiting for me at the exit.

"You're giving me a personal ride home? I gotta say I'm touched."

"Shad-up and follow me to my car. I'll fill you in on what we learned from the prints we pulled."

We settled in the car and Sullivan continued. "The goon who tried to use you for batting practice is one Willie Wetherly, out of Pendleton's facility just four months. Did time for armed robbery and assault and battery which sent him up six years back."

"Yeah, and I'm betting they'll go for a big heist on Halloween, when people will be in costume all over the city."

IN THE FINAL days before Halloween, Sullivan and his team learned the biggest Halloween party was to be held at the Athenaeum on East Michigan Street. The event was on the 30th, since the 31st came on a Sunday. Every available man would be there to put an end to the

Masked Bandits. If they put in an appearance, they were going to be finally stopped.

Assured that Sullivan had things in hand, I returned to my work at the department store. Saturday morning, taking the day off, I drove down to my barber on East Michigan Street just off Sherman Drive. While Jeffries clipped my hair, we talked about the autumn holiday.

"I understand there's going to be a costume party at Governor Gates' mansion on Meridian," he mentioned.

"Really?"

"Nothing like the big party downtown, though."

I made a note to mention it to Sullivan and then promptly forgot it on the drive home.

I put on the porch light around five and set up a bowl of candy bars for the kids who'd come by for trick-or-treat. Around six forty-five, my phone rang.

"Keagan, here."

"Mr. Keagan, the security guard for the department store?" A young woman's voice.

"Yes."

"It's me—Maggie. I'm the shop girl at the costume place."

"Yes, Maggie, I remember you."

"Remember the man my boss told you wanted something for his boss' party, but didn't buy anything? He just left the shop a little bit ago. Said he needed masks for a party. I told him that because of the big party at the governor's place, we didn't have much left. When I asked if he was going to the party, he told me, 'Something like that.' He pointed to two masks hanging on the wall, and I sold them to him."

"What sort of masks?"

"One was Groucho Marx and the other was his brother, Harpo. I remembered what you'd said and called the department store. Someone there gave me your number."

I thanked Maggie and immediately called police headquarters, asking for Sullivan.

"I know where there's going to be a robbery by the Masked Bandits."

"Yeah, we know. We've got it taken care of," the cop at the phone desk said, and hung up.

I repeatedly called the Athenaeum but only got busy signals. I tried to call the Governor's Mansion, but with the same results. If someone was going to try and stop those goons, it would have to be me.

I packed my piece, jumped into my car, and headed north of downtown. The block where the mansion was located was packed with parked cars. I found a spot one street away and hurried to the mansion with my bum hip.

At the entrance way I was blocked by a modern-day Friar Tuck dressed in robes and sandals. "I'm sorry. You can't enter without a costume."

"I need to get in there. Everyone is in danger! Is there anyone in charge of security here?"

"I repeat, you must be in . . . "

I pushed my way past him just as I heard a voice cry out.

"Don't none of you make a move. This is a robbery. You try to stop me, and I'll blow your head off!"

"Willie!" I called out and the man in the Groucho mask spun around. He raised his gun in my direction but I fired first. His body jerked as a red hole appeared on the white shirt over his chest. He staggered for a moment and then collapsed to the carpet. "Harpo" looked back at me and dropped his handgun.

"Don't shoot! I give up!"

I spotted Governor Gates who looked wide-eyed and for once, speechless.

"Call for the police," I instructed. "Tell them that the Masked Bandits have tried to pull their last heist and failed."

"Has anyone ever told you, that you're one crazy so-and-so?" Sullivan ranted as he paced back and forth in the governor's study. He and half a dozen uniformed officers had arrived twenty minutes earlier, taken Harpo in for questioning, and sent Wetherly's body to the morgue.

I shrugged. "On several occasions."

"Why didn't you try to get a hold of me?"

"I was told you were busy and not to be disturbed. Something about catching the Masked Bandits."

I filled him in on what I'd first learned from my barber, Maggie's phone call, and my arrival at the party.

"You do know that the governor is very impressed with you. He may well put pressure on the department to give you back your old job on the force."

I shook my head. "With this hip of mine, I'd be side-lined doing paperwork all day. That's not for me. I'll leave battling the underworld for younger men like you."

I started to leave when he called me back.

"It's ironical, you know."

"What is?"

"You're ridding this city of scum like Wetherly. Do you ever listen to Groucho Marx on the radio?"

"No, I've never been a big fan of the Marx Brothers."

"Well, Wetherly was dressed as Groucho, and for the past year, the real Groucho's had his own radio show, *You Bet Your Life*."

"So?"

"Looks to me as though this Groucho bet his life and lost it, thanks to you."

I never did appreciate Sullivan's weak attempts at humor. However, I did appreciate the three grand reward for my efforts.

AN EERIE BUMP IN THE ROAD

BY MARY ANN KOONTZ

"Amber, your date's here!"

I jumped at Mom's booming voice echoing through every inch of the house. A rush of heat rose from my neck to my cheeks. Grabbing my purse and jacket, I hurried down the hall, biting my lip and praying the night wouldn't be a total disaster.

When I reached the living room, the latest episode of *M*A*S*H* was playing loudly on TV as my date tried to converse with my parents above the noise. He was dressed like every guy I knew—bell-bottom jeans, Rolling Stones t-shirt, and jean jacket. Not as typical was his short-cropped red beard that failed to match his long sandy brown hair. I turned the volume knob down.

Noticing I'd entered the room, he greeted me with a smile.

"Hi," I replied, then stumbled over his name calling him Mack. It earned me a sideways glance from my date.

"It's Jack," he smirked. I'd either amused or annoyed him.

"Right . . . Jack." I stabbed a finger in the air to prove I knew it. His green eyes focused on me for an uncomfortable moment longer than necessary. "Sorry," I added. The night was not off to a great start, but little did I know that it would soon get much worse.

Once outside, Jack shot a raised eyebrow in my direction, then gestured toward the driveway. I led the way down the sidewalk, walking further and further from the circle of porch light until we reached the driveway. I stared at the rusty blue Chevy. Its door protested with a grating squeak as he opened it for me. My sentiments exactly, I thought, as I plopped into the passenger side seat of the sixties' ride that had seen better days.

I didn't really have time for dating. Between working to pay for classes at a local college and studying in order to stay in school, dating was low on my list of priorities. It was in a sleep-deprived moment of weakness that I'd caved and said yes to my dear friend's matchmaking attempt. *Ugh!* I shivered, whether due to nerves or the cool October night was anybody's guess. I rubbed my arms.

"Cold?" Jack asked. My teeth chattered 'yes' in what sounded like Morse code. Reaching over to the controls, Jack slid a lever to the "on" position. The heater responded with a moan, followed by a funky smell, but within minutes a radiance of warmth surrounded me. Okay, he scored points for chivalry, I thought, but the night was young. At least we were going to a dance, so there wouldn't be an awkward silence to fill.

"You know how to get to Hillside, right?" I asked. The dance venue opened in 1970, and now four years later, was the most popular in northeast Indiana.

He nodded. "Know anyone else who's going?"

"Not really," I replied. I thought how great it would be to see a familiar face, and if this didn't go well, I could at least get a ride home.

My two-word sentences didn't deter this guy though, and soon I was rambling on about school, work, and family. Jack's head swiveled back and forth between the road and me as he spoke. Before long, I found myself easing into a degree of comfort with him.

Jack steered the clunker left off of Bluffton Road onto Engle Road and we were engulfed in darkness. Nonfunctional street lights stood along the road like dark, imposing sentinels. It wasn't a power outage though, because I noticed lights on in several houses. Jack's single headlight kept him focused more on the black road with its faded markings than on conversation with me.

We both saw him too late. Perhaps if I hadn't been thinking ahead to the dance, I'd have noticed the body sooner and been able to warn Jack. But the car's beam illuminated it too late. The figure was lying face-down a few yards in front of the vehicle when Jack swerved sharply. A sickening *thump, thump* lifted us off our seats. I couldn't breathe.

"I think I only ran over his legs!" Jack shouted, then repeated it, as though it were a mantra.

I struggled in vain to grasp what had happened. My thoughts became jumbled, and the sour bile rising in my throat burned. I covered my face to shut out the fear, to shut out the sickening image of what we'd done.

Jack was talking to me, but my brain refused to acknowledge or make sense of it. My ears rang. I whimpered, keeping my face hidden from the reality of it all with my trembling hands. Please let this be a horrible nightmare, nothing more. I felt his hand on my shoulder, shaking me gently, then firmly.

"Amber! Amber! You've got to pull it together. I need your help."

I slid my hands ever so slowly away from my eyes. Glancing out the window, I noticed we were parked along the side of the road now, much closer to the houses with the light escaping from behind closed curtains. I turned to Jack. His green eyes darted back and forth, and I found my earlier feeling of ease I'd had around him was gone. I pulled away, the back of my head sliding up against the cold car door window. It jolted my brain into functioning again.

"Why was that man lying in the middle of the road?" I asked. Flashes of his plaid shirt in the headlight brought up more bile. "Do you think someone else could've run over him before us, but took off, and then we ran over him again?" I started to gag, then swallowed hard. "Do you think he's dead?" My eyes opened wider. "Did we kill him? I think I'm going to be sick." I forced open the heavy car door and dry heaved. This date was officially beyond a bungling disaster.

"Amber, we need to call the police."

Yes. Yes, that's what we needed to do.

"I need you to get help while I check on the body. I don't think he was moving, but until an ambulance gets here, I need to see what I can do. At the very least, I can direct cars around him so no one else hits him."

Jack pointed past me to the homes on the north side of the street. "Look. See where the lights are on in the house over there? See if they will let you in to call the police. Go! Now!"

I couldn't remember getting out of the car, but soon I found myself stumbling in the direction of the nearest house. My legs responded with all the stiffness of a zombie's gait from some horror movie. I glanced back to see Jack running into the street, but it was too dark to see the body from here. Turning back to my destination, I arrived at a door painted a country blue. With a trembling finger, I pushed the doorbell. I rang several times but no one came to the door.

In a panic, I ran to the next house. I stared at the peeling gray paint on the siding and listened to the chimes ringing an off-key tune inside the home. Only then did I realize that I must have already pushed the doorbell. It'll be okay, I told myself. The man in the street could still be alive. After all, Jack only ran over his legs. Surely, whoever lived here would let me call the police. They'll send an ambulance. Moments went by, though, without an answer. As I turned to leave, I heard the lock turn and an elderly couple in their pj's and tattered robes opened the door.

I was so relieved that I began blurting out my story about how my date and I had run over some guy we hadn't seen lying in the road. The woman began to back away, shoving her husband forward. I begged them to let me inside their home to use the phone. The elderly man ran his fingers through his untamed white hair. In spite of the wife's not-so-subtle head shaking and tugging on her husband's sleeve in warning, the guy took a step back. He opened their door and let me inside.

"I'm Amber," I said. "Thank you. I'll try to make it quick."

"Sam and Edna Gravely," he replied. I glanced at the small living area to the right, where the TV was blaring. Three trays with dirty plates and glasses remained in front of a couch and a recliner. A crooked smile from the elderly man revealed yellow teeth with a gaping hole at the center. "The phone is on the wall in the kitchen," he said.

I followed him through the living room, his wife trailing behind me, into a dismal kitchen with wallpaper as neglected as the outside of the house. He motioned to the phone, then held up a wrinkled hand with darkened fingernails.

"No long-distance calls, you hear?"

I nodded. "I'm just calling the local police."

The call went about as expected. I heard doubt in the voice of the police dispatcher, who had probably handled a number of Halloween prank calls already. Still, the dispatcher was obliged to take the information and promised to send a squad car to the location. I hung up.

"Didn't believe ya, did he?" The man chuckled and winked at his wife. She giggled.

Stuttering, I thanked them for letting me use their phone, then ran out the door. I peered into the dark, then headed toward the street in search of Jack. At the edge of the road, I nearly collided with him. He was breathing hard.

"Amber, where'd you go? Did you call the police?"

I nodded. "They're sending someone."

He bent over, resting his hands on his thighs in an attempt to catch his breath. "I tried to stop you." Jack looked up. "I went to the house where I'd told you to go. I figured you were still there calling the police. The door was unlocked, so I walked on in. I only wanted to stop you. A woman wearing a bathrobe with a towel wrapped around her hair came around the corner from the hallway. She screamed bloody murder at me, yelling at me to get out. I tried to explain, but she only screamed louder."

"I went to that house first, but no one answered the door," I said, realizing that the woman must've been in the shower at the time. "So, I went to the next house. Why were you trying to stop me? What's going on?"

Jack rubbed his hands over his face. "He's gone. The body's gone."

"Gone? You ran over his legs. He couldn't get up and walk away."

"I know. The thing is, I saw him, and then I didn't."

"You're not making any sense, Jack. When did you see the body last?"

"I grabbed a flashlight from the car, then went to check on him. He had no pulse and was ice cold."

Jack took a breath. "That's when I saw headlights further down the road. I ran toward them to flag down the car, but the headlights disappeared. I looked for the car, but it's really dark over there. Then, just as I decided to return to the body, the headlights reappeared. I was jogging toward them when they vanished into total darkness again. I waited awhile but they didn't reappear. It was so weird. When I got back to the body it was gone."

I looked at Jack in disbelief. Disappearing headlights? Disappearing body? Was he telling the truth? Jack's entire body was shaking and his eyes were wide with fright. I had to believe him.

"Jack, are you as scared as I am? What if a murderer moved the body and is watching us now?" Jack and I looked into the surrounding darkness. It was impossible to know if that was true.

"Either that or someone's playing a cruel trick," Jack said. "Did you see anyone right after I ran over the guy's legs?"

"No, but I was so shook up then, that I don't think I would've noticed if a murderer was standing three feet from us—or closer."

The police car approached us with flashers on but no siren. It pulled off to the side of the road opposite us. A police officer got out and sauntered across the road.

"Not a good sign," I whispered to Jack. "It looks like he's already doubtful."

"Our news of the missing body isn't going to help," Jack whispered back.

Without a hello, the officer said, "I'll need to see your license and registration."

I stood next to Jack's open car door as he scrambled to retrieve his registration from the glove box. He handed it over along with his license. The police officer scrutinized both with his flashlight before returning them. "Okay. Now I'd like you to walk a straight line, turn and walk back."

Jack scowled as though about to protest this latest demand, but seemed to have decided it would only make matters worse.

"Now can I show you where the body was lying in the road?" Jack asked, after he'd passed the sobriety test. The officer nodded, and Jack led the way back down the road. He recounted the whole story, from running over the body to finding it missing. I noticed he failed to mention the disappearing headlights. He probably thought it was hard enough to get the officer to believe a body was missing, without stating that he'd seen vanishing headlights, too. The officer scribbled down notes as Jack spoke, interrupting only with an occasional "uh-huh." He completed a cursory check of the road where the body, in his words, "was alleged to have been," then shook his head.

"At least your story explains a woman's call from this neighborhood about an intruder who'd insisted his girlfriend was in her house. As far as the body you supposedly ran over, this could be your lucky day. Without a body, there's no crime to report. However, if a dead guy in a flannel shirt happens to turn up, I'll be sure to call you. Happy Halloween." He walked back to his car, then pulled away in his cruiser, making a wide U-turn that forced us to take a step back. I could just make out the silhouette of his head shaking side to side in disbelief.

"Huh," I said. "You can't exactly blame him for not believing us."

I grabbed the flashlight from Jack's hand and clicked it on. Aimed it at the road, I then walked toward the houses and the car. Jack followed me in a sullen silence until I stopped abruptly.

"Do you see this?" I pointed to marks that ended at the sidewalk. "They dragged the body through here." We searched the area, but no new tracks appeared.

"There's nothing more we can do," Jack said. "What do you say we skip the dance and get some coffee instead?"

I'd completely forgotten about the dance. Tonight's fiasco had killed the mood on that for sure. If there was a murderer or someone trying to play a sick joke on us, maybe a brightly lit place that was apt to have lots of people around would be best. "How about the McDonald's in Waynedale?" I suggested. Waynedale was considered a small suburb of Fort Wayne, and the McDonald's there was one of the few places to get a cup of coffee at night. Chances were good we wouldn't be alone.

"That works. Let's get out of here."

I started to lead the way down the sidewalk toward the car, trying not to trip over its raised chunks of concrete pushed up by surfacing tree roots. We hadn't gone far when the flashlight flickered then went off completely. I held it up and swung around suddenly asking, "Jack do you . . . ?" But I'd turned too quickly for Jack's forward momentum, causing the flashlight to smack him soundly on the nose. He howled, covered his nose, and squeezed his eyes closed in obvious pain. A grating noise interrupted the sound of Jack's moans, but before I could mention it, Jack exploded.

"What are you trying to do, kill me?" He snatched the flashlight from me.

"I'm so sorry," I said. "I was just going to ask if you had extra batteries in the car. Are you okay?"

"I'll be fine," he muttered.

He slapped the flashlight against his palm. Immediately, it turned on, revealing an ugly red welt across the bridge of his nose. I winced.

"I'll take the lead this time," Jack insisted.

"I really am sorry," I said, meaning it. "By the way, I don't suppose you heard that grating sound while you were hopping around in pain? It sounded like your car door."

"My car!" Jack shouted.

We veered off the sidewalk, rushing gingerly across the uneven ground that was only slightly safer to walk on. When we reached the old Chevy, Jack's flashlight beam revealed nothing unusual. Both doors were closed with no one in sight. Jack shrugged.

"I guess you imagined the sound."

"I know what I heard," I said between clenched teeth. I pursed my lips and grabbed the flashlight from Jack, squeezing it so tight the ridges on its hard rubber handle were digging into my palm.

"Okay, geeze. Sorry," he said, raising both hands in surrender.

Turning in a huff, I stomped around to the passenger side, then stopped cold. Next to the car's door were more marks in the gravel. Something or someone had been dragged to our parked car.

Jack had already climbed inside the car and slammed his door shut. My throat went dry at what I glimpsed in the few brief seconds the dome light was on. It was useless to try to speak through the unopened door, useless to try to warn him. I slid a foot back, away from the car, but Jack had grown impatient and reached over, shoving the door open for me. This time the dome light stayed on, illuminating the horror.

My eyes bulged and I stifled a scream. I pointed a shaky finger toward the back seat of the car. Confused, Jack twisted around to see what had frightened me. His legs hit the steering wheel hard as he clawed at the door handle in a desperate attempt to escape the gruesome sight. Finally, I found my own legs and sprinted around to the driver's side, just in time to collide with Jack as he flew out of the car.

"What the hell!" Jack shouted.

I realized Jack could have had ample time to move the body while I was phoning the police. "Did you do this? Did you put that body in there?" I immediately regretted the accusation.

"No! Are you kidding? What do you think I am, some psycho?" Jack retorted. "Besides, you were with me when I got the car's registration. Did you see a body then?"

I shook my head back and forth, wishing I'd thought of that before accusing him. Of course he hadn't put the dead body in the back seat of his own car, but someone did. Why? It made no sense.

Jack began to pace back and forth. "If this is someone's idea of a joke, it sucks!"

Moments ticked by before we got up the courage to take a second peek. Jack opened the car door cautiously. In the glare of the dome light, we could see a dead body wearing a flannel shirt. It was lying across the back seat on its side, in the same position we'd found it when we ran over it.

"Quick, close the door!" I said. "We don't need anyone else seeing the body. They'll think we killed him. We need to cover it up. Do you have a blanket?"

Jack unlocked the trunk and grabbed a thick gray blanket. He hesitated. "Maybe we can put him in the trunk."

"No. We need a more permanent solution. Besides, I'm not touching him unless it's to hide him somewhere else."

Jack threw the blanket over the body, while I looked around. Out of the corner of my eye, I thought I saw movement at the house with the peeling paint. Had one of the Gravelys been spying on us from the front window?

"I feel like someone's watching us. I hate to say this, but I think we need to get back in the car and get out of here."

We no sooner climbed in the car when the stench of the corpse hit us. Gagging, we attempted to roll the windows down, but they jammed half-way. "Nice car," I gasped. Jack ignored the insult as he pulled his t-shirt up over his nose, and pulled out into the street.

"We need to get rid of this body," Jack said, after a block. "Like the officer said, if there isn't a body, there's no crime. As long as they don't find the body with us, we can't be accused of his murder."

"You've got a point, but we can't just dump him alongside the road. I'm not okay with that, plus someone might see us." Jack and I both went quiet.

"Wait," I said. "There's a cemetery next to a church a little further down Engle Road. I remember seeing it during the day when I've passed by here. No one would see us leave a body back there, and at least we can leave him in a good resting place."

Jack spotted the church, then turned into the lane just past it that led to a cemetery in a wooded area. He drove along the narrow road until we were near the back of the graveyard and parked the car. "Now what?"

"First, can you turn your dome light off? We'll use the flashlight, but only when necessary." I studied the blanket and shivered knowing that there was a corpse lying beneath it. "How are we going to get him out of the back seat?"

Jack chewed on a lip. "If we can roll him onto the blanket, then we can use the blanket to lift him out."

Squeezing between the seats and door jams of the two-door car, we spread the blanket on the back floor. I shivered at the icy touch of the stiff corpse as Jack and I rolled it off the seat and onto the blanket.

"How did the killer manage to get the body into this back seat by himself?" I asked. "Do you think he had help?"

Jack shrugged. "Maybe."

Once we'd successfully removed the body from the car, we drug it across the ground on the blanket, weaving between ghost-gray head-stones. We stopped at a monument that stood nearly as tall as me, with names and dates barely visible from erosion. The crumbling structure loomed over nearby graves, far from the drive, a perfect spot to leave the body.

We rolled the rigid corpse off the blanket. I wanted to cover the guy with it, but Jack insisted we get rid of the blanket elsewhere. He didn't want to risk it leading back to him. My only consolation was that at least the body appeared to be lying in restful slumber.

"What about animals?" I asked. "We'll have to report finding the body anonymously, maybe from a public phone, so they can find it before the animals do."

"Not until we get out of here and get rid of this blanket."

Jack balled up the blanket and tucked it under an arm. I led the way back to the car careful to keep the flashlight beam focused low to the ground. I never thought I'd be so relieved to see the old Chevy.

Suddenly, I heard Jack rattle off a string of curses. Then I spied the source of his ranting. The left rear tire was flat. Not only that, but it appeared to have been slashed! I spun around, peering into the dark-ness in every direction.

"Jack!" I choked out his name, but he didn't hear me. He kicked the flat and punched the air with his fists. I grabbed one of his arms. "Jack!" I followed up with a shove and spoke in a low, tense voice. "Someone's coming up the drive!" Finally, I had his attention.

Jack stuffed the blanket under the driver's seat. "Who could that be?" Sweat had begun to mat his hair to his forehead, some escaping down into his red beard.

I stared at the dark figure. There was something familiar about it.

A crop of wild white hair came into view. I recognized his tattered bathrobe.

"You kids need some help?"

I whispered to Jack. "That's the guy from the house where I called the police."

"What's he doing here?" Jack whispered back.

"I thought I heard some commotion over here and thought I'd check it out," he said. He shook Jack's hand. "Sam Gravely. I'm the caretaker here. It's my job to look after the place." He paused to spit in the grass. "I recognize your car. Saw it parked on our road earlier. Looks like you got a flat now."

I wasn't sure if I should be relieved or not. How much had he heard, or worse yet, how much had he seen?

"You must have the hearing of a bat." Jack scowled.

"Well, you got me there," Gravely said. He seemed to be looking past us. "Actually, it was my son, Bones, who heard something and called me." Gravely made a summoning gesture, and a figure, slightly taller than his own six-foot frame, stepped out from behind a large oak tree. He wore overalls and a flannel shirt similar to our corpse's, and carried a pocketknife in a bandaged hand. Its blade glinted in the flashlight's beam.

"I saw where they hid the body, Pa. Did you like what I did with their tire?"

Gravely smiled and patted his son's shoulder. "You got a little carried away, Bones."

Jack sneered. "Bones Gravely? You've got to be kidding me. Who'd give their kid a name like that?"

What was Jack doing, trying to get us killed? I gave him a sharp elbow to the ribs.

Now it was Gravely's turn to scowl, but Bones spoke up before he could reply. "I like our Halloween games. Worked real good this year, didn't it, Pa?"

I looked from Bones back to Gravely. "What's he mean, 'Halloween games?'"

He ignored my question. "Bones, why don't you go bury the body for good this time?" Gravely produced a shovel that had been hidden by his robe and handed it to Bones.

"Is the game over now, Pa?" Bones said as he took the shovel.

"Yes, son. We're all done."

Bones' shoulders slumped as he turned and headed toward the monument where we'd left the body in peaceful slumber. My head was spinning with questions.

"We didn't mean any harm," Gravely said. "I never expected you to call the police, let alone from my own home."

"So why did you let me?" I asked, then answered my own question. "You knew the police wouldn't believe us when there wasn't a body to be found. But how could you have moved it when you were in the house with me and your wife?"

"Bones did that. He's as strong as an ox, but maybe not as smart. He got the body off the road, and after you nearly collided with your friend here, Bones was already heading for your car with it. By the time I got to him, the body was half-way in the back seat, so I figured I'd better help him finish the job before you got back to the car."

I blinked. This was their idea of a Halloween prank? I was furious. "We could've hit an oncoming car head-on when we tried to swerve at the last minute!" I was about to say more when Jack interrupted.

"So, the headlights I saw in the road that vanished were just a coincidence?"

Gravely looked down and formed a circle in the dirt with his boot. "Not exactly. Bones helped me set up a couple battery-operated flood lights on the side of the road earlier. I used a remote control to turn them on and off while Amber was using our phone. It gave Bones time to move the body off the road."

Jack opened the trunk and grabbed the spare tire and car jack. He set to work replacing the tire, while I continued seeking answers to this Halloween fiasco.

"And the body?" I asked.

"From here," Gravely said, as though it was the most normal thing in the world to borrow a dead body from the cemetery where he was employed, all for a Halloween prank. "The guy didn't have any kin," Gravely added. "Figured we weren't hurting anyone."

Unbelievable, I thought.

"I'm pretty sure that messing with a corpse is a serious crime," I said.

Gravely's face turned stern. "I'm sure it is, kind of like you hauling one around in your car and hiding it in this cemetery."

He had us.

Jack finished replacing the slashed tire and threw the car jack back in the trunk. "Ready to go?"

We wasted no time jumping into the car. I checked the back seat. Clear. I could hear the scrape of Bones' shovel hitting dirt and rock in the distance. "I've never been more ready."

Jack made a U-turn, then peeled off down the lane.

This had definitely been the strangest blind date I'd ever been on. I glanced over at Jack. His jaw was set as he held a death grip on the steering wheel. Still, I might consider going out with him again. After all, things couldn't possibly get any weirder, but then I guess there was only one way to find out.

MAYBE IT'S IN THE GENES

BY B.K. HART

"How are you feeling, Mama?"

Lacy rubbed her mother's shoulders feeling for tension and knots along her thin neck. She wished her mama wouldn't sleep in the recliner night after night, but no amount of saying so would change the habit. Though her mama's eyes had been closed, Lacy could tell from the breathing that she was awake.

"Out all night, Lacy?"

"I just got in. You want some breakfast?" Lacy slipped off her jacket and dropped it on the end of their ratty couch. She would have spent some of the money to make the place nice, but Mama said no. No sense in prettying something up when they weren't gonna be there long.

"Working?" Mama turned her pale blue eyes on her daughter with shrewd assessment. "You always been better than I was."

"Why do you say that? You don't know what I've been doing."

She nodded her head knowingly. "Cause, I know how your mind works, girl. How many times did you drive the route, walk the floor-plan? I might have made a pass at it once or twice, but I bet you counted steps."

"Ah, hush." Lacy blushed, slightly unnerved that her mother knew her so well. From day to day, she could never be sure if her mother would be lucid or murky. "You taught me everything I know."

"That might be so. But you always been better."

Lacy opened the refrigerator and removed eggs and cheese for an omelet. As the coffee brewed, the kitchen took on a homey feel, even though she could never really consider this type of place a real home. It was the smell and feel of comfort. She could hear Mama battling to get out of the recliner and smiled. The chair was a brown leather monstrosity. Big, bulky, and comfortable. But you needed muscle power to push it into a recline position and nearly as much grit and determination to get out of it. Mama was slight, but she was fierce.

Lacy set a plate on the counter as her mama climbed onto a stool at the breakfast bar. She placed a short glass of orange juice in front of the plate and a black cup of coffee next to the juice. Mama always added her own cream and sugar, so Lacy nudged the bowl over with a tiny spoon and put the carton of half-and-half next to it.

"Did the payment come through?" Lacy asked as she folded the egg over in the pan creating a half-moon shape. When cut in two, it would be the perfect portions for them to share.

"Yep." Mama stirred her coffee, taking her time with it. "I already transferred it to the Bermuda account. Most important assignment of our lives. You all set for tonight?"

"I spent most of the night at the Carlton. Liberated a uniform and checked out the ballroom, hallways, and bathrooms. They have a corridor under construction on the second floor. If I run into any issues tonight, that area could be useful."

After sliding the omelet onto their plates, she placed the skillet back on the stovetop.

"Good to be thorough. I put your invitation to the fancy costume party on the table next to the door. I can't see that you will have any problems getting in. It's some of my best work, even if I do say so myself." Mama grinned and stabbed a piece of omelet with her fork and nodded. "Forgery. That's where I should have made my mark."

Lacy shook her head, knowing better than to encourage her mother down the lane of what might have been. She pulled her own stool over and sat while she angled the laptop so she could check her emails and map the route one more time. As Lacy ate and surfed, she watched Mama. She almost didn't even look sick today. This took a huge weight off her shoulders as she needed to be focused on the job this evening. Keeping her emotions in check was the only way Lacy had learned to do this type of work over the years.

"I don't know if I ever said I was sorry."

Lacy raised her eyes. Blue meeting blue.

"For what, Mama?" Lacy asked softly.

"This life I gave you." Mama waved her hand at the protest. "This ain't no life. Not really. Yeah, we go places and see some things. But we're always moving. We have to. You know that."

"I do. I know. No need to be sorry."

"But you didn't get a choice. I had a choice. Until they took your daddy . . . "

Lacy waited.

Mama rarely talked about their past. Lacy pieced together a history from small details over the years. Mama was a sharpshooter, ex-military. Daddy worked security for an ambassador. Both had been expert riflemen. The agency had pressured her mother into doing the first assignment. Using her father's job as leverage to *encourage* her mother to work for the Stateside Procurement Agency.

Lacy hadn't seen her father since she was six. He was just a vague image in her memory these days. He died defending his ambassador a few months after Mama took the first "job." At least, that was what they were told. Mama didn't believe the official narrative. The SPA, as the agency was commonly referred to, was heavy on secrets and light on truth.

It wasn't easy to find out information on SPA, but Lacy was excellent with computers. Stateside Procurement was established in 1789 as a purchasing arm for the English ruling class. Over the years, the agency grew into a US run entity. Its duties morphing over time, becoming responsible for the retrieval of "lost" items. Typically, long out of use bearer bonds that seemed to reappear every few years. Lacy's research told her SPA was not in the business of assassination. But a *bad seed* managed to work his way to the top of the food chain. This bad seed was responsible for her father's death and he would be at the party tonight.

Mama still believed the agency didn't know about Lacy. Oh, but they knew. Lacy introduced herself to their handler and put them on notice to steer clear of her mother. She wasn't worried about any government agency tracking them down. Not really. She could bounce a signal to Mumbai and back if she needed to conceal their location. Lacy excelled at disguises and anything related to computers.

Mama was better at creating fake IDs and planning. Their jobs always came in with an itinerary, sometimes months in advance. Mama usually picked the location. Since Daddy had been born in Indiana, Mama thought it was a nice place to finish. At least, that was the intention. Do this last job and be done with it.

"Your daddy would have been proud of you."

"Why are you telling me this now?" Lacy began a slow rhythmic tap of her foot. She was tired and felt grubby, and she needed her head in the game tonight. Thinking about her family history, and why she was even doing this kind of work made her emotional. She couldn't afford to be sloppy when she had an assignment.

Mama snapped, "Because I know you hate this life. Lugging around your old lady. Moving place to place. Living in shitholes."

"We don't have to live this way. We have money in the bank."

"Yes, we do, young lady, and that's where it's going to stay. In the bank. Hidden deep enough that these doctors don't get their hands on it."

It wasn't even a reasonable argument. As far as the doctors getting their hands on anything, they never kept the same personas long enough for a bill collector to track them down.

"You know there are treatments," Lacy reasoned, reigning in her own anger. It didn't make sense to react to her mother when the attitude would change in the next breath. "I read about an experimental treatment in Switzerland, and light therapy using a UV wand in Hong Kong. There are things we can try, Mama."

"No sense in wasting money on voodoo remedies. That money is your nest egg, so you never have to do this again. I see the research you do on beach houses. Before I die, I want to make sure you have enough money that you don't live on the run anymore."

"It's not like that, Mama. I can do this work as long as we need it." Lacy reached out and rested her hand on her mother's wrinkled and aged arm. "It's worth it to me to have you around another year, or week, or even just a day. Besides, we're the good guys. You read the dossiers. These are arms dealers, pedophiles, terrorists, and politicians."

Her mama's eyes filled as she took a deep breath.

"You're just trying to make me feel better now. We never get any politicians."

"Some hit the profile. I'm surprised they haven't shown up on the list," Lacy admitted.

"Tonight is special though, not just because of how much it pays," Mama explained then abruptly changed direction, "You know that last doctor in Houston said the beach climate might be beneficial to me. Maybe we could get a house in Florida as a more permanent residence, or a long-term rental?"

Lacy gave her mama a sad smile. "Let's do it. Maybe for a short while. We shouldn't really stop in one place for very long. Not yet." Lacy changed the subject. "Are you putting a costume on for the evening?"

"You betcha. Gonna watch the kiddies running up and down Washington Boulevard. Think I'll do the nurse routine. I still got the uniform. I can roll out the wheelchair the hospital loaned us on the last series of treatments. The candy cannon will be useful so I can . . . " Mama tilted her head as her eyes grew distant and confused, "*shoot* the kids without them having to come up the steps."

"You look like an old hag in that outfit."

"I am an old hag," Mama confirmed, seeming to come back to herself. "If you help me, I can fix my eyes up like a zombie. Maybe shred my shirt and make it look a bit bloody. Kids love zombie stuff these days."

"Oh, I can blacken your eye all right," Lacy teased. She stood up and started clearing the counter.

"You stop that," Mama said, leveraging herself off her stool. "You need to get some rest if you're working tonight. I'll put this breakfast away. As much as I can manage. You can finish it later if I run out of steam."

"All right, Mama." Lacy gave her a peck on the cheek. "I need a shower, then I'll get a few hours of sleep. I have a lot of work to put into my costume for this evening, so I can't sleep all day. If you don't see me up by five, make sure you holler."

"I'll see if I can't find us a nice little place. One with a patio and beachfront access. And little geckoes running about the place. We can head out tomorrow."

"And a hot tub. It'll be November, so unless it's southern Florida we won't want to get in the water."

"Oh yeah," Mama called after her. "Maybe we need to go further south? Mexico, the Caribbean?"

～

"WHEN WAS the last time you were on the range, Lacy?"

"Over the weekend. Little place up near Kokomo. Discreet, remote. I was getting good readings on the shots. I'm all set."

"Next time you go, maybe I could get some practice in as well."

Lacy eyed her mother's slender body. There was still muscle. Positioned correctly, the rifle wouldn't create much kick, but it would certainly leave a bruise on her bony shoulder. Besides which, Mama didn't have any reason to need practice these days.

Lacy grabbed her mother's chin and repositioned her face.

"You need to sit still so I can finish this black eye. The bloody rip on your face looks realistic. Did you fix yourself a squirt gun with some red food coloring so you can spray your face every few minutes and keep it looking fresh?"

"I did. I wasn't born yesterday."

"No, you weren't. However, disguises are my forte, just as yours is forgery, so just checking."

Mama grinned at her, then patted her on the leg. "You always been better."

Lacy shook her head, lips pressed to hide the smile. She thought it was the medication causing the repetition, as if Mama didn't remember she had already said this. Lacy hoped it was just the drugs. She didn't know if her family had any Alzheimer history. But the chemo caused episodes of forgetfulness and confusion, sometimes accompanied by an agitated state. And, her mother's accent seemed to revert to her Alabama roots on some days. Mama hadn't lived there in nearly thirty years.

"I learned everything I know from you, Mama."

"That might be so. But you always been better."

"Can you line around my eyes in some black? I want to make it pop out more." Lacy invited her mother to work on the makeup keeping her engaged as she studied her. She wanted to assess how much the treatment the day before was still affecting her mother.

"I don't know why you want to mess up your pretty face with all this crap," Mama said, but she picked up the liner and dutifully traced around her daughter's eyes. "And why do you have to smear this red lipstick all down your chin like that? It looks messy."

"Harley Quinn is messy. It's the character."

"Well, she looks trashy and bruised." Mama clicked her tongue. "And these pigtails. Makes you look like a child."

"The paint hides my face so I can move freely tonight."

"I suppose the torn hose is in character too?"

Lacy laughed then. A long belly laugh. And Mama smiled. Lacy felt the tension curling in her belly all morning release. Every job did this to her, pressure forming from the time they received the assignment until it was complete. She couldn't focus on anything but the end goal. She never thought about the future because she couldn't be sure there would be one.

"I'm sorry, honey. It hardly makes you look grown at all. I guess it's bringing out my protective nature."

"Let's get you set up on the porch so I can finish my costume. Are you sure you feel up to sitting outside for the trick-or-treaters?"

"I feel great right now." Mama's hand drifted up to the fake blood on her face, then patted her purposefully matted hair. She drew in a deep sigh. "Maybe just a little tired. You go on now, I can push the wheelchair onto the porch. Get my candy cannon armed and ready for action."

Lacy watched her shuffle out of the bedroom then turned back to her own outfit.

The short-shorts, the long boots, the barely-covering-her-belly t-shirt. She snapped on some thick bangles and carefully smeared one side of her painted-on mask down to her jawline. She affixed a black choker collar in thick leather, which she found surprisingly comfortable. She had purchased a half-blue half-red jacket specifically for this job. Since the temperature was predicted to drop this evening, she was glad she had. She assembled a backpack with warmer clothing so she could change once the job was done, even if she couldn't fix her face right away.

Lacy phoned their neighbor.

Then, she checked her email for any last-minute changes to the arrangements.

She picked up her bag and her oversized mallet and gave herself one more look in the mirror. Trampy, but perfectly crafted.

She joined her mother on the front porch. Halloween was Mama's favorite holiday precisely because she got to dress up and hand out treats to the kids. It didn't matter where they were, or if they were on a job, Mama always dressed for the occasion.

They had spent some time decorating the wide concrete porch. A black hairy spider perched in the corner. Ghostly lanterns and hanging sheets were placed strategically throughout the bushes and trees. The walk was lined with tea lanterns leading visitors along the path. Children would find the candy cannon, surrounded by cobwebs upon which a green goblin perched.

"Good Lord, Lacy. Are you trying to look like a tart?"

"Yes," Lacy grinned. "I called Mabel, and she'll join you on the porch in the next hour or so. She'll get you inside if you get too tired. And, she'll be good company."

"Why you want to bother our neighbors, girl? I can manage," Mama protested.

"You would deny Mabel the joy of watching the terror on these kids' faces as they come up the walk for candy?" Lacy teased.

"What's that you got there?" Mama pointed at the costume prop.

"Ah, this is ingenious really," Lacy said and set down her bag then placed the mallet in her lap. "The top of the hammer here snaps off. The reason I picked this costume was because Harley carries an over-sized wooden mallet in many of the comics. With tweaking you can conceal about anything."

Lacy popped open the fasteners and looked quickly around to confirm nobody was within viewing distance, then she opened the head of the mallet. Laying in the foam casing was the stock of a rifle. The barrel fit smoothly into the handle of the oversized hammer. One side of the carved-out casing held space for an additional magazine round.

"M28 bolt action?"

"Yep. Needed something accurate in close range that didn't need to be calibrated before the job. It worked fine on the range last week, so I trust it for tonight. Heavy as hell though. It's top-heavy and makes the balance off."

"How you planning to shoot that thing?"

"The end cap pops off." Lacy demonstrated, fully removing the fake mallet casing. Then she popped an access panel on the scope mount. "Ready to go in like ten seconds. Another ten to lock on to the target, and maybe five seconds to reassemble."

"Hmm, normally about eight pounds for this rifle. What is it? Fifteen with this getup?"

"About that. It's a bit awkward. I had to use PVC piping around the barrel. Good thing this was painted in red and white to match the costume. Tape and paint conceal a lot."

Lacy quickly began restoring her prop to its original condition. No sense in scaring the kids with the real stuff if they started showing up early.

Suddenly, Mama grabbed her by the wrist and leaned in close.

"Don't you ever let them get their hands on you, girl. You stay clean and safe." She hissed. "I made the new ID so tight they will never track you down. Anything ever happens to me, you take it and go."

Lacy's heart leapt in her chest and began to pound. She scanned the area around the house and both directions on Washington Boulevard. She could see nothing out of place. What caught Mama's attention this time? Or was this another episode?

"Don't talk like that, Mama. We've been fine all these years. Nothing's going to happen to you."

"You don't know that. I worked with our government a long time. I sometimes think the only reason the agency hasn't found us yet is because they didn't have a reason to come looking. Tonight, just might give them the reason." Mama waved her hand at the mallet. "No one knows you do all the hard parts now. And I don't want them to find out either. They would use me to get to you. Just like they used your daddy."

"There's no reason for them to know you don't work in the field anymore. I got this," Lacy said slowly bending over to pick up her bag. "I'm not a child anymore. They can't take me anywhere I don't want to go. When I cut off the head of the snake tonight, the agency will be in chaos. No one's going to spend energy looking for us."

It scared Lacy when Mama went off on a rant. Some days, the chemo treatments made her moods unpredictable. It never seemed to last long. A moment of anger, or paranoia. Luckily, Mabel knew about her mother's condition. If there ever came a time when Mama let something slip, Lacy would be able to blame that on her medications.

Mama nodded slowly and settled back in her wheelchair. Lacy waited, watching to see which way her mother would go. She needed to leave so she had one last time to assess the hotel. Do a final run before the hit. But she didn't want to leave Mama as she was.

"Mabel should be over in the next hour or so," Lacy finally said.

Mama smiled at her. "I found us a nice little place in Gulf Shores. I decided not to go so far south. It is on the beach though, with a hot tub, like you wanted. We can take off tomorrow and drive down. I booked it starting next week, so we can take our time on the drive."

Alabama. Lacy knew how her mom's mind worked. The job in Indiana bringing her father's death full circle. Her mother had chosen to go back to where she was born. Back to her roots. Iron control snapped in place over Lacy's heart.

Later. She would think about this later.

"That'll be nice." Lacy said, shifting from her left to her right foot.

"You know how proud I am of you, Lacy?" Mama picked at the edge of her soiled nurse's uniform. "Maybe we can look at that program in Switzerland. Can't take that contraption," Mama said waving her hand at the sledgehammer.

"No, we certainly can't. I would like you to consider more progressive treatment." She kissed her mama on the cheek and headed down the steps.

"You look pitiful," Mama clucked, her gaze suddenly distant, as she melted far away in thought. "That man took your daddy from us, Lacy. Tonight, that bill comes due. You always been better than me."

"You taught me everything I know," Lacy said, backing watchfully down the sidewalk. "You okay?"

"Go on now." Her mother made a shooing motion with her hands.

Lacy nodded, turned and disappeared down the block.

Her mother's eyes cleared and became calculating.

"But you always been better," Mama whispered.

THREE SIMPLE RULES

BY ELIZABETH PERONA

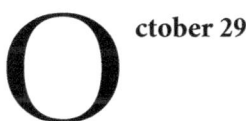ctober 29

"I LOVE THIS COMMERCIAL!" Charlotte Reinhardt told her friend Francine McNamara. It was during a commercial break of the latest *Bachelorette* episode, one they'd missed because they'd been playing bridge with their septuagenarian group, the Summer Ridge Bridge Club, the night before. This afternoon they were streaming the missed episode on Hulu.

It would be more accurate to say Charlotte was streaming the show. Francine knitted a sweater for her granddaughter Mariah.

"You certainly are in stitches," Francine said, looking up. "What's it a commercial for?"

"I have no idea, but there are a bunch of teenagers trying to escape from a chain-saw-wielding killer in a horror movie and they keep making all these dumb choices. Someone just suggested they hide in the basement. Hilarious!" she cackled.

Francine returned to her knitting.

Charlotte continued to laugh out loud. She slapped her knee. "Did you hear that? Now they're hiding in the cemetery!"

Francine gave her a half-hearted smile.

"Don't you think it's funny?" Charlotte asked.

Francine shrugged. "There are three simple rules that get violated in every horror film, and it always leads to the untimely demise of the characters."

"Since when did you become an aficionado of horror films? You never watch them on television with me when I suggest it. How would you know about any rules?"

Francine set her knitting aside. "I made them up one time when Jonathan binged on horror movies. It was shortly after we got Netflix, and he'd watch just about anything. Drove him nuts that I could predict what was going to happen two scenes later. He finally banished me from the room."

"Well, don't keep me in suspense. What are the three rules?"

Francine ticked them off on her fingers. "One, don't go in a haunted house. That's the one that always gets violated first. Two, if you go in and find a dead body, never touch it. Too often it's not as dead as you think. And three, if you go in, under no circumstances should you investigate the basement. It never turns out well."

"Seems like pretty good rules not to violate."

"Amazingly enough, the writers make it look natural when they do." Francine chuckled to herself. "Probably because they're always teens. No self-respecting older adult would fall for that."

Charlotte's eyes lit up. "You'd be surprised. You're a rule follower. Not everyone, even older adults, always act so sensible. One of these days Francine, I'm going to catch you doing something totally irrational and call you on it."

Francine was about to make a follow-up comment when *The Bachelorette* came back on. Charlotte turned to watch it and Francine resumed knitting. When it was over, Charlotte turned the television off. "Let's have some tea," she said.

Francine checked her watch. Four o'clock on the dot. Sometimes Charlotte was predictable, even though she liked to think of herself as spontaneous and always living in the moment. Though, Francine had to admit, some days Charlotte didn't have tea. Some days she had Happy Hour. She was okay with either.

The two got up and went into the kitchen. Being so close to Halloween, Charlotte was wearing an ugly Halloween sweater—black and orange with scary-looking jack-o'-lanterns all over it. Francine found their eerie smiles creepy, but she hated it when too much emphasis was placed on horror rather than fun. She thought Halloween night belonged to the kids.

Charlotte put the kettle on to boil while Francine took a seat at Charlotte's dining room table. When the kettle began whistling, Charlotte set teabags into mugs and poured boiling water into them.

"Seeing this boiling water makes me think of what's going on with the Liebermans," Charlotte said. She set one mug in front of Francine and another where she intended to sit. "Did you hear what Alice said about them last night at bridge? She lives two doors away and saw Liza chase Harold around the yard with a hatchet."

Francine frowned. She hadn't heard Alice say anything of the sort. Maybe it was when she'd gone to the bathroom. "Really?"

Charlotte nodded enthusiastically. "There's so much drama over there I can't believe they're still doing a haunted house for the neighborhood this year."

"Well, no one does Halloween quite like the Liebermans." Francine used her spoon to chase the tea bag around the insides of the mug. While she wasn't a haunted house aficionado, Francine did admire the effort the Liebermans put into making their home a scary place. They'd been at it for a decade.

Charlotte returned from the kitchen with a plate of Halloween sugar cookies Francine had brought over. "Halloween may be the only thing left that unites them. You've no doubt heard the rumors they're getting a divorce."

Francine took off her large, black-framed glasses and set them next to her tea. "No!" she said. As she aged into her seventies, Francine was feeling more and more out of the mainstream. None of the latest movies interested her and listening to current music only made her cringe. But neighborhood rumors? Surely her bridge club buddies would keep her up-to-date on those! "How long has this been going on?"

"A couple of months."

Stunned, Francine picked up a pumpkin shaped sugar cookie swathed in orange icing and sprinkled with red and yellow sanding sugar. Her visiting grandkids had decorated them over the weekend. She took a bite, and though it was overly sweet, it made her smile.

Charlotte settled into her chair. "So, are you going to the Lieberman's haunted house this year? I'm going with Alice. This will be her first time with the lights out. I can't wait to see how she does. She was traumatized when she visited the Necropolis in Indy back in her thirties and she hasn't been in a haunted house since, even though she's got "Haunted House" on her bucket list."

Francine knew of Alice's aversion to haunted houses. The Liebermans put on a pretty scary show during their "haunted hours" from six until nine. Afterwards, they put on a very nice open house (with lights on) for the neighbors until late in the evening. That was when Alice would show up. "I always thought her bucket list item meant going to a real haunted house, not one created by humans."

"It might be haunted by the time Halloween gets here." Charlotte rummaged through the cookies and selected a bat with chocolate-iced wings. "Liza may have killed him by then."

Francine breathed in the aroma emanating from her tea—cinnamon spice, a fragrant scent so much like autumn she practically felt a chill in the air. Or maybe it was Charlotte's insinuation that there might be a murder at the Lieberman house. "If the rumors have been going on for only a couple of months, I can't help but wonder if it's all part of their shtick. Any yelling and screaming is probably just a setup for the atmosphere they're trying to create with the haunted house. And I can't believe you didn't tell me about the rumors!"

"I thought for sure you knew. And I don't think the hatchet chase was a put-on. Alice swears she hasn't seen Harold since." Charlotte hoisted the cookie near her face so she could examine the icing. The thick frosting must have passed muster because she bit into it, closed her eyes and concentrated on the flavors as she chewed. "This is so good. I love the chocolate."

"Credit my grandchildren. They did the decorations. I'm making more cookies tomorrow afternoon so I can take a big tray of them over to the Lieberman's as my contribution to the open house."

"I'm providing my usual two gallons of apple cider. That's one thing I did plan ahead for. I bought them a few days ago at Beasley's Orchard. I have an idea. Why don't we both take them over to the Lieberman's tomorrow afternoon after you finish the cookies? That way we can scout around the place for Harold. Maybe ask a few prying questions if we don't see him."

Francine actually thought it was a good idea. Once Charlotte got thoughts of murder in her head, she didn't let go of them until she was proven wrong. And Francine didn't want her going on and on about it for long. "Sounds good. Though I'm sure there's a reasonable explanation for Alice not seeing him. Maybe she's done something to alienate him. You know how pushy she can get sometimes."

"Especially if she's trying to sell a house," Charlotte said, snickering. While they all loved Alice, she was still working as a realtor and could be seen as a little too forceful when in business mode.

"Don't pretend she's the only one who has that effect on people. You've been known to alienate a few in your time."

Charlotte scrunched up her face. "Name one."

"Jud Judson." Jud was a detective with the Brownsburg Police Department, and Francine knew he worked hard at tolerating Charlotte. Of course, it would help if they weren't tripping over dead bodies all the time.

"Okay, I'll give you that one. Maybe. I mean, don't you think he's putting on an act? We've single-handedly solved a number of murder cases for him. He should be grateful."

Francine demurred. "I could see where he thinks we get in the way."

"Nonsense."

She shrugged her shoulders. "I should have the cookies finished and ready to go about four o'clock tomorrow. Why don't you come over to my home then and we'll take everything over?"

OCTOBER 30

IT WASN'T FAR from Francine's house to the Lieberman's, but as cold as it was, they decided to drive over. Francine briefly considered that she might have overdone the sugar cookie production, but Halloween at the Lieberman's was a neighborhood party. Everyone came in droves. She reasoned that her formidably-sized tray of cookies wouldn't last a half hour.

The Lieberman's two-story house was well-kept-up, so from the outside it looked nothing like a haunted house. The shutters were painted and attached securely, the bushes were neatly trimmed and the landscaping impeccable, and no ivy grew up the sides of the red brick façade. Francine did notice, though, that the draperies were drawn in every window.

She leveraged the tray she was carrying against the side of the house and rang the doorbell. Instead of the usual ringtone, it loudly rang out Vincent Price's evil laugh from Michael Jackson's "Thriller."

Francine nearly dropped her tray.

"That was spooky!" Charlotte said.

Francine quickly wrestled the shaking tray into submission, grasping it white-knuckled before any of the cookies spilled out. "They may have outdone themselves this year."

They waited. No one came to the door, causing Francine to rebalance the platter to free up a hand, and this time she knocked. The barn-red door creaked open.

The women looked at each other. "Should we go in?" Francine asked.

"You decide. I'm the one with an overactive imagination, and I've seen too many slasher movies with this exact same premise."

She peered inside. "Liza? Harold? It's Francine and Charlotte. We've brought the cookies and cider for tomorrow night!"

There was no response.

"It's dark in there," she told Charlotte.

"I'll go check to see if their cars are in the garage." Charlotte stepped off the porch and walked around to the side door of the garage where she stared through the beveled window pane. "The image is distorted, but I can see that both her car and his truck are there." She returned to the front porch, still carrying her cider jugs.

Francine hesitated.

"Why don't we go in and drop off our contributions?" Charlotte suggested. "We can leave a note saying we were here and the door wasn't quite closed. We can't just leave it unlocked."

That seemed reasonable to Francine. She nudged the door fully open with her elbow and they went in. Having the front door open provided just enough light that she could see into the den, which was the first room to the right. "Liza? Harold?" she called.

Still no answer.

Charlotte flicked the light switch up and down, but nothing happened. The darkness remained.

"Maybe we should put our stuff down," Francine said. "I know there's a table in the den here somewhere. They may have moved it to make way for the haunted house props. I can leave my cookies on it and we can lock the door on our way out."

"That's all well and good for you, but my cider needs to be refrigerated." Charlotte put her jugs on the floor and whipped out her cell phone. She turned on the flashlight app. She shined it into the room. "There's your end table."

Francine moved toward it and set her tray down. Charlotte waved her cell phone a bit further and began exploring the room.

"What are you looking for?" Francine asked.

"Paper and a pen, to write a note with."

"Good idea. I want to get out of here."

"Looks like they've got this room ready for tomorrow night."

"What do you mean?"

"I mean the cobwebs in the corners of the room, the black drapes blotting out the daylight, this coffin in the corner."

Francine looked to where Charlotte had pointed her flashlight. "That can't be a coffin," she said skeptically.

"Then what is it?"

Francine pulled out her own cell phone and used her flashlight app to help illuminate the corner Charlotte was pointing at. The two women approached the object. "You're right!" Francine said. "It is a coffin." She thumped on the wood and it made a hollow sound.

"Let's open it," Charlotte said.

"No!"

"It's still daylight. Any self-respecting vampire would be asleep in his or her coffin. A shaft of light could cause instant vaporization."

Francine put her hands on her hips. "That's all well and good, but all we've got is a cell phone flashlight app."

"Probably just make him squint, then."

Francine laughed. "The Liebermans haven't spared any expense this year. Coffins are not cheap, even a rustic model like this one." She set her hand on the coffin but couldn't bring herself to open it. "What if something jumps out at us?"

"Then the person inside won't be dead." Charlotte threw open the lid.

They both peered inside. There was a hatchet lying inside where the chest of a corpse would be. The blade edged a pool of something liquidy. "It's empty. But is that blood?" Francine asked. As relieved as she was nothing was in the coffin to surprise them, the sight of blood, even if it wasn't real, was disturbing.

Charlotte pointed to the floor. "It trickles out on this side of the coffin. Maybe our vampire is somewhere in the house."

Francine noticed that the blood, which she presumed was fake, trailed across the large area rug. "I wonder if that stain will come out? This is an expensive rug, even if it's not authentically Persian."

"It leads toward the kitchen. We have to go there anyway." Charlotte picked up her cider and started back across the room.

"I'm sure this is just part of Liza and Harold's haunted house exhibit," Francine reasoned, "and they've left the house to do something and forgotten to lock the front door." She threw back her shoulders as if everything was okay. "Since we're already headed to the kitchen, I'll drop the cookies off there. We can leave a note and then get out of here."

"Good idea," Charlotte said.

On their way, they tried every light switch they could find. None worked. Charlotte forged ahead using her cell phone.

The darkness continued to unnerve Francine. "If there was a power outage, shouldn't we have known about it? Wouldn't it have affected the whole neighborhood?"

"I would think so," Charlotte said.

The kitchen was on the backside of the house on the bottom floor. Charlotte and Francine eased into the dark room and set their goods on the large island in the middle. Francine looked to where she knew the windows were over the sink. "Ah, that's why it's so dark in here. Blackout film's been attached to the windows."

"They know how to go all out for haunted houses, don't they?" Charlotte said.

Francine didn't respond. She dug a pad of paper out of a drawer along with a pen. She started writing her note to the Liebermans while Charlotte followed the blood trail. It led to the pantry door.

Charlotte threw the door open. "There you are," she said, crossing her arms over her chest. "Nice job on making this place creepy."

"Who are you talking to?"

Charlotte turned to Francine. "Liza." She turned back. "You can stop with the dead act now. We love what we've seen, and yes, you scared us in the front room." She nudged Liza with her foot. "Liza! Liza! C'mon, I know you're faking it."

Francine didn't like where this was going. She dropped the pen and hustled over. Charlotte was bent over the body, having taken Liza by the shoulders and given her a few good shakes. Liza continued to slump.

Francine felt her heart jump in her chest. This could not be happening. "Liza!" She bumped Charlotte aside and felt for a pulse. There was none.

"Call 911," she told Charlotte.

"I wouldn't do that," a voice said.

The women looked around. The voice was distorted, disembodied, and decidedly female. "That's not Harold's voice," Charlotte whispered to Francine.

"Because I'm not Harold," it continued. The voice sounded like it went through a speech modulator and had rapidly changing variations in pitch. The effect made Francine think of Cher's song, "Believe."

"Where's Harold?" Francine asked. "Have you done something to him, too?"

"You might want to check the basement."

Francine bent down so her mouth was right next to Charlotte's ear. "You go down into the basement. Make enough noise for both of us. I'll stay up here and see if I can figure out what's going on. Liza may not have a pulse, but she's not bleeding, either, and her body's not cold."

"Maybe she's been poisoned," Charlotte whispered back.

"What are you whispering about?" the voice asked.

"What did you do to Liza?" Charlotte asked.

"Why do you need to know?"

"I hate it when someone answers a question with a question," she retorted. "What did you do to Liza?"

"The same thing I will do to you if you don't follow my instructions, Charlotte. Now open the door to the basement."

The door was on the far end of the kitchen. Francine prodded Charlotte toward it.

Charlotte reached the door and threw it open. "It's dark down there." She flipped the light switch several times in vain. "I can't see anything."

"Use the cell phone like you've been doing exploring the rest of the house," said the voice. "Francine, you'll need to go with her."

Francine was on edge knowing whoever this was could see her. "How do you know our names?"

"I know everything about you, including how nosey you are. I didn't think you'd be here today. But since you are, I will have to do something about it."

A light flickered momentarily in the basement. Though it was brief, there was definitely a body lying face down on the floor.

Charlotte gasped. "That looked like Harold!" She tromped down the stairs.

"Don't go in the basement!" Francine shouted. This was like a bad horror movie. It suddenly hit her they were making every mistake the teenage victim would make. They'd entered the haunted house. They'd stuck around after they found the dead body. And now they were headed into the basement.

But she couldn't let Charlotte go down there alone.

The Vincent Price laugh went off again.

Was the haunted house a cover for killing Liza? But who would want her dead, other than Harold? He appeared to have gotten it too.

Francine hustled down the stairs.

Charlotte had reached the bottom and was now bent over the body they presumed to be Harold. Francine grabbed her by the shoulder and turned her around. She intended to haul her back upstairs but when she saw Charlotte's face, it was anything but terrified. Charlotte was laughing.

"Got ya," she said.

The presumably incapacitated Harold sat up. He was smiling as well.

"What is this?" Francine demanded.

Alice appeared at the top of the stairs. "You were right, Charlotte. Under the right circumstances, she'd fail the three simple rules." Liza, not dead, holding some kind of theatrical neck prosthetic, was behind her, grinning.

Francine's face reddened. "What are you doing here?" she asked Alice.

"Checking another box off my bucket list."

"But this isn't a real haunted house! And you're not going through it, you're just setting it up. Getting me to play the fool."

Alice smiled broadly. "My bucket list just says "Haunted House." It doesn't specify the level of participation. And when Charlotte suggested it, I couldn't resist."

"Charlotte, how could you?" Francine stomped up the stairs. Liza and Alice backed away.

Charlotte followed right behind her. "Don't be mad, Francine. You're the sensible one. I told you one of these days I'd catch you doing something irrational and call you on it. And when you described your three simple rules yesterday, I couldn't resist."

"Oh, Charlotte," Francine said, shaking her head. She plopped down in a chair in the kitchen. "You're always talking me into doing irrational things. How many murder investigations have we done?"

Charlotte tallied five or six on her fingers. "Six, I guess. If you count those as irrational."

"I do. Not that I don't take some satisfaction in seeing justice served, mind you. But you're always getting me out of my comfort zone."

"I am?"

"And I love you for it. But if you try this ever again, I'll . . . "

"You'll what?"

Francine thought a moment. And in that moment, she had to laugh at herself. "I'll stop being such a rule-follower and give you all a worse heart attack than the one you've just given me."

Charlotte's eyes lit up. "I like the sound of that. You're on!"

WHICH WITCH?

BY DIANA CATT

The waxing crescent moon passed behind a rain-laden cloud casting my yard into deep darkness. I sat on the front porch swing having transformed my twenty-five-year-old self into seventy-eight-year-old Granny Mossman. I donned this disguise every Halloween as an homage to my grandmother and all her idiosyncrasies that earned her the legendary title of Old Witch Mossman of Crab Apple Street. She's been gone now for ten years, but the annual challenge to knock on the witch's door continues. So, I sat in the shadows. Drank my wine. Waited patiently to scare the kiddies. They always came.

The next morning, I took down the new motion-sensor activated lights I'd mounted on my front gate and sidewalk for last night's festivities. I planned to store them in Granny's former workshop out back. Her menagerie of potion jars, dried plants, roots, and notes still filled the shelves. Though the building was old it was solid, had a good roof, and I had plans for using it as the base for my own greenhouse business in the near future.

I wasn't expecting the door to be ajar. Maybe I left it open yesterday. Just in case the teenagers had started a different assault tactic, I looked around. The thick layer of dust and cobwebs appeared to be undisturbed. I thought back to the previous night and remembered my Rottweiler, Coco, had raised a ruckus a couple hours after dark. I'd assumed she'd detected a raccoon or possum and hadn't worried. She couldn't escape the yard, but had easy access in and out of the house through the rear doggie door. If any of the neighborhood kids had jumped the fence to raid Old Witch Mossman's workshop, they risked getting bitten. I had Beware of Dog signs everywhere for their protection. And mine.

I locked the workshop and returned to the house, leaving Coco sniffing around the perimeter fence. I fixed a sandwich and a cup of hot tea and turned on the family room TV to continue my binge of old *House* episodes. Coco's never-ending appetite brought her back indoors and to my side, mouth drooling, watching intently for sandwich crumbs to fall. The sound of footsteps on my front porch switched Coco to guard mode. I pulled on my cardigan and made it to the front door by the third knock. I recognized Joe McKay's voice when he called out "Dani, open up. It's the police."

Coco was barking and ready to defend to the death, so I left the chain on the door and peeked through the gap. There he was, in uniform, the guy I had hardly spoken to since our senior prom fiasco. He stood next to a similarly-uniformed petite blonde I didn't recognize.

"Joe? What the hell kind of an announcement was that? You could have phoned ahead."

"Sorry, Dani. It's just . . . well, it's important. We need to ask you some questions. Can we come in?"

"Well, sure, I guess."

"Chain up that dog, first," he said.

"No worries. I'll just put Coco in her cage and clear off some chairs."

Coco followed my command and waited on high alert in her cage. My cats, Fluffy and Lightning, protested a bit as I moved them from their favorite napping sites. They leave hair on everything. I placed clean afghans over the hairy chairs and invited the officers to sit. I held out my bowl of left-over Halloween candy.

"Help yourselves. I over-bought this year. Want some coffee or tea?"

They both turned down the offers. I plucked out a Snickers and sat on the sofa. "Well?"

"Dani, this is Officer Meadows. I don't know if you've met. She's Janine's little sister."

I studied her face. "One of the bratty little twins, right?"

She laughed. "Helen. And, guilty as charged. Addy and I were pretty awful to Janine's friends. Sorry."

"Accepted. Now, what's this all about?"

"Where were you last night between eight and ten?"

"Hell, Joe. I was right where I am every year on Halloween. Sitting on my porch. Entertaining the neighborhood kids who want to get their thrills by doing mischief at the home of the legendary witch."

Joe laughed. "I remember sitting out there with you in the dark, waiting for some kid to take a dare and try to knock on the door. We scared the shit out of Zach Jacobs one year."

He motioned to Helen. "You know Zach. He's the young guy on the city council." Her eyes widened.

"There's a version of Zach that comes by every year," I said. "Never fails."

"And last night?"

"Same thing. I dressed up in my Granny Mossman costume and waited for dark."

I turned to Helen and explained. "I stick a big wart on my cheek, wear a gray curly wig, a long dress, a fringed shawl, and carry a cane. That's how I remember my dear old Granny. She was the infamous neighborhood witch."

Helen jotted that down in her little notebook.

"Had quite a reputation," Joe said.

"True. People came around to her little shop out back for all sorts of potions and oils. You'd have enjoyed it this year, Joe. I added some new techno stuff." I was grinning at the recollection. "I rigged up a motion sensor light that turned on whenever someone entered the gate. It illuminated a sign that said 'Take one treat if you dare, or risk a scare.' I had plenty of candy in a bucket by the sign. Also, I created a pentagram out of tiny lights on the sidewalk right behind the candy that also lit up with the motion sensor. It was freakin' awesome."

"Trick-or-Treating ended at nine," Helen said.

"Also true, but the teenagers are just getting started about then. They're after thrills, not so much candy. I always stay out there until after midnight or I will get the inevitable footsteps, the giggles, and the knocks at the door. I usually go through a bottle of wine and enjoy the stars. It's become a . . . nice . . . Halloween tradition."

I raised an eyebrow at Joe. "Is that enough of an alibi for you? Are you going to tell me what's happened?"

"Allie Anderson was found dead in a ditch a couple of hours ago. At the edge of St. Mary's Cemetery," Joe said.

"I don't understand. I don't know any Allie Anderson."

"She was fourteen. She bled to death from a botched abortion attempt."

I sucked in a deep breath and my hand went to my chest. "Oh, no! That poor child." I looked from Joe to Helen and back to Joe.

"Why are you here, then?" Of course, I knew, but I wanted him to say it.

Joe had the grace to look at the floor. "Sorry, Dani. Really sorry. But word around town is someone looking to have a cheap abortion would find help here. Because of Granny Mossman."

"I didn't take up Granny's business, Joe. I can't believe you'd think that."

"Her herb garden is still out back, right? It's also rumored her potions are still in her workshop," Joe said. "Moreover, Helen found *your* address in a text message on the girl's phone. I told her it was probably just related to Halloween, nothing else. Nothing related to the girl's death."

Helen sent him an annoyed glance then said to me, "We still had to check it out."

"Of course, I only meant . . . " Joe started.

"It means nothing," I said. "Kids share this address every year. They meet up here. You know, Joe. That witch of a Granny has given me twenty-five years of innuendo, rumor, and ridicule. Everyone knows our names. No one leaves us alone."

"Us?" Helen asked. "Are you living here with someone?"

I sighed. "No, that was hyperbole. I inherited the place when mom died last year. It's just me now."

"Do you have your Granny's recipes for her potions?" Helen asked.

I paused for a minute and took a bite of my Snickers bar. I had copies, not the originals, but they didn't need to know. "No, my cousin Laura wanted them. That's all she wanted from Granny. She's going to compile them into a thesis for her graduate studies in local mythology."

Helen looked up from her notebook with a question on her face.

"My cousin, Laura Mossman," I explained. "She's pursuing an anthropology degree at Purdue. She spent summers here when we were growing up. Joe knows her. She hasn't been down much since she got out of high school, but we still keep in touch."

"What would you do if someone came around for a potion? Granny's Love Potion, say?" Joe asked.

"I'd say 'Get the f off my property' or something to that effect. I told you, I didn't go into Granny's business."

"How about if they wanted an abortion?"

"Granny called that 'Love Potion, The Sequel.' But the answer would be the same. No luck here. Besides, I think a Google search will probably tell someone what plant the old crony likely used. I honestly don't know and don't want to know."

"How about Laura? Could she look up the recipe your Granny used and find the active ingredient in The Sequel? We can compare it to what forensics finds in Allie."

I sighed. "I'll give you her number." I pulled out my phone, found Laura's number but instead of showing Joe, I pushed her message icon, then the mic icon. Voice-to-text usually ends up wonky because of my Southern Indiana accent, but Laura could probably get the gist. I looked up from the phone and met Joe's eyes. "Really though, Officer Joe, you can't possibly believe my cousin is making and selling Granny Mossman's potions. That old witch gave us both enough grief to last a lifetime. Besides, it wasn't a money-making enterprise, I can assure you. Neither Laura nor I have the same calling that drove Granny." I looked back at my phone and slid my thumb over to the send arrow, then read her number off out loud. Helen jotted it down.

"Any more questions?" I asked.

"No. Sorry to bother you, Dani, but we had to check you off the list," Helen said.

I walked them to the front door, past Coco who was emitting menacing growls from her cage. I made small talk hoping they wouldn't notice and write me a ticket for having a dangerous pet.

"Helen, what is Janine up to these days?"

"She and Tom had twin girls, three months old tomorrow. So, she's doing all the mommy stuff . . . at twice the pace. Mom is staying there to help out."

"Who'd she marry? Someone from here?"

"Tom Black," Joe said.

I looked at Joe in surprise. "The same Tom Black from high school?"

He grinned and nodded. "The one and only."

"What was Tom like in high school?" Helen asked.

"My mom called him rake-ish," I said. "But she said that about you, too, Joe."

"He liked the girls and the girls liked him," Joe said. "All the guys were envious."

"Well, he's over the moon with his girls, now," Helen laughed. "And they have his good looks."

"Well, tell her I said congratulations on the twins and good luck with Tom. Hey, Joe. You know, Allie might have located a plant that would induce an abortion and accidently took too much. I'm thinking the real bad guy here is whoever got an underage teen pregnant in the first place. Are you looking for him?"

"We're on it," he said. "Good to see you, Dani." He leaned in close. "Your life might have been different if Granny's Love Potion had really worked. Remember prom night?"

Officer Helen's eyebrows shot up to her hairline. I winked at her. "The dress stayed on."

"You never could take a joke, could you, Mossman?" Joe said with a laugh.

Helen turned a fetching shade of pink. Good luck with that one, Joe, I thought as she hurried to the car.

WHEN MOM PASSED LAST YEAR, I received a tidy insurance sum and I'd been making plans to put it to good use by opening a greenhouse business. I supposed I'd inherited some of my granny's green thumb and love of flowers and herbs, but instead of making medicinal concoctions, I intended to market to landscaping firms and others via the Internet. My research into the topic was promising and this was a good time to get started on the construction. I'd found a young man with an excellent reference from a friend of mine and made an appointment to discuss my project.

"I'm planning to fix up the old workshop in my backyard," I explained to Jeff Bynum, the owner of Bynum Construction. I had to tilt my head back pretty far to meet the eyes of this giant. "I want to add a greenhouse to the east side. I have an old herb garden I'll use for starter stock for the greenhouse and expand from there. I have a big yard that needs a bit of landscaping, too." I showed him the layout I'd sketched of my vision.

"I can handle that. Are you taking up where Old Witch Mossman left off? Making and selling potions? You're the same Mossman, right?" Jeff asked.

I sighed. "You've heard about my Granny? I thought since you were new to the area . . ."

Jeff smirked. "She's still famous among the younger set. Especially this time of year."

That comment gave me pause. I'm only eight years out of high school. What younger set is he hanging out with? Maybe I'm too sensitive to age-related comments.

"Her legend has magnified over the years," I said. "She was really just a sweet old lady who dabbled in herbal teas. She thought she could cure stomach aches and headaches, stuff like that."

"How about I stop by tomorrow afternoon about two, look the place over, and write up a quote?"

"Works for me."

THE NEXT AFTERNOON, I stood at the edge of Granny's herb garden, studying her map of its layout and comparing the autumnal remnants to pictures in my wildflower and herb book. A few of the plants had died out over the years, others were unidentifiable without flowers, but there were several perennials still intact this late into the season—rue, club moss, feverfew, pennyroyal, oregano, marsh rosemary, and blue cohosh just to name a few. I wished I had taken care of the plot instead of letting it overgrow. That would change next spring when I would have better luck figuring out what was a weed and what was worth cultivating.

I noticed a spot where the soil had been disturbed toward the back of the plot. I stepped in for a closer look and realized a plant had been uprooted recently from the area of the map indicating blue cohosh growth. There was a footprint in the dirt that was not mine, and a lot of Coco's prints all over the place. I became alarmed though, when I found drops of blood on the adjacent, intact plants. I immediately thought of Coco's ruckus on Halloween night and the open workshop door. Someone may have been bitten that night while robbing my garden and trying to enter the workshop. I took a picture, then pulled up one of the blood-splattered plants and sealed it in a plastic baggie. Then as an afterthought, I decided I'd better call Joe and explain what I'd found.

"Did Allie have a dog bite?" I asked him. I fervently hoped not. But a determined girl might have braved the witch's dark garden for the necessary herb.

"I'll check with the coroner and be over soon to collect that blood sample for comparison."

True to his word, Joe showed up fifteen minutes later at the back gate.

"Where's Helen?" I asked.

"I didn't need her for this. I'll just grab some of the blood sample and run it over to the lab." He bent down and pulled up all the plants with visible blood splatters and put them in an evidence bag.

"But don't you need photographs? Look for footprints? That sort of stuff?"

"That's just TV policing. I got a picture on my phone. That'll be good enough. It'll probably turn out to be animal blood anyway."

Just then, Coco shoved herself through the doggie door and raced towards us, barking and growling. Joe ran toward the back gate but couldn't work the latch fast enough. I yelled at Coco to stop while Joe bailed over the fence. He fell awkwardly to the ground on the safe side.

"Keep the damn dog on a leash or I'll shoot her," Joe yelled, holding his wrist. "I think I sprained something, damn it."

"Sorry, Joe. I don't know what's got her all worked up. She always obeys my commands."

"Well, that's not true anymore, is it? Consider this your first warning."

What could I say? Coco is big enough to really hurt someone if she wanted to. I should have caged her before letting Joe come into the back yard. Now Jeff Bynum was due to arrive. I ordered Coco back to the house. She went, but not until Joe was out of sight.

The carpenter arrived a few minutes later. I took him through the house to the back yard. As we passed Coco's cage, she went ballistic. Jeff said, "Nice doggy," and veered wide around the cage. "Hope that lock holds," he added.

"She's having a bad day," I said. "Don't worry. She can't get out."

I left Jeff to take measurements and do his calculations and went back inside to get Coco some water. She stuck her nose through the cage bars and nipped at my jacket pocket, growling all the while. I reached into the pocket and pulled out the baggie with the blood-splattered plant. Her growl changed to a high-pitched whine. She didn't like whatever had left that blood trail.

I took the baggie into the kitchen and realized I'd forgotten to ask Joe what he found out about Allie having a recent dog bite. I called the police station but he wasn't there so I asked to speak to Helen.

"Hi Dani," she said. "I was going to call you. Your cousin, Laura, confirmed the ingredient in The Sequel as blue cohosh. Granny Mossman's directions were to grind up the roots and make a tea to drink six times a day until achieving the desired result. Do you know that plant? A large quantity was found in Allie's stomach contents."

"I think that's what was taken from my herb garden where I found all that blood."

"What are you talking about?"

"I called earlier and Joe came over to get a sample for the lab. I think my dog must have bitten someone in my garden on Halloween night. The ground is disturbed in the cohosh growth area. Looks like someone pulled a plant and then Coco got them. I forgot to ask Joe what the coroner said about Allie having a dog bite. It could have been her."

I heard paper rustling. Finally, Helen spoke. "No mention of any wounds on Allie. It wasn't her."

"Whoever it was has a fresh bite. And Coco has vicious teeth. With all that blood loss, they might have needed stitches."

"Ah, good thinking, Dani. I'll call around to the ER and clinics, see if they stitched anyone up that night."

By the time Jeff finished up his quote, Helen and a team of officers were in my back yard collecting samples from the cohosh patch all the way to the fence. Joe wasn't with them.

"What's happened, Helen?" I asked.

"The samples Joe collected never made it to the lab and he's not answering his phone. Also, he got twelve stitches to his wrist that night. He told the ER doctor he'd been on a run to a domestic quarrel and their dog bit him as he tried to stop the husband from beating up his wife."

"Joe? Are you kidding me?"

"No. We're hoping to find trace samples of his blood here at the scene."

"I saved one of the blood-splattered plants. Can you use that?"

"You what?"

"Yeah, I was afraid I'd get sued for having a mean dog and I might need evidence that someone trespassed. I took a picture, too."

Helen pursed her eyebrows. "Go get it. We might have some chain of custody issue, but if the lab can verify the plant is the same one from the photo and we can match the blood to Joe, we got him."

I walked slowly to the house, stunned by the actions of my childhood friend. I thought back to our senior prom night and Joe's drunken admission that I was too old for him at seventeen. Later, he tried to pass it off as a joke, accusing me of not having a sense of humor. Our friendship was never the same after that night, though. Sadly, I realized I should listen to people when they tell me who they are.

I let Coco out of her cage and gave her a big hug for her role in solving the crime, and for some good feels. She licked my face in response. It wasn't enough, though, to get poor Allie's fate out of my mind. She might still be alive if she'd had Granny's directions to follow, and made tea from the roots instead of eating the plant. Perhaps I'd rethink my position on Granny's medicinal herb business. Maybe Laura could sell her book of Old Witch Mossman's recipes and I'd stock the necessary plants in my greenhouse. Potion ingredients for a do-it-yourselfer might have a market.

I jostled Coco's muzzle. "A little witchcraft on the side couldn't hurt my greenhouse business, right girl?" Coco licked my face again as if in agreement.

AUTHOR BIOGRAPHIES

Teri Barnett is the author of the Bijoux Mystery Series and the upcoming Lac Voo Mystery Series—both set in the Lake Michigan region. In a past life, she also wrote historical time-travel/paranormal romance. Born and raised in Michigan, Teri currently resides in Indiana where she writes books, makes cool art, crochets too many shawls and afghans, and hangs out with Black Cat Lou, her bossy black cat who has earned her own hashtag #theblackcatlou. You can visit Teri online at www.teribarnett.com to learn more about her books, contact her, and/or subscribe to her newsletter.

Joan Bruce is a pseudonym for D.B. Reddick, a short story writer with more than a dozen published stories to his credit. He is a former newspaper reporter/editor and an insurance industry professional. He and his wife, Rebecca, live in Camby, IN.

J. Paul Burroughs is a retired English teacher after 44 years in Indianapolis Public Schools. He is a member of Sisters in Crime. His stories have been published in *Homicide for the Holidays* and *Murder 20/20*. His novel, *Karma and Crime,* was published in 2020. He and his wife of 38 years, Ronda, live in a historic home in Greenfield, Indiana with their adorable (but mischievous) pug, Pip.

Ross Carley - Murder and mayhem by malware . . . Bits and bytes that steal and kill . . .
Ross Carley's first four novels feature PI and computer hacker Wolf Ruger, an Iraq vet with PTSD. *Dead Drive* (2016) and *Formula*

Murder, set in the formula racing industry (2017) are murder mysteries. Cyberthrillers *Cyberkill* (2018) and *Cryptokill* (2020), are books one and two of the *Cybercode Chronicles*. His fifth novel, *The Three-Legged Assassin*, featuring assassin Lance Garrett, will be released in late 2021. Ross is a computational intelligence and cybersecurity consultant. He and Francie split their time between Indiana and Florida.

Website: www.RossCarleyBooks.com,
Instagram: @rosscarleyauthor
Facebook: www.Facebook.com/RossCarleyBooks

Diana Catt (www.dianacatt.com) is an author, editor, and daytime scientist. She has 20 short stories appearing in anthologies published by Blue River Press, Red Coyote Press, Pill Hill Press, Wolfmont Press, The Four Horseman Press, Speed City Press and Level Best Books. Her collection, *Below the Line*, is available on Amazon. She is co-editor of *The Fine Art of Murder* (2016, Blue River Press) and *Homicide for the Holidays* (2018, Blue River Press) and *Trick or Treats: Tales of All Hallows' Eve* (Speed City Press). She is married with three kids, three grandkids, and three pets. She thinks good things come in three.

B.K. Hart is an American writer of humor, mystery, and horror. B.K.'s short stories have been published in mystery anthologies, with **Speed City Indiana Sisters In Crime**, and in several independent horror anthologies. B.K. currently resides in Indiana.

Shari Held is an Indianapolis-based freelance journalist, editor, and author. Her short stories have been published in *Hoosier Noir* magazine and numerous anthologies, including: *The Fine Art of Murder* (2016), *Homicide for the Holidays* (2018), *Circle City Crime* (2019), *Murder 20/20* (2020), for which she also served as co-editor, and *The Big Fang* (2021). When not writing, she cares for feral cats and other wildlife, knits, and thinks up imaginative ways for her characters to get into all manner of Trouble!

Ramona G. Henderson is a former assistant professor of nursing who has always had a passion for writing. Her stories are fiction and historical fiction that are mostly mysteries. She is also a playwright, and her comedy *Operation Farley* was performed at the 2018 Divafest. Her mystery story "The Release" appears in *Murder 20/20*. She gets inspiration for her stories from her native southwestern Indiana and places where she has traveled. She is a member of the Indiana Writers Center, The Indiana Playwrights Circle, and Sisters in Crime National. She is currently serving as a board member of Speed City Sisters in Crime.

Mary Ann Koontz - This is the second short story that Mary Ann Koontz has had published in a Speed City Sisters in Crime anthology. Her first was "The 20/20 Club" published in *Murder 20/20, A Speed City Crime Writers Anthology*. She has also had short stories and articles appear in both newspapers and magazines. Under the name M. A. Koontz, she has authored books including *Shards of Trust* and its stand-alone sequel, *The Cry Beyond the Door*. Koontz has also co-authored *Maybe, Just Maybe*, a children's chapter book, with her granddaughter, Hailey Landreth. Koontz resides in Indiana.

Website: www.makoontz.com
Facebook: @makoontz27/
Twitter: @makoontzFW

C. J. Nelson is a contemporary paranormal romance novelist (*Ghost of a Chance* and *Mystic Images*) and mystery short story author, an avid reader of suspense-filled romance and cozy mysteries. She's a devoted football fan and mother of three grown children—and grandmother of an adorable grandson. She participates in writer's groups and Midwest Writers Workshops. She is a member of SINC and Speed City SINC. She loves to haunt estate sales for oldies, but goodies. Ms. Nelson resides in the Midwest with her happily-ever-after husband.

C.A. Paddock wrote her first mystery, *Mystery Adventure of Jimmy Hashburger*, as a first grader. Although it was never published, the story was featured during the classroom reading hour. She has two short stories published in Speed City Sisters in Crime anthologies: "The Making of a Masterpiece" in *The Fine Art of Murder* (2016, Blue River Press) and "Into the Light Darkness Falls" in *Homicide for the Holidays* (2018, Blue River Press). She is a member of the Indiana Writers Center and Sisters in Crime. She has worked in communications, event management, and leadership development for corporations and nonprofits. She lives in Indianapolis with her husband, Steve.

Elizabeth Perona is the father/daughter writing team of Tony Perona and Liz Dombrosky. Tony is the author of the Nick Bertetto mystery series, the standalone thriller, *The Final Mayan Prophecy*, and co-editor of the anthologies *Racing Can Be Murder* (2007, Blue River Press), *Hoosier Hoops & Hijinks* (2010, Blue River Press) and now *Trick or Treats: Tales of All Hallows' Eve* (Speed City Press). Tony is a member of Mystery Writers of America and Sisters in Crime. Liz Dombrosky graduated from Ball State University in the Honors College with a degree in teaching. With her dad, she writes the *Bucket List* mysteries. She is currently a stay-at-home mom and serves as an administrator for her church. She also is a member of Mystery Writers of America and Sisters in Crime. See more at https://elizabethperona.com/

Karen Phillips lives in Granite Bay, California, where she enjoys writing mysteries, MG/YA fantasy, and poetry. She has several short stories published in various anthologies and is working on a full-length novel. She is also a published author of non-fiction articles such as "Vetting the Tevis – A brief history of the use of veterinarians for the Western States Trail Ride." She is a member of both Speed City and Capitol Crimes chapters of Sisters In Crime.

Elizabeth A. San Miguel is a new, if not young, writer who lives in Indianapolis, Indiana. She graduated a long time ago from Indiana University, Bloomington with degrees in Journalism, History, and Fine Arts and a minor in Art History. She also received a Certificate of Applied Computer Science from Indiana University-Purdue University at Indianapolis (IUPUI). Her father is a native Spanish speaker but Elizabeth grew up in Indianapolis with a British mother. In Spanish she excels at inquiries on library location. (Not that she could understand the answer.) Otherwise, she spends her days coding in the statistical database language SAS and her evenings and weekends amusing herself by thinking up fun ways to kill people, literarily and not literally.

C. L. Shore has always loved mysteries, reading her first Nancy Drew novels in the second grade. She started taking writing seriously after joining Sisters in Crime and published her first mystery novel, *A Murder in May*, in 2017. The prequel, *Maiden Murders*, followed in 2018. Her women's fiction novel, *Cherry Blossom Temple*, was published in 2020. Additionally, Shore has authored multiple short stories that have appeared in Speed City anthologies and online mystery publications. She hopes to complete another novel by early 2022 and continues to entertain her fantasy of living in Ireland for a year.

Stephen M. Terrell - Recently retired from his law practice, Stephen Terrell is a writer and columnist for the American Bar Association's *Experience Magazine*. His most recent novel, *LAST TRAIN TO STRATTON*, tells the story of Zach Carlson, a Chicago crime beat reporter who moves to a small Indiana town in hope of finding a healing balm for his shattered life. Stephen is also the author of two tense legal thrillers: *STARS FALL* and *THE FIRST RULE*. His short stories have appeared in several Sisters in Crime anthologies. He has also written articles for various legal publications. Stephen is an avid motorcyclist.

Janet E. Williams has been writing her entire life, first as a child making her own books and later as an award-winning journalist for newspapers in Pittsburgh and Indianapolis. She has always believed that journalism is, at its heart, strong storytelling. Today, she uses her experiences covering courts, crime, and politics to create her fiction. Before retiring in late 2020, Janet worked with Franklin College journalism students and now she is developing her fiction-writing skills with short stories as she works on her novel.

Speed City Sisters in Crime is the Indiana chapter of the world-wide mystery/crime writers' association *Sisters in Crime*. The Speed City chapter was founded in 2005. Members of the organization are published mystery and crime authors, writers working on mysteries and thrillers, and readers and fans of the literary genre. There are currently 40+ members who live in Indiana or the Midwest.

https://www.speedcitysistersincrime.org/

 facebook.com/speedcitysistersincrime
twitter.com/sincspeed
instagram.com/sincspeed

www.ingramcontent.com/pod-product-compliance
Lightning Source LLC
Chambersburg PA
CBHW070447120726
47910CB00003B/953